There was her face—her familiar face, ash pale now with shock, gazing in utter disbelief out of the glass. And there, lifting high behind her shoulders, was a pair of irides⸱⸱⸱⸱⸱⸱⸱⸱ gs.

Anita ⸱⸱⸱⸱⸱⸱ d⸱⸱⸱⸱⸱⸱ ⸱o beautiful and fine and ⸱⸱⸱⸱⸱⸱, ⸱⸱⸱ ⸱⸱⸱⸱⸱ ⸱⸱⸱⸱⸱⸱ her like the wings of a dragonfly. She saw her reflection rise in the mirror and felt the rim of the sink fall away from her hands. She looked down and saw that her feet had lifted clear of the floor.

"I'm flying!" she screamed.

The FAERIE PATH

FREWIN JONES

eos

An Imprint of HarperCollins*Publishers*

For Rod

Thanks to Susannah Drazin for the recipe

for Hopie's medicine in Chapter VIII, and to Rob Rudderham

for letting me use the first verse of his song "Far From Here"

at the beginning of Chapter XV.

Eos is an imprint of HarperCollins Publishers.

The Faerie Path
Copyright © 2007 by Working Partners Limited
Series created by Working Partners Limited
All rights reserved. Printed in the United States of America.
No part of this book may be used or reproduced in any manner whatsoever without
written permission except in the case of brief quotations embodied in critical articles
and reviews. For information address HarperCollins Children's Books, a division
of HarperCollins Publishers, 1350 Avenue of the Americas, New York, NY 10019.
www.harperteen.com

Library of Congress Cataloging-in-Publication Data
Jones, Frewin.
    The faerie path / Frewin Jones.— 1st ed.
        p.   cm.
    Summary: Anita, an ordinary sixteen-year-old girl, is transported from modern-day
London to the realm of Faerie where she discovers that she is Princess Tania, the long-lost
daughter of King Oberon and Queen Titania.
    ISBN 978-0-06-087104-8 (pbk.)
    [1. Fairies—Fiction. 2. Identity—Fiction. 3. Fantasy.] I. Title.
PZ7.J71Fae 2007   2006018955
[Fic]—dc22   CIP
                                                                        AC

Typography by Al Cetta
❖
First paperback edition, 2008

Faeries tread the faerie path
Amber-trapped though moth-wing light they be
Mortals stay in mortal world
Iron-clad with half-blind eyes they see

One alone will walk both worlds
Daughter last of daughters seven
With her true love by her side
Honest hand in true love given

YNIS BOREAL ➤

Tongue
Hob's
Tongue
Highmost
Voltar
Rhoth
Ynis
Maw
Fidach Ren
Gallowshead
Beroald Sound
Caer Liel
Reganfal
R. Lych
WEIR
PRYDEIN
Caer
Circinn
MINNITH
BANNWG
LLYR
Caer Rivor

The Cloud
Scudder

The
IMMORTAL
Realm of
FAERIE

Part One: Anita

I

Anita Palmer stepped out of the shower and reached for the bath towel. Wrapping it around herself, she padded over to the mirror. She lifted her hand and swept a clear path across the misted glass before leaning forward to look at her reflection.

Her long red hair clung to her head like seaweed to a rock, framing her heart-shaped face with its wide mouth and high cheekbones. She leaned closer, staring into her mirrored eyes. The irises were a smoky green. Nothing particularly remarkable about them.

Or was there?

She leaned even closer.

Gold flecks deep in the green irises—that was what she was looking for.

Evan had said that if he looked into her eyes for long enough, he could see gold dust in them.

Anita grinned.

Gold dust in her eyes.

Sometimes when she was with Evan she could almost believe she had gold dust in her eyes.

She frowned.

It was quite scary—the feelings that Evan Thomas was stirring up in her.

Were they real? They felt real enough. Over the past few weeks thinking about Evan had somehow become the default setting of her brain. And she kept seeing his face—in the swirls of a freshly stirred cup of coffee. In shadows and light. In clouds. In the darkness behind her closed eyelids.

She recalled lines from the play they had been rehearsing for the end-of-term performance. Shakespeare. *Romeo and Juliet.*

She could hear Evan's voice in her head.

"But, soft! What light through yonder window breaks? It is the east, and Juliet is my sun!"

She'd said to him, "That's not right, Evan. Romeo says, '*and Juliet is* the *sun*' not '*my* sun.'"

He'd smiled and said, "No—you're Juliet, and you're definitely *my* sun."

And the way he had looked into her eyes right then had made her feel like the whole world was turning upside down and inside out all around her.

She laughed into the mirror, shaking her head to dislodge the memory. Still grinning, she threw the towel up over her head and rubbed vigorously at her wet hair. She didn't want to be late meeting Evan today—*especially* not today.

She winced as the towel scraped against the two itchy points on her back. She lowered the towel and angled her bare back to the mirror, craning to see over her shoulder. Something had bitten her. Twice. There was an angry red point on each shoulder blade. They had been there for a few days now. Very irritating, and in such an awkward place to scratch. She'd have to wear something that covered her back—the last thing she wanted was for Evan to think she was crawling with fleas.

She looked into the mirror again.

Did she really love Evan, or was she just getting tangled up in the fact that she had to *act* as if she loved him in the play? No, she was sure that it was much more than that. She had felt a strange, thrilling flutter in her stomach when she had been chosen to play Juliet opposite his Romeo, and over the weeks of rehearsals, as she had gotten to know him better, that thrill had just kept getting more and more intense.

She thought back to the auditions. Everyone had been surprised that Evan had shown up at all. He had only been at the school for six months, and he had always seemed so reserved and self-contained, not the type of person who'd want a major part in the school production. He was amiable enough in class, but he hadn't made any close friends and the other students mostly thought of him as something of a loner. No one had ever been invited to his home, and he didn't hang out with them on weekends or go to any parties.

Anita could remember exactly when Evan had

first turned up. It had been on the same day as the school trip to Hampton Court.

It had been a weird day. She knew it was called déjà vu when you have vivid memories of a place you've never been to, and that's how she had felt from the moment the bus had driven up to the parking lot and she had first set eyes on the sixteenth-century palace at Hampton Court—the feeling that she'd been there before. The sturdy red-brick Tudor towers and buildings with their cream-colored stone battlements and ornamentations, and the cobbled courtyards and wide, formal gardens—they had all seemed strangely familiar. But when she mentioned this later to her parents, assuming she'd visited the palace when she was much younger, they said they'd never taken her there.

The strangest thing of all had been the world-famous maze. It was a large triangular block of tall hedges, grown close together to create a warren of narrow winding corridors. Pretty much every visitor to the palace wanted to put their sense of direction to the test and find their way to the center. Everyone from the school bus had bundled in there, the boys boasting that they'd get to the middle first. It had been total chaos—most of them got hopelessly lost and had to be guided through by the people shouting from the wooden viewing platforms.

At first Anita had hung back. The green tunnels of the hedges had given her a creepy feeling that she couldn't explain. But then her best friend, Jade, had grabbed her arm and dragged her in—and once she was in the maze, the oddest thing had happened. Somehow she had known the path, and made her way to the little statue in the center without taking a single wrong turn. "How about that?" she'd said to Jade, laughing. "Am I a genius, or what?" But Jade had said it was just luck.

That same afternoon, she had seen him for the first time. The most gorgeous boy she had ever set eyes on in her entire life, standing outside the school gates when the bus pulled up. Evan Thomas—a new student who had just moved into the area.

And here she was, six months later, not only playing Juliet to his Romeo, but—more stunning yet— with Evan as her first-ever boyfriend.

At the early rehearsals, Anita had been nervous about getting the complicated words wrong or falling over her feet, but Evan had been friendly and helpful to her. And he turned out to have a great sense of humor. In the death scene at the end, she had to throw herself across him as he lay on the floor, but he kept giggling, which would start her off, and often the rehearsals would end up with the pair of them laughing hopelessly.

That was really when they had started to bond— that, and lunches together in the school cafeteria to discuss the play. Except that the more they met, the less they talked about *Romeo and Juliet*. After a couple of weeks, it had seemed perfectly natural for them to go to a café together after school. She could still vividly remember sitting across the table from him that first time—just sitting there gazing into his eyes and not hearing a single word he was saying.

She had found it so easy to tell him about all her secret wishes and desires—things she had never told anyone else. Like the fact that, if she did well in her exams, she planned to fill a backpack and tour Europe or America. Then go to college, and maybe have a career as an investigative journalist. And afterward— well, the rest of her life. Traveling the world. Having adventures. Always with a home to come back to, of course—a white house perched on high cliffs over-looking the sea. A husband. Children.

And she had wanted to know every detail of his life. But he would just shrug and say it was too boring to talk about. He had relatives in Wales, but he didn't really get on with them. He had come to London to escape—and he'd found her! And that's when his life had really started, or so he had said.

"That's just silly!" she'd told him, but it had made her feel special to believe he really thought that way.

He always wore a broad leather strap around his wrist, tied with two thin leather cords. Set into the leather band was a small, flat black stone. He told her it was a family heirloom, the only part of his family that he would never part with. "Why's that?" she had asked, intrigued. "What's the significance?"

But he had just smiled. "I'll tell you one day," he'd said. "Not now, but soon. I promise." Very mys-terious! Anita liked that—the feeling that there was so much more to find out about him.

Of course, Jade and the others wanted all the details of her private time with Evan—what had happened? Did he walk her home? Had he kissed her? Were they an item? *We talked, that's all, and he bought me a coffee. Yes, he walked me home. No, we didn't kiss. Not then, anyway. Are we an item? I don't know . . . yet.*

Anita looked into the mirror. Their first kiss had been pretty amazing. That was when he had told her about the gold dust in her eyes—and at that moment she had believed him.

A couple of days ago he had revealed that he had arranged something for her birthday. She was going to be sixteen tomorrow. A lunchtime barbecue with all her friends had been organized at her house for tomorrow, but Evan said he wanted to do something really special the day before, just for the two of them. When Anita asked him what he had planned, he told her she'd have to wait and see.

Maybe he would take her to some romantic place and tell her he loved her.

She gazed at her reflection. How would she feel about that? No one had ever said anything like that to her before. The idea of Evan saying that he loved her was huge and kind of scary—but it was pretty exciting too.

And she had the overwhelming feeling that she'd want to tell him the same thing right back.

She stared at herself in the mirror and mouthed the words silently: *I love you, Evan.* Her eyes widened.

She didn't know whether to yell with laughter or scream in panic.

A sudden flare up of itchiness on her shoulder blades broke into her thoughts and she opened the bathroom cabinet to look for some antihistamine cream.

It was half an hour later that she ran down the hall, shouting good-bye to her mum and dad as she passed the open living room door.

"You're late!" her father called. "Evan will probably have got fed up waiting. He'll be long gone by the time you arrive."

"Thanks for the vote of confidence, Dad!" Anita called back, grinning. "I think he'll be a bit more patient than that."

She bounded down the front steps, swinging on the railings and running down the pavement toward the Camden Town Underground Station. All that effort to look good for Evan, and now she was going arrive sweaty and breathless and late.

Now is the sun upon the highmost hill of this long day's journey . . . it is three long hours—yet she is not come . . .

Anita let out a yell of exhilaration as the speedboat skimmed the water and the wind whipped her hair against her cheeks.

"What do you think of your birthday surprise so far?" Evan shouted over the roar of the engine and the slap and smash of the keel on the water. "Like it?"

"Like it? I *love* it!" She let out another yell as the prow dipped and rose, cutting the rippling surface of the river like a hot knife. Fine spray stung her face. "This is the best present I've ever had!"

He smiled at her, lifting one hand off the wheel and reaching out to stroke her hair. Trembling a little at his touch, she took his hand. She kissed it and pressed it to her cheek. She was so happy that she felt like she was about to burst right out of her skin. She looked at Evan, her heart pounding. His dark blonde hair was flying back off his face. His wide chestnut brown eyes were narrowed against the wind, his lips spread in that gorgeous smile.

Evan guided the boat under one of the curved arches of Westminster Bridge. They were in shade for a heartbeat, then they shot out into bright sunlight again. To the right, Anita could see the Gothic spires of the Houses of Parliament, backed by the office blocks and towers of London, glittering against the clear blue sky.

"This is just the start of it," he went on. "We're going all the way up to Richmond. We can have something to eat and hang by the river for a while. Then I'm going to bring you back to town for some heavy-duty clubbing." He smiled at her. "Are you up for that?"

"You bet!"

Evan had not said a single word of complaint when she had turned up half an hour late at Monument Tube Station. He had simply kissed her hello, then taken her hand and led her down to the river. They had walked along a bobbing jetty and down to the small, sleek speedboat that he had hired for the day.

A few minutes later they had been speeding along the Thames with their curved wake lifting like a swan's wing behind them.

"Where did you learn to drive a boat?" Anita called.

Evan grinned at her. "Are you impressed?"

"Very!"

Evan laughed. "I'm multitalented—didn't you know?" He wiggled the steering wheel from side to side and the boat did a little jig on the water.

"Don't!" Anita gasped. She grabbed the metal rail. "Ow!" she exclaimed, snatching her hand back.

"What's wrong?" Evan called.

Anita rubbed her fingers. "I got a shock from the metal rail."

"It's your electric personality," he said, slowing down the boat as they passed a water taxi.

She frowned at him. "Don't make fun—it stings!" She was able to speak at a more natural level now that they weren't moving so fast. "It's been going on for a couple of weeks now. Every time I touch something metal, I get a shock. Dad says it's static electricity."

Evan shrugged. "So stop touching metal things."

"That's easier said than done," Anita pointed out. "How do I eat if I can't hold a knife and fork? It's very annoying. If it carries on, I'm going to have to start wearing gloves all the time." She shook her head. "It would happen to me!"

"Do weird things often happen to you, then?" Evan asked, looking at her sideways with an amused gleam in his eyes.

"Not weird, just awkward," Anita said. "Mum says I'm accident-prone. Dad says I was probably born under an unlucky star."

"I don't think that's true," Evan said.

Ahead of them, Lambeth Bridge was getting rapidly closer.

"I certainly don't feel unlucky right now," Anita said. She grinned.

"Good." He glanced at her again, suddenly looking more serious. "Anita? There's something important I have to tell you."

A buzz of nervous excitement went through her, and her stomach seemed to flip right over. She looked at him, half scared and half thrilled by what he might be about to say.

Call me but love, and I'll be new baptized . . .

But before Evan could say anything, a chill shadow swept over them, as if a dark hand had covered the sun. Anita looked up—the sky was cloudless.

Evan's head turned quickly and his eyes widened. A look of alarm twisted his face.

Anita gazed across the river, trying to make out what it was that had startled him. For a split second, she thought she saw a long, heavy dark shape wallowing low in the water.

"No!" Evan snarled between gritted teeth. "He can't have found us. Not now, of all times!"

Anita stared at him in confusion. What was he talking about?

He spun the wheel. The boat turned sharply, tipping on the water so that Anita staggered sideways, falling against Evan. Cold water dashed into her face, making her gasp for breath.

"Evan! Stop!" she shouted.

"No!" he howled, his voice wild and cracked. "He'll know we're here. He'll take you away from me!"

"What are you talking about? Evan, *please!*"

From the corner of her eye, she saw something huge and dark looming toward them. She just had time to turn her head as one of the stone pillars of Lambeth Bridge filled her vision.

A moment later, a violent impact sent her hurtling forward. Her ears filled with a brain-shredding noise. The sky whirled like a kaleidoscope. Then there was the deadly, freezing embrace of deep water. Red flames rimmed her sight and everything went black.

II

At first there was just the voice.

A man's voice, speaking soft and low, very close to her head.

" . . . mortals stay in mortal world, iron-clad with half-blind eyes they see . . ."

"Dad?"

No, not her father's voice.

It faded.

Then there were lights—bright white lights on a bright white ceiling. Concerned faces swam in and out of her line of vision.

She was lying on her back. There was pain—but it felt far away, as if it had nothing to do with her.

Soothing voices asked odd questions:

"Do you know where you are?"

"Can you tell me what day it is, Anita?"

"Squeeze my hand, Anita, as hard as you can.

That's good. That's just fine."

And then a different voice, distant but quite clear.

"She's a very lucky girl, Mrs. Palmer. If that police launch hadn't been nearby—well, it's doubtful she would have survived for more than a couple of minutes."

She heard her mother's voice.

"Oh, Clive, look at her—look at our poor girl. . . ."

And she was vaguely aware of her own voice, sounding weak and strained. "Evan? Is Evan all right . . . ? Please, I have to know. . . ."

Her father: "What's she saying?"

"She's asking about Evan."

Then the lights blurred and whirled and the voices faded away.

Lights again. Voices. The sensation of movement. The distant squeak of wheels. A gray-tiled ceiling sliding above her head. Someone holding her hand. Her mother's voice.

Cool sheets and a soft pillow for her head.

Floating away again.

Memories of the auditions for the school play came bubbling into her mind. Evan had surprised everyone. He was good—very good. He could make Shakespeare sound like everyday conversation.

Mrs. Wiseman had organized the first read-throughs of the play. Knowing her luck, Anita had guessed she'd end up playing the old nurse, especially as it was so obvious who was going to be playing Romeo.

All the same, she had learned a whole speech of Juliet's.

O Romeo, Romeo! Wherefore art thou, Romeo?

Voices again.

"Do you know what's she saying, Mrs. Palmer?"

"It's some of her lines from the play they've been rehearsing."

"Will she be out of hospital in time for that?"

"Oh, I should think so. She's had a bad concussion but she should be fine after a few days' rest. There's no real damage, just a few nasty bruises. She was lucky to be thrown clear when the boat hit the pillar."

"Mum?"

"Yes, honey, I'm here." A warm hand in hers.

"Where's Evan?"

Her father's voice. "He's okay, there's no need for you to worry about him."

"Dad?"

"We're both here. You're going to be fine."

"My eyes . . . so heavy . . . can't open them . . ."

"You've had a bang on the head, sweetheart," came her mum's voice. "Go to sleep now. We'll still be here when you wake up."

"How's Evan?"

"He's fine."

A third voice—a woman's, soft and gentle. "She'll probably sleep for a few hours. There's a vending machine in the hall outside the ward. It has soup and tea and coffee but it all tastes the same, so it doesn't matter which button you press."

"Will the boy be all right?"

"The doctors will know more in a few hours," the woman said. "We didn't find any personal information with his belongings. Do you know how we could contact his parents?"

"I'm sorry, we don't," said her mum. "I know it sounds ridiculous, but I'm not even sure where he lives."

"Do you know how the accident happened?"

"He hired a motorboat. He must have lost control of it as they were going under a bridge. They crashed into one of the pillars. . . ."

A black velvet curtain swept in across Anita's mind and oblivion took her.

Anita woke up to the subdued bustle of the hospital ward. She sat up, her head throbbing and spinning. The lights seemed very bright.

A pretty nurse with long curling red hair and a face full of freckles came over to her bed. "Steady now," she said, an Irish lilt in her voice. "Don't try to do too much too soon."

Anita blinked at her. "What time is it?"

"Four thirty," the nurse said. "You've been asleep all afternoon."

"How's Evan?" Her mouth was dry and there was a strange, bitter taste on her tongue.

"Your friend?" the nurse asked. "He's doing fine." She turned and pointed. "There he is."

Anita frowned to get her eyes to focus. Her bed

was at one end of a room that held five other beds. Across a stretch of gray linoleum, in the end bed on the opposite side of the bay, she saw a figure lying flat and still under the sheets. Evan's pale face was on the pillow, his eyes closed.

"Is he hurt badly?" Anita whispered.

"Not very badly," said the nurse. "He's sleeping."

"Is he going to die?" Anita heard her voice cracking and she felt tears sting her eyes.

"Hush, now, of course not," said the nurse. "He's been unconscious since the both of you were brought in here. But the doctors say there's nothing seriously wrong with him." She smiled. "It's like his brain has shut down for a while so he can heal himself. He could wake up anytime." She looked at Anita. "Are you thirsty? Can I bring you a drink?"

"My head hurts."

"Ah, it will when you go head-butting bridges, Anita," the nurse said with a smile. "What were you thinking?"

"It was a birthday present," Anita said, propping herself on her elbow to get a better look at Evan's face. "The boat ride, I mean."

"Is it your birthday, then?" said the nurse. She gave a wry smile. "Well, this is a fine place for a girl to spend her birthday!"

"No. It's tomorrow," Anita said. "My birthday's tomorrow." She looked into the nurse's kind face. "I don't really remember what happened."

"The boat went out of control and hit one of the

supports of Lambeth Bridge, so I'm told."

Anita threw her hands up over her face, over-whelmed by a flashback of stonework hurtling toward her. "Oh, yes!" She gasped. "We hit the bridge."

She took a deep breath and lowered her hands. "Can I go and speak to him?" she asked.

"Later, maybe. Right now you need to rest."

"Nurse!" It was a voice from a bed at the other end of the ward.

"I'm coming." The nurse gently pressed Anita back down onto the pillow. "Try and get some sleep," she said. She pointed to a button that dangled from a wire at the head of the bed. "Press that if you need anything."

"Yes. I will," Anita breathed as the nurse walked away. "Thank you."

She lay back, her head twisted on the pillow so she could see Evan's bed across the room.

What a mess. And everything had been so perfect.

Large, slow tears ran down into her hair, but inside she just felt numb and empty.

It was just before midnight. The curtains had been drawn around Anita's bed. Her mother and father were sitting on chairs pulled close together. They had been given special permission to be with her after nor-mal visiting hours, as long as they were quiet and didn't disturb any of the other patients.

It would be Anita's sixteenth birthday in exactly four and a half minutes.

Some birthday!

"We've called everyone," Mrs. Palmer said. "The party's postponed until you're back home."

Anita was sitting up, propped against her bunched-up pillows. She was feeling a little better— her head was clearer and the worst of the pain in her arms, legs, and back had faded, but she couldn't stop worrying about Evan. He still hadn't woken up.

The Irish nurse had told her there was nothing physically wrong with him. So why wouldn't he wake up?

"It's a shame about the party," her dad said, breaking into her thoughts. "I was looking forward to dancing the afternoon away in the garden."

"You're not invited," Anita joked. "If you think I'm going to be known in school as the girl with the world's most embarrassing dad, you can think again."

"But I've been practicing the Hustle especially," her father said. "Shall I give you a demonstration?"

"No, I don't think so," Anita said. "Mum, stop him."

"Clive, sit. Behave yourself."

A brief stab of pain in her head made Anita wince.

Mr. Palmer leaned forward, his eyes filled with concern. "How are you doing, my little girl?"

Anita clutched his hand. "I ache all over," she whispered. "And every time I close my eyes I see the bridge coming at us." She frowned. "I don't understand why Evan doesn't wake up. They say he's fine, but how can he be fine if he won't wake up?"

"They know what they're doing, honey," her mother said. "I'm sure he'll wake up when he's good and ready." She gave a smile full of sympathy. "By the way, Jade sends her love."

Anita nodded. "That's nice. Have you phoned everyone to put the party off?"

"Yes," her mother said. "I just told you that."

"Did you? Sorry. I'm a bit fuzzy right now."

"It's the concussion," her father said. "That's why they want to keep you in here overnight. When someone's been knocked out, they like to make sure nothing unexpected is going on in the old brain box." He stroked her hair. "Although I could've told them that there's never anything going on in yours—not a thing."

Anita smiled weakly. "Thanks, Dad."

"Don't mention it. Now then, is there anything we can do for you? There's a shop downstairs. We could get you some magazines, chocolates, a drink? I think they had some fruit too—fancy a few grapes?"

"They'll be closed at this time of night," Anita said. "And you know I hate grapes."

"That's not the point. You're in hospital—you have to have grapes."

Anita knew he was trying to make her laugh, but she couldn't—not yet. She rested her head back on the pillow.

"We should go soon," Mrs. Palmer said softly.

"Not before she gets her present," said her father. He looked at his watch. "It's midnight." He leaned over her and kissed her forehead. "Happy birthday, sweet sixteen."

"Thanks, Dad."

Her parents had gone home in the evening to freshen up and to fetch her some pajamas, and they had brought back one birthday present for her to open.

She knew it wasn't *their* present—they had told her their gift was too big to bring into the hospital. They wouldn't say what it was, but she hoped it was the new computer she'd mentioned about fifty times in the past few months.

"We've brought you something that came in the mail this morning," said her father.

Mrs. Palmer reached down and picked up a large, padded manila envelope."We assumed it must be a birthday present," she said, handing the envelope to Anita. It felt heavy and solid in her hands. "There's no return address, but the postmark is Richmond."

Anita looked at the bulky package. Her name and address were written in handwriting she didn't recognize. She frowned. Richmond? That was in West London.

"I don't know anyone who lives in Richmond," she said.

"Well, someone in Richmond obviously knows you," her father said. "Go on—open it up. I want to see what you've got."

Puzzled, Anita opened the envelope. Whatever was inside was wrapped in blue tissue paper. She reached in and carefully drew it out.

She peeled back the tissue.

"Oh, wow!" she breathed. It was a book—a very old-looking, leather-bound book with red and green tooling on the spine and inlaid emerald-colored decoration around the binding. It was worn and faded and there was a pearly glaze on the leather, as if generations of hands had polished it to a glowing sheen.

"Is there a letter or a card or anything with it?" her father asked.

Anita peered into the envelope. "No, nothing."

"What about inside the book?" her mother suggested.

Anita rested the book in her lap and opened the cover. Nothing. She turned the thick, ivory-colored pages.

The book was blank. Anita gave her parents a puzzled look. "It's lovely," she said. "But it's a weird thing to give someone." A book with no writing in it? And sent anonymously too.

"It's beautiful, though, isn't it?" her father said, running a finger along the leather binding. "Amazing workmanship. It looks like an antique. It's probably valuable."

Anita looked suspiciously at her parents. "Are you absolutely certain you don't know who it's from?"

"No, honey," her mother promised. "We haven't a clue. Maybe Evan sent it as a surprise?"

"I don't see why he would," Anita said. "Besides, the boat trip was my present."

"You should ask him when he wakes up," said her father.

"Yes, I'll do that." She carefully turned more of the old pages. All were blank.

"You could use it as a notebook for school," her mother suggested. "Or as a diary."

"That's a good idea," Anita said. She closed the book and rested her hands on the smooth, cool leather. She smiled. "First entry: Dear diary, who in the world could have sent me this mysterious book?"

"You shouldn't use a ballpoint pen, though," her father warned. "That book is far too grand for anything like that." He grinned. "What you really need is a quill. I'll see if the ducks in the park can spare a wing feather or two."

"You leave those ducks alone," Anita said. "I'll buy a really posh fountain pen the minute I get out of here."

"That's the idea," her father said. "And now I think it's time we went home. You need to sleep." He leaned over and kissed her forehead. "Look after yourself."

"I will."

Her mother leaned over her for a kiss. "Don't worry about Evan," she whispered as their cheeks touched. "I'm sure he'll wake up soon."

They drew the curtains back from around her bed and walked quietly away along the dimly lit ward. Her dad turned to smile and wave before he vanished through the double doors. Anita tried to wave back, but her limbs felt as heavy as stone and her head was beginning to ache again.

She lay back in the cradle of pillows, her hands resting on the book, her head turned to look at Evan's darkened bed. She just wanted him to wake up so she could look into his eyes and know he was all right.

Why wouldn't he wake up?

She tried to remember how the accident had happened.

She saw them speeding along under a clear blue sky.

He had said something.

Her head throbbed.

"There's something important I have to tell you."

Yes. That was it.

And then?

She remembered a shadow over the sun.

Panic in his voice. He was shouting something but she couldn't remember what.

There was something dim and indistinct in the water. Something big, right in front of them. Not the bridge, something else. Like . . . like . . . no! It was gone.

Then the bridge rushing forward.

And then nothing.

Nothing.

It was the maddening itching in her back that woke her up. It was those two stupid bites on her shoulder blades again—only they seemed to have gotten a lot worse.

It was some time in the middle of the night. The ward was quiet and only dimly lit. Soft footsteps sounded in the distance. Evan's bed was shrouded in darkness.

Anita twisted her arm up behind herself to try and scratch. Through the white satin of her pajama top she could feel distinct lumps under her fingertips. No, not lumps. Ridges. Two raised parallel ridges running down her shoulder blades.

She sat up, alarmed now and wide awake. She forced her hand down inside the back of her pajama jacket, straining to touch one of the ridges.

The welt felt tender and sore. There was a warm wetness on her fingers—the skin was broken. She pulled her hand out and held her fingers up close to her face in the half-dark. She had expected to see blood—but the wetness was clear and thick and slippery.

She looked around at the sleeping figures in the nearby beds. She didn't want to call a nurse. The whole thing seemed absurd, almost unreal. The bathroom was only a little way off. There were mirrors in there, and she would be able to see what was going on with her back.

She drew the covers down and slipped out of bed. She stood at her bedside, swaying a little and feeling very peculiar. Light-headed.

No, not just light-headed.

Her whole body felt light. Insubstantial—as if she was in a dream.

She took a step forward and felt herself almost float across the floor.

She smiled, enjoying the weird sensation.

Light as a feather, she glided across the floor. A black-haired nurse sat at the desk in a small pool of bright light. She looked up. Anita indicated that she was heading for the bathroom. The nurse nodded and lowered her head again.

Anita drifted forward. She pushed open the bathroom door and floated through.

The lights were much brighter in here. There was a row of sinks opposite the toilet stalls. Over each sink was a square mirror.

She felt suddenly dizzy and grabbed the edge of a sink to stop herself from falling. It felt like there were whirlwinds spinning through her body. She closed her eyes. Now it felt as if she was moving at enormous speed, racing through the air, breathless and unable to stop.

She opened her eyes, gasping.

She reached for a tap, needing a splash of cold water on her face.

As she touched the tap, an arc of blue fire flared from her fingertips and a fizzing, burning pain shot up to her shoulder. She let out a cry, cradling her arm against herself.

And then a pain hit her that blotted out everything else. She screamed as two bolts of intense agony stabbed her in the back. The pain dragged downward, as if someone was slashing her shoulder blades with razors.

She fell to her knees, doubled over.

Something pushed against the back of her pajama top.

There was a tearing sound.

There was something *growing* on her back—two things that flexed and expanded like the opening of long-fingered hands.

The pain wasn't like scalpels digging into her flesh now—it was like when she had sat with her legs curled up under her for too long. The exquisitely unbearable feeling of pins and needles as the blood begins to course again. Except that it wasn't in a leg—it was in something else.

Anita was on her hands and knees on the floor, her limbs folded under her, her head in her arms, her eyes tightly shut.

And she could feel these things—these two unbelievable growths that had sprouted from her back. They were unfolding and spreading and expanding.

She lay huddled on the cold floor for several minutes, too scared to move, almost too scared to breathe. Gradually the discomfort faded and the fear loosened its grip on her.

She lifted her head.

Strange new muscles flexed on her back and she felt the air stir. She drew herself up onto her hands and knees. There was no pain now. Grasping the rim of the sink, she pulled herself to her feet.

She turned to face the mirror.

"What the . . . ?"

There was her face—her familiar face, ash pale now with shock, gazing in utter disbelief out of the glass. And there, lifting high behind her shoulders, was a pair of iridescent gossamer-light wings.

Anita stared at them. They were so beautiful and fine and delicate, stretching behind her like the wings of a dragonfly. She flexed her shoulders and the wings quivered, changing color constantly as the harsh yellow light struck them.

"I've got wings . . ." she breathed. Her face split into a wide, radiant smile as the wings beat faster, whipping her hair around her face.

She saw her reflection rise in the mirror and felt the rim of the sink fall away from her hands. She looked down and saw that her feet had lifted clear of the floor.

As easy as a feather floating on the breeze, she glided toward the window. It was closed and locked, but when she touched the lock with her fingertips, it clicked open and the window sprang wide.

Cool night air wafted over her.

Without thinking what she was doing, Anita dived headfirst through the window and soared up into the clear night sky.

She looked down at the lights of the city. They twinkled and sparkled beneath her, lovely but somehow remote, like things seen from an airplane. Cars moved in ribbons on the canyon streets—ribbons of white and ribbons of red. She could see necklaces of light framing the sinuous shape of the River Thames. Bridges cut across the indigo water, lit up like party decorations. Boats shone and shimmered, casting their shattered images down onto the inky river.

Anita spread her arms, lifting her face to the stars and to the slender crescent moon, arching her back as she flew higher.

"I'm flying!" she screamed.

As a child, she had often dreamed of flying. Small dreams of swishing through the treetops and of grazing the chimney—swooping and diving while her friends watched her, breathless with envy.

And the weirdest thing of all was that now it was really happening, it didn't feel the least bit strange.

The night wind fluttered through her pajamas and tugged at her hair as she pirouetted above the rooftops.

"I must look like an angel," she said aloud. She spun and dived, gazing down as she swooped low over the streets.

Can anyone see me?

She waved. "Hey! Up here!"

But no one was looking up into the sky.

She frowned. "How am I going to explain this to Mum?"

The world below her rippled like a reflection when a stone is dropped into black water. The streets and buildings of the city wavered and trembled and then, in an instant, all the lights of London went out.

For a moment Anita was so startled that she forgot to beat her wings.

She fell halfway to the ground before she remembered to fly again. She brought her new muscles into play, her wings scooping the air. The action felt as natural as moving an arm or a leg, and she seemed instinctively to understand how to angle her body to get lift and balance.

The city had gone!

The stars still glittered above her, but below her there was only a deep empty darkness.

Beating her wings, Anita wheeled around to look at the round face of the full moon.

It had not been like that before. The moon over London had been just a sliver—a new moon on its second or third night.

But now it was full, and so close that she could see the shadows that scarred its white face.

She looked down, her eyes adjusting to the shadows.

The River Thames still looped and coiled its way through the land. But the bright lights of London had vanished. And the night seemed less dark—it was more of a blue-gray twilight, rich and deep and sleepy.

On the northern banks of the river lay a vast palace. She looked down on turrets and keeps and gatehouses and courtyards, on towers and battlements and colonnades that seemed to stretch on forever. And there were bridges over the river, and more clusters of buildings that hugged the south bank. And beyond them, there was a dark, dense forest.

Fascinated, Anita glided lower, drawn toward the points of light that glowed here and there, like candles flickering in glassless windows.

But as she came closer, she saw that many of the walls and buildings were smashed and broken. Troubled, she swooped over the river. She came to a bridge, but it was half destroyed, its arches all fallen down into ruin. Hunks of masonry jutted out of the black water like jagged teeth.

She flew over the palace. The roofs of great halls were slumped and cracked, the soaring towers torn open and hollowed out.

It was as if warfare had passed over the land and left only decay and desolation.

Tears pricked Anita's eyes. It shouldn't be like this. *This was not how she remembered it.*

"No!" She turned and flew back up into the twilight sky. *"No!"*

There should have been lights—thousands of blazing lights, each outdoing the other to banish every shadow. There should have been music and laughter and dancing and singing. There should have been barges and launches and wherries on the river.

There should be life!

But as she soared skyward, with tears flooding down her cheeks and a sense of wrenching loss in her heart, she felt the strength fading from her wings.

The muscles seemed to waste away on her back.

She glanced in alarm over her shoulder: The rainbow-colored gauze of her wings had become dull, and the glorious gossamer spread was shriveling and withering.

And even as she looked, the wings shredded and fell away from her back.

She clawed the air in terror, tried to remember which muscles she had flexed to lift her.

But she no longer had the power of flight.

Her wings were gone.

Turning over and over in the air, she plunged earthward like a stone.

III

"Anita? Come on, dear—up you get."

She felt chilled to the bone. She was sprawled face down on a cold, hard surface.

Gentle but strong hands lifted her and turned her so that she was sitting up.

She opened her eyes. The night nurse was crouched at her side, holding her shoulders. She was back in the hospital bathroom.

"What happened?" she asked.

"You fainted, Anita," said the nurse. "Can you stand on your own, or should I call someone?"

"No, I think I can get up." Using the nurse's shoulder as a support, Anita got to her feet.

"You should have called someone if you were feeling giddy," said the nurse, looking closely at her.

"I didn't," Anita said. She blinked, still woolly-headed. "Feel giddy, I mean. How long have I been in here?"

"Ten minutes at most," said the nurse. "You seemed to be taking a long time, so I came to check. Do you still need to go?"

"Sorry?"

The nurse nodded toward the stalls.

Anita shook her head. She twisted her head to look at the window. It was closed and locked.

She let out a breath of astonished laughter.

It had been so real.

She glanced at herself in the mirror.

No wings.

Of course not. Are you out of your mind?

"Let's get you back to bed," said the nurse. She put an arm around Anita's back. "What's happened here?" she exclaimed, drawing back. "You've made a real mess of your pajama top."

Anita stiffened. "What do you mean?"

"There are two long tears," said the nurse, running her finger down the ripped fabric. "What a shame. You must have done it when you fell over."

Anita looked at the nurse. "That's where my wings came through," she said.

The nurse gazed quizzically at her. "Well, that would certainly explain it," she said. "Shall we get you back to bed?"

"Is there anything on my back?"

The nurse smiled. "You don't have wings, if that's what you mean."

"No. Anything. Red marks."

The nurse opened the tears in the top and examined her back. "There's nothing there," she reported. "Clean as a whistle."

Anita turned and looked into her eyes. "What's it like when you go insane?" she asked softly.

The nurse studied her for a long moment. "You've had quite a rough day," she said. "Come on, let's get you back to bed." She guided Anita out of the bathroom and across to her bed.

Anita held her gaze. "Will you tell me the truth about something?"

"Certainly, if I can," the nurse said.

"Is Evan going to be all right?"

The nurse gave her a thoughtful look. "The doctors are a bit puzzled that he hasn't woken up yet," she admitted finally. "He's had a CT scan and there's nothing wrong that they can see."

"A CT scan?"

"It means that they've had a good look at his brain. It's working fine, as far as they can tell, but he doesn't seem to want to wake up just yet."

Anita swallowed. "I heard somewhere that the longer a person is in a coma, the more chance there is for something to go wrong inside their head."

"That's generally true," the nurse agreed. "But your boyfriend isn't in a coma. He's just fast asleep." She smiled. "He could wake up at any minute."

"Really?"

The nurse nodded. "Really." She drew back the

sheets for Anita to climb into bed. "It's your birthday today, isn't it? We found something among Evan's things you might like to see. Just wait a moment."

She was gone for less than a minute. She came back with a small package in her hand. She drew the curtains around Anita's bed and switched on the over-bed light.

The package was wrapped in red paper and there was a gift tag attached.

For Anita. Wishing you the very happiest of birthdays. Love, Evan.

"He must have meant to give this to me yesterday," Anita said quietly, turning the package over in her hands. "Maybe I should wait until he wakes up before I open it."

"Oh, I don't think he'd mind," the nurse said. "Go on, open it."

Anita carefully peeled off the sticky tape and unfolded the scarlet wrapping paper. Inside was a black box. She lifted the lid and opened layers of white tissue.

Just when she was beginning to think the box was empty, she saw a pendant nestled in the tissue paper, suspended from a fine chain that looked as if it had been made from spun glass. The pendant was shaped like a long-tailed teardrop, amber in color and as lustrous as a pearl.

Anita bit her lip. She drew the chain up and lifted the pendant from the box. It hung heavy in the air, glowing with light.

"Well, isn't that lovely," said the nurse.

"Yes," Anita whispered. "It's absolutely beautiful."

She raised her arm, bringing the pendant closer to her face. Deep in the heart of the amber teardrop, she could see a leaf of dark light that moved like a trapped flame.

"Could you help me put it on?"

She leaned forward and the nurse closed the clasp at the back of her neck. The pendant was warm against her skin. Anita felt a desperate, urgent need to be with Evan—even if only for a few seconds.

"I have to thank him, even if he can't hear me," she pleaded. "Can I go and sit with him? Just for a minute or two?"

"In the morning you can," the nurse said. "He might even be up and about himself by then." She smiled down at Anita. "Now then, get some sleep."

Anita settled back into the pillows, one hand cradling the pendant. The nurse arranged the sheets around her shoulders. "Press the button if you need me." She switched off the light and slipped through the curtains.

Anita's eyes began to close, her eyelids suddenly as heavy as lead.

Good night, good night! Parting is such sweet sorrow, that I should say good night till it be morrow.

Anita awoke into the same quiet darkness. Her fingers still held the amber pendant. She smiled. Evan's lovely gift. She reached out and felt for her watch on the bedside table. The luminous dial showed that it was only five thirty in the morning, but she felt oddly awake and alert.

She drew herself up and switched on the over-bed lamp. A bright pool of light flooded down onto her.

She didn't know what to think about the previous night. About the wings and all that. It was all quite crazy. Except she didn't *feel* as if she was going crazy. Surely she'd be able to tell?

She leaned over and picked up her new book from the bedside table. She rested it in her lap, stroking the supple leather. As soon as she got herself a good pen, she was going to write down everything she could remember about her flight. It didn't matter whether or not it was real—it had been totally amazing.

She opened the front cover. The ivory-colored pages were thick and textured like cloth. She ran her hand over the paper.

She turned the first crisp, heavy leaf.

The last time she had looked, the page had been quite blank, she was absolutely certain of that; but now the page held lines of clear, dark writing printed in an ornate, gothic script.

> *Faeries tread the faerie path*
> *Amber-trapped though moth-wing light*
>   *they be*
> *Mortals stay in mortal world*
> *Iron-clad with half-blind eyes they see*

One alone will walk both worlds
Daughter last of daughters seven
With her true love by her side
Honest hand in true love given

Anita had no idea what the words meant, but they sounded Shakespearean.

She felt strangely distracted and remote from reality. "I must be dreaming again," she murmured. "Just like last night."

Smiling, she turned the page.

There was more writing. A lot more.

On this day was born Princess Tania, the seventh daughter of our glorious King Oberon and our blessed Queen Titania. And the bells rang out throughout the Realm at the joyful news.

It sounded like a fairy story, yet it was written in archaic, flowery language that a child would struggle to understand. A fairy story for grown-ups, perhaps?

Frowning, Anita read on. There were long descriptions of celebrations and visits by important people and endless domestic details about the first few days of the baby's life. The writing began to swim in front of her eyes. Anita yawned and her hand slipped off the book. She was shaken back into wakefulness as the pages began to turn on their own. As she watched, her eyes wide in alarm, the book settled into stillness a few dozen pages on, where a new chapter started.

Upon the eve of her sixteenth birthday, Princess Tania prepared herself for her marriage to the young Lord Gabriel

Drake of Caer Liel in Weir. She was glad and joyful, for he was high-born and handsome and filled with grace.

That sounded more interesting. Anita settled back in the bunched-up pillows and began to read.

On the night before her wedding day, Princess Tania's bed was strewn with rose petals and with perfumes of sandalwood and evening primrose, so that her dreams should be blessed and sweet. Then she was left alone to sleep one final time in the bedchamber she had known since childhood.

Anita smiled as she read the description of Tania sitting up in her massive four-poster bed, holding a red rose that her fiancé had given her, and gazing happily out of her casement window at the full moon.

And in the quiet hour before midnight, there came upon Princess Tania's door a soft knocking. Princess Tania bade the person to enter. It was her sister Princess Rathina, come to spend a few last moments with her. They spoke together and made merry, but their bliss was destroyed when Princess Tania all of a sudden vanished without trace from her bedchamber.

Anita blinked in surprise. She went back and read that section a second time just to make sure she hadn't misunderstood.

No, Princess Tania had definitely vanished.

Princess Rathina was greatly distressed at the disappearance of her beloved sister, and she ran from room to room of the Royal Apartments, awaking everyone with her cries. Soon all the palace was astir and word spread from chamber to chamber, from tower to tower, from battlement to battlement, even to the most far-flung regions of the Great Palace—Princess Tania was lost.

Anita turned the page.

And at dawn the next day, the day that should have been his wedding day, the youthful Lord Drake knelt before King Oberon and made a vow that he would not cease searching for his lost love, even if his quest took him seven times seventy years.

And that was it. The story stopped dead halfway down the page. Anita turned the next page, and the next, and the next, but there was nothing else. The rest of the book was blank. She read the last paragraph again, wondering if she'd missed something.

She looked up in surprise. A soft male voice had started to speak the words aloud as she was reading them. A gentle, murmuring voice that seemed to be coming from very close to her head.

But there was no one there.

"Who are you?" she whispered.

There was no reply.

"What's happening?"

Silence.

"I'm not scared," Anita said to the empty air. "I just want to know what's going on."

A voice echoed her words. "What's going on?"

But it wasn't the man's voice; it was a brisk, lowered female voice, and it came from beyond the curtains that surrounded Anita's bed.

"I don't know, Sister. He was there a few minutes ago." Anita recognized the second voice as the nurse who had picked her up off the bathroom floor.

"I'll check the men's bathroom," the first voice said. "He can't have gone far."

Anita heard footsteps moving rapidly out of the room. She put down her book and slipped out from between the sheets. She drew open the curtains. The night nurse was standing at the foot of Evan's bed.

The covers had been thrown back.

The bed was empty.

Anita felt a sudden rush of joy. Evan had woken up! He was all right. The relief made her feel dizzy.

She padded over to where the nurse was standing.

"Where is he?" she asked.

The nurse looked at her. "Quiet, now. We don't want to wake everyone up," she said. "And you shouldn't be out of bed at this hour."

"I want to see Evan," Anita said. She looked around, expecting him to be standing somewhere nearby. "Where is he?"

Before the nurse had the time to reply, there was the sharp click of heels along the floor. The Ward Sister approached them. "He's not in the bathroom," she reported. "I'll stay on the ward, nurse. You go and find him—quickly, please. We can't have patients wandering around the hospital unattended."

The nurse nodded and vanished into the shadowy corridor.

Anita stared at the Ward Sister. Where was Evan?

"We'll find him, don't you worry," the Ward Sister said. "Meanwhile, I think you'd be better off back in bed."

Anita allowed herself to be shepherded across the room, but she was too excited to sleep, or even to lie down.

She leaned against her pillows, fingering her amber pendant and waiting for the moment when Evan would appear at her bedside and everything would be all right again.

Anita was sitting up in her bed, staring at the far wall, her fist tightly clutching the amber pendant.

It was three hours later. Evan had not been found.

The Irish nurse sat on the edge of the bed, holding Anita's free hand in both of hers.

"Where is he?" Anita murmured. She gazed bewildered at the nurse. "Where could he have gone?"

"Don't worry," the nurse said. "He couldn't have gone far. None of his clothes are missing."

"But he could be lying unconscious somewhere," Anita said. "He could be hurt."

"Don't start imagining the worst," the nurse chided her. "I expect he woke up feeling a bit disorientated and wandered off in a daze. The police have been told to keep a lookout for him just in case he got out of the building. If he's tottering about the streets in a hospital gown, he'll soon be found and brought back."

Anita bit her lip. "I hope so."

The nurse stood up, slipping her hand out of Anita's. She smiled. "They'll find him, don't you worry."

Anita gazed after her as she walked out of the room, trying not to imagine Evan wandering the corridors confused and in pain, his head throbbing so much that he couldn't think straight.

She turned her head to stare out of the window at the far end of the ward.

It was a bright, sunny day out there.

It was a bright, sunny day and Evan was stumbling around after a serious accident. He could fall and injure himself. He could walk in front of a car.

Anita shook her head. She had to keep believing that Evan would be found safe and sound, that he would be brought back to her and everything would be all right.

She closed her eyes and saw the bleached image of the window floating on the inside of her eyelids.

She leaned back into the pillows, watching the drifting white stain behind her closed eyes.

She frowned. Instead of blurring and fading, the fuzzy light-stain seemed to be shrinking and altering and taking on a definite shape.

It became the white silhouette of a person hovering behind her eyelids. It was featureless and two-dimensional, but it was definitely the outline of a human being—a man.

Evan?

As she watched, the figure walked forward and reached out a hand to her.

With a gasp, Anita opened her eyes.

It wasn't Evan.

The man stood about twenty feet away from her, dressed in the sort of clothes they would be using for the school play, clothes from the time of Elizabeth I— a long, black fur-lined cloak, a doublet and hose of dark red material, and knee-high leather boots. He smiled and gave a slight bow. He was handsome, with high cheekbones, deep-set eyes, and dark hair drawn back off his face. Anita could see that he was only a few years older than she was.

But there was still something wrong with the image. He was grainy and slightly out of focus like a poorly recorded video, and Anita could see the walls through him.

"Come to me."

It was the same low, melodic voice that she had heard reading aloud from her book.

"Who are you?" she breathed.

"Come to me and all will be revealed." The young man's image flickered and faded for a moment and a new note of urgency entered his voice. "There is little time, my lady. You must come to me."

Convinced that she was dreaming again, Anita got out of bed.

She walked toward him, but although his legs didn't move, he drifted away from her.

Now he was holding both hands out toward her.

She padded across the cold floor, but again, he floated back.

She followed him to the end of the ward, to a door that led to a television lounge. He passed right through the closed door.

"Come to me."

"I'm *trying*."

She opened the door to the lounge. A few people looked up at her without interest. But none of them looked at the man, even though he was standing right in front of the television.

The man glided backward to an outer door that led onto a small balcony.

Anita opened the door and stepped outside into the bright sunshine. There were a few armchairs pulled up to small plastic tables, but there were no other patients out there.

The beckoning figure was even harder to see now.

"Attend me closely, my lady." His voice was just a murmur. "You have the power. You must reach for me. Dismiss from your mind all other thoughts. Reach out and touch my hand. Think of nothing else."

Anita concentrated hard on his outstretched hand. She moved toward him, and this time he did not drift away from her. She came closer, staring at his hand.

None of this is real, she told herself.

It was nothing as exciting as her flying dream, but all the same, there was something intriguing about the handsome young man, and she wanted to know where he was taking her.

Only a couple of feet separated them now.

"Come, my lady," he urged again.

He was leaning forward, his arm stretched to its full length, his fingers straining toward her.

With a final effort, she lunged at him.

Their hands touched.

He gave a triumphant shout and his eyes flashed. His long fingers closed around her wrist and he pulled hard.

Anita let out a yelp of pain as she was jerked off her feet.

And as she stumbled forward, the hospital balcony and the nearby buildings and the blue sky and the white sun all evaporated in front of her eyes and she was plunged into a deep, velvet darkness.

"Where am I?" Anita's voice echoed in her ears.

"Home, my lady," said the man, draping his cloak around her shoulders to cover her pajamas. "Your long exile is at an end."

Anita turned to him. "I'm sorry," she said. "Who exactly do you think I am?"

"You are Princess Tania, seventh daughter of King Oberon and Queen Titania," he announced.

She smiled crookedly. Either this was the most vivid dream she had ever experienced, or she was going completely crazy.

"I see," she said. "And you would be . . . ?"

He bowed low. "I am Gabriel Drake, the Duke of Weir."

The leather-bound book! She was inside the fairy tale! Gabriel Drake was the man who had been going to marry the lost princess.

"This is cool," Anita said. "What a shame that I'm going to wake up back in hospital any moment now."

"You are not asleep." He took her by the elbow and gently turned her around. "Behold your birth-place—behold the Royal Palace of Faerie."

They were standing on a wooden wharf that jutted out over a wide, dark river. On the far banks, under a blue-gray sky draped with a lacework of stars, lay a vast palace that stretched as far as she could see in both directions. Every room, every tower, every wall was adorned with lights—thousands of lights, throwing their dancing reflections onto the river.

The river was filled with boats, festooned with bobbing lanterns. Music drifted across the water, the sound of harps and flutes and rattling tambourines accompanied by singing and laughter.

Rising in a long, slender span to their left was an ornate bridge of white stone with tall towers at either end. The bridge was lit with flickering torches along its whole length, so that its arc was mirrored in the rippling black water.

Anita knew where she was in an instant. It was the same river and castle that she had seen in her flight the previous night, except that now it was whole and filled with life.

Just as she remembered.

"Yes!" she breathed. "*That's* what it should look like!"

"Permit me to escort you, my lady." Gabriel Drake

offered his hand to her. She took it and he led her toward the bridge.

They climbed a set of stone steps onto the bridge. She walked across the river, hand in hand with the young lord, breathing in the smell of flowers that hung in baskets all along the bridge. She knew some of the aromas—her mother was a keen gardener and often filled the house with fresh-cut flowers. Among other, stranger perfumes, she recognized night-scented stock and evening primrose and moonflower.

She glanced at Gabriel Drake's face. He was very good-looking, she thought, although his deep-set silver eyes were a bit disconcerting. She wondered for a moment why he looked so very happy—then it struck her that it must be because he thought he'd found his long-lost bride.

She hesitated, wondering where this astounding dream would take her next. Not to the altar, she hoped. She wasn't too keen on the idea of getting married to a total stranger—even if he was strikingly attractive and this was only a dream.

"What do I call you?" she asked him. "Duke? Your Lordship? Mr. Drake?"

He raised his eyebrows very slightly. "You may name me your most devoted servant."

"I can hardly call you that all the time."

"Once, you called me beloved," he said.

She wrinkled her nose. "I don't think I can call you that, either, if you don't mind. I'm a princess, right?"

"Verily."

"I'll take that as a yes," Anita said. "In that case, I'll call you Gabriel." She frowned. "This is incredible," she said. "I mean, look at this place! Who'd have thought my imagination would come up with all this?"

"The realm and dominion of your gracious father has lasted for eternity, my lady," Gabriel said.

"If you say so."

At the end of the bridge, a long tongue of white flagstones led to an archway in a high wall. Beyond the arch was a square courtyard. A hundred windows cast light onto them as they crossed the courtyard, Gabriel's boots ringing on the cobbles. He led her up a short flight of stairs and through an arched doorway.

They walked along a candlelit corridor with oak-paneled walls and tall, mullioned windows. Paintings hung on the walls—portraits of beautiful people in fabulous clothes. Anita noticed that the children in these pictures had fine shining wings, just like the wings she had in her other dream. The adults were all wingless.

Beyond closed doors, she could hear the sound of tinkling music and of voices, but the corridor itself was empty.

They passed through a series of rooms lit by candelabras and filled with such a display of ornate furniture and elegant statuary and exquisite tapestries and artworks that it was like walking through a museum.

"If I'd known I was capable of dreaming up stuff

like this, I'd have spent a lot more time in bed," Anita said. She looked at Gabriel. "Where are we going?"

"To the Great Hall, my lady."

He drew her through a low doorway that led to a narrow spiral staircase. At the top there was another door. Through it, Anita could hear the sound of more laughter and of bright, chiming music that came from stringed instruments.

"Sounds like someone's having a party," she said.

"It is the feast of the White Hart."

Gabriel threw open the door and the noise suddenly became much louder. He ushered her onto a high gallery overlooking a huge hall with a high, elaborately vaulted wooden roof and dark-paneled walls hung with tapestries. Flickering yellow candles set in sconces between the tapestries and two chandeliers, also lit with candles, hung from the ceiling. Anita gazed down over the balustrade. The hall was full of people, all dressed in dazzling Elizabethan clothes. At the far end of the hall was a long, wide table filled with trays and bowls and dishes of food. Anita could smell the roast meat. And she could see a small band of musicians gathered in a corner, playing curious, old-fashioned instruments. At the center of the table were two thrones under a scarlet awning. Seated side by side on the thrones were a man and a woman.

The man was dressed in a fur-trimmed black doublet, which was covered in white embroidery and had puffed sleeves that were slashed to show flashes of a white lining. There was a white ruff at his neck and a simple white crown on his golden hair, encrusted with black jewels. He had a close-cut beard and mustache; high, slanted cheekbones; and deep, piercingly blue eyes.

The woman was wearing a pale blue dress with a lacework of white embroidery over the bodice and the long, slashed sleeves. She had a high ruff that sparkled as if there were white jewels sewn into it. She had bright, wide-set green eyes, snow white skin, and vividly red lips. Set among the curls of her up-drawn red hair was a sapphire-colored coronet set with black stones that flashed in the candlelight.

As Anita gazed down at them, she felt as if she was teetering on the brink of a great dark ocean of memories.

A few others sat at the table, but most of the people were dancing. The steps of the dance were slow and intricate; the men and women weaving in and out of one another in an elaborate pattern that never faltered.

There was a huge stone fireplace, but the fire was not lit and the hearth was filled with vases of flowers.

"It's beautiful," she whispered.

But then a solitary, unmoving figure caught her attention.

He was sitting on a stool beside the fireplace. His elbows were on his knees and his head was in his hands, as if he was unaware of the revelries going on all around him. He had long golden hair and he was wearing a green doublet and hose trimmed with yellow thread. But there was something about him—something in the way his hair curled, something in his posture—that Anita felt sure she recognized.

"Who's that?" she asked, pulling her hand away from Gabriel's as she leaned farther out over the banister rail. "I know him."

The moment she let go of Gabriel's hand, everything changed.

The hall was plunged into a yellowish half-light. The dancers all dissolved away. The music stopped abruptly. The scent of roasted meat was gone. The long table was bare and the chairs and the two thrones were empty. A coldness wafted up from the hall, along with the musty smell of damp decay.

The only remaining light came from a few yellow candles set on the mantelpiece.

The only person left in the hall was the man in green.

As Anita stared down at him, he lifted his head out of his hands and looked up at her, and in the flickering light she saw his face.

It was Evan.

IV

For a few moments, Anita gazed down in sheer astonishment. Then a relieved smile spread across her face.

She'd found Evan and he was perfectly safe.

"Evan!" she called. "Where have you been? Everyone's looking for you."

He glanced up at her for a moment, his face totally expressionless. Then he looked away again.

Puzzled, Anita turned to Gabriel. He was standing beside her, one hand on the polished wooden banister, looking down at Evan with a faint smile on his face.

Evan's voice came up to them. "Well met, my lord."

"Our enterprise has met with success, Edric," Gabriel said. "The lost one has been found, due in no small part to your endeavors."

Edric? Who's Edric? Wait, this doesn't make sense.

Evan bowed his head. "Your eternal servant, my lord," he said.

"Evan?" Anita called down. "What's going on? Why are you talking like that?"

"My lady." Gabriel touched her arm. "The man you knew as Evan is my bonded servant, Edric Chanticleer. I sent him into the Mortal World to find you and bring you home to your rightful place."

Anita gave a breathless laugh. "No, you've got it all wrong," she said. "He's my boyfriend."

Gabriel gazed at her with his deep silvery eyes and she felt a shiver of unease. What was going on? Her dream was getting out of hand. This wasn't how it should be.

She put her hand to her head, struggling to clear her thoughts. "Listen," she said. "I'm not a princess. This place isn't real. That guy down there is my boyfriend, and his name is Evan Thomas." She stared hard at Gabriel. "And I'd really like to wake up now, please, before this gets any weirder."

Gabriel smiled at her, his gray eyes filled with compassion. "My lady, you have lived too long in the nightmare of the Mortal World. It is time for you to wake and remember who you truly are."

Anita shook her head. "No," she insisted. "Evan and I had an accident, and I think maybe my brain got a bit scrambled. Or it could be the painkillers they gave me, which might be giving me these crazy dreams." She looked straight into Gabriel's eyes. "Either way, you're not real. Evan is my boyfriend, and just before the boat hit the bridge, he was going to tell me he loved me."

Gabriel shook his head. "Not so," he said softly. "He was going to tell you who you really are—Princess Tania, seventh daughter of King Oberon and Queen Titania—and that he had been sent to bring you home."

Anita turned away from him and leaned over the banister. "Tell him the truth, Evan!" she begged.

The man in green lifted his head and looked at her. *Looked at her with Evan's eyes*. "The truth is as Lord Drake has told you," he said. "I am but his lordship's servant, sent to bring you back to Faerie."

"No!" Anita shouted. "You love me and I love you. Please, Evan, don't do this to me."

She felt as if the dream was spiraling away from her, darkening and warping and changing into a terrifying, spiteful nightmare. Why would her mind do this to her?

Evan turned to Gabriel. "Do I have your leave to depart, my lord?"

"Yes, you may go," Gabriel said. "You have done well."

Evan stood up, bowed, and walked the length of the hall to a pair of wide doors that stood open. Anita stared after him, too miserable and disturbed to speak. At the doorway, Evan turned and gave one final bow before stepping back and drawing the doors closed behind him.

The echoing boom of the closing doors struck

Anita like a blow to her stomach. Her mind was flooded with feelings of hurt and betrayal. Could this be true? Did this mean that Evan had never loved her? Had it all been pretense?

In a shadowy corner of her mind, a small voice screamed that none of this could possibly be real. But it *felt* real—it felt all too real, and the emotions that burned through her were as intense as anything she had ever known in her life.

"Why am I here?" she whispered. "Why is this happening?" She closed her eyes and leaned on the wooden rail.

Her thoughts were broken by that familiar soft, velvet voice. "By your leave, my lady, I would like to take you to your father."

Anita opened her eyes and stared at him in surprise. "My dad? He's here?"

"He has waited long for your return, my lady."

"Not *that* long," Anita pointed out. "I saw him only last night."

"Not for five times a hundred years have you beheld your father, the High King Oberon," Gabriel said.

"Oh, right, *him*," Anita said. "I thought you meant— Well, never mind." She straightened up. "Okay, Gabriel, since I seem to be stuck in this dream for the time being, I might as well go along with it. Take me to the King."

Gabriel lifted a candle from a sconce on the wall and opened the small door that led down from the gallery. "After you, my lady."

She raised one eyebrow. "Too right, after me," she said. "Who's the princess around here?"

The palace that Gabriel led her through looked very different now. The rooms and hallways were dark and silent and lifeless. All the bright lights and the sound of happy voices were gone. There was a musty, sour smell in the air. The tapestries and paintings hung shrouded in deep, brooding shadows. A dark, gloomy sky stretched away beyond the dusty, cobwebbed windows. There were no stars.

They walked silently in a pool of flickering candlelight. The darkness opened grudgingly in front of them and closed bleakly at their backs.

Anita shivered. "Where did everyone go? It wasn't like this when we arrived."

"What you saw then was only an illusion," Gabriel said. "I wished to show you the Royal Palace as you had known it." There was deep sadness in his eyes. "Few now live in the palace, and none are merry."

"Why's that?" Anita asked.

"Time froze in Faerie when your father heard about the death of your mother, Queen Titania," Gabriel said. "She died tragically, soon after your own vanishing." He walked to the window and cracked it open. Cold air wafted in from the gloom. "It has been twilight here for five hundred years. The whole of Faerie shares in Oberon's grief." He looked at her, and now his eyes were shining. "It is my hope that the joy of your return will lift the King's long despair." He smiled. "We may yet see a glorious sunrise. And then you will witness such sights, my lady, such marvelous sights!"

Anita smiled back. "That would be nice," she said. "So the Queen is dead, is that what you said?"

"Indeed. Your mother drowned, my lady."

"That's sad," Anita said. "But she wasn't my mother. My mum can swim like a fish; she won medals for it when she was a girl. Breaststroke, butterfly, freestyle." She looked at Gabriel. "You haven't got a clue what I'm talking about, have you?"

"Your speech is sometimes strange to me, my lady," Gabriel said.

"*My* speech?" Anita said. "You've got to be kidding me."

Gabriel inclined his head with a smile. They had come to a large arched door. He twisted the black handle and pushed it open, then stepped aside to allow Anita through.

She found herself in a long courtyard. Tall, dark, red-brick buildings crowded all around her. She could see square battlements, jet black against the sky. Ahead of them, an arched gateway led into darkness.

Gabriel guided her across the courtyard and through the gateway. It led to an open area of long lawns and cobbled paths. Now that she was away from the musty smell and the sad silence of the empty palace, Anita began to feel better. Walking beside Gabriel under the twilit sky, she felt a dreamy excitement wash over her. This was only a dream, and now she was being taken to see the King of Faerie. How cool was that?

The lawn-flanked path sloped gently away from them. Anita heard the soft ripple of water and realized they were approaching a river. Away to her right stood the pale white towers of the bridge over which she and Gabriel had first come.

The river lay deep and wide and drowsy between the banks. Anita saw a jetty, a tongue of darkness that stretched out over the black water.

She turned to look at Gabriel. His eyes were glowing like moons. Behind him, the angled shapes of the palace were outlined against the horizon—turrets and towers, battlemented walls, great spires and steeples of stone, black against the perpetual evening of Faerie.

On the far bank of the river, wharves and jetties and low-roofed buildings bit into a forest of tall trees. No leaf stirred. No bird sang.

Anita became aware of a huge wooden barge moored at the far end of the jetty, lapped by the bloated belly of the silent river. A single lantern hung at its high prow, but the light it gave off was sickly and yellow. More torches lined the bows, but none were lit.

Gabriel stepped down into the barge. He held out a hand. Anita took it and climbed down next to him. She felt a thrill of amazement as she looked around. The wooden barge was covered all over with intricate carvings—stylized shapes of intertwined leaves and branches and flowers. An awning made of heavy dark cloth shrouded the rear half of the barge. Figures of people and animals were woven into the material. She couldn't make out the shapes very clearly in the flickering, greasy lantern light, but she thought she glimpsed a unicorn, and maybe even a winged lion.

"The King's *here*?" Anita whispered.

Gabriel nodded. He drew aside a curtain of the dense material. Anita saw that candles were lit within. The light was dim and smoky.

"Here goes nothing." Taking a deep breath, she ducked under the awning.

At the far end of the barge, deep in shadows, Anita saw a seated man. She caught her breath; the air thrilled in her lungs as though charged with electricity.

The King of Faerie was sitting on an ornately carved chair with a high arched back and padded leather arms. He was dressed in similar clothes to Gabriel, except that his doublet and hose were black, fur-trimmed, and lined with white satin. His doublet was embroidered with white threads and beaded with jewels.

His head rested against threadbare velvet cushions. His golden hair hung around a lean, care-lined face. Anita had seen that face before, just for a few moments, when she had first stepped onto the gallery above the Great Hall. It was the man she had seen on the throne, the man with the neat beard and mustache, with the sharp, angled cheekbones and the flashing blue eyes. Except now his expression was filled with sadness and his eyes were hooded, as if he was lost in deep, heartbreaking memories.

"Your Grace." Gabriel's voice startled Anita. For a moment she had been totally lost in that sad, noble face.

The King looked up.

Anita felt a shiver of something between apprehension and delight as those bright eyes came to rest on her face. As she watched, the King's eyes widened and a look of astonishment spread over his face.

"Hi there," Anita said tentatively.

The King suddenly leaned forward, his hands gripping the arms of his chair. "It cannot be!" he murmured, his voice a low, rumbling growl. He rose from his chair and his face slowly transformed, at first with disbelief, and then with absolute bliss.

"Tania!"

"Well, not exactly—" Anita began, but she had no time to say anything else as the King surged up out of his throne and wrapped his arms around her, pulling her against him in a fierce, breathtaking embrace.

Anita stood stiffly in his arms, feeling embarrassed and awkward, her feet almost clear of the floor. His fur collar was right in her face, filling her nose and mouth.

"Uh, excuse me." She gasped. "I can't breathe!"

The arms relaxed and the King's hands came up to cup her cheeks. She felt even more uncomfortable as he stared into her face with an expression of such absolute happiness that all she could do was hang there and smile uncertainly up at him.

"My daughter!" he said, his voice amazed. "Tania. Dear heart. Are you truly here, or is this but an illusion?"

"It's definitely me," Anita said. "Sort of."

"I must see you more clearly," said the King. Anita allowed herself to be led out into the open. Again, he scrutinized her face with wide, ecstatic eyes. "It is you, indeed," he said. "And you are as I remembered—the very image and reflection of your mother."

Anita smiled at this. All her life people had commented on the fact that she looked nothing like her parents. Now she understood why—her real parents were Faeries! Why hadn't she thought of that before?

Because you've never been in such a crazy dream before, that's why!

Oberon stepped away from her, his face transformed with elation. He tilted his head back, his mouth opening to let out a shout of pure joy. He lifted his arms up to the sky, his voice ringing out like a peal of bells.

A sphere of light appeared in his cupped hands, and as Anita stared up in amazement, the light surged out from between his fingers, bright and piercing, flashing like sapphires, burning like blue flame.

As the echo of his voice rolled back from the walls and battlements, Oberon slowly spread his arms, and as he did so the brightness poured up from him in a fountain of brilliant blue fire. The column of light gushed upward, fanning out, spreading rapidly over the dark sky. It lifted like a great wave, curling and breaking at its peak, scattering and cascading down from horizon to horizon, banishing the darkness, bathing the whole world in a glorious burst of daylight.

Anita staggered backward, lifting her arms to shield her eyes.

She heard a sound like laughter rising around her. Deep, rumbling laughter, as if mountains were laughing; high, keening laughter that was like the cry of seagulls; a silvery, shivering laughter as of running water; and a sibilant, gusty laughter like the wind in tall trees.

Her ears still ringing, she stared around. The dull gray twilight world had been transformed. The sun was riding high in a clear, blue sky. The river sparkled as it ran swiftly between its banks. Sunlight glinted on the red-brick walls of the palace. The forest was a field of glittering emerald leaves, rustling gently, filled with birdsong. The heat of the sun warmed her face and a warm breeze ruffled her hair.

And at the center of this new-waked universe stood the Faerie King, smiling down at Anita as if she was the brightest thing in this bright new world.

She gasped. "How did you do that?"

"I am Oberon," he said, as if that explained everything.

She turned in a slow circle. It was unbelievable. Stunning. Now she almost *could* believe that she was in the Realm of Faerie.

Gabriel was standing behind her. "Not alone did the King reawaken the light," he said gently. "It is you, my lady, who is at the heart of this miracle."

"And it was you, Lord Drake, who returned my daughter to me," Oberon said. "Your rewards shall be as great as it is in my power to bestow."

Gabriel dropped to one knee. "I ask nothing more than to be your most devoted servant," he said, lowering his head. "All that I have done was done for your sake, and for the eternal Realm of Faerie."

Oberon stepped forward and rested his hand on Gabriel's head. "This I believe to be true," he said, then his tone grew a little grimmer. "And in gratitude, I shall not ask by what dark arts you returned my daughter to me." As Gabriel looked up at the King, Anita glimpsed a flash of apprehension in his silver-gray eyes.

"Rise, Lord Drake," Oberon said. "In recognition of your service to me and to Faerie, I grant you the Earldom of Sinadon. From henceforward you shall be Lord Chancellor and sit at my right hand in my Council."

"Your Grace honors me far beyond my desires or my merits," Gabriel breathed as he rose to his feet.

"And now," Oberon said, turning to Anita, "I wish to speak with my daughter." He called out, "Wardens, throw back the shrouds, and bring food and wine."

Men in holly green uniforms appeared out of the shadows, and the heavy draperies were rolled up and tied back so that the new sunlight was able to flood into the covered cabin at the back of the barge.

Oberon rested an arm around Anita's shoulders and drew her under the awning once more. He sat on the carved wooden chair and gestured for her to sit on a padded stool at his feet. Gabriel followed them and stood quietly behind the King's chair.

For what seemed to Anita like a very long time, the King sat there gazing at her. Gradually, as the thrill of what had just happened became less overwhelming, she began to feel awkward and uncomfortable. She glanced up at Gabriel and he smiled reassuringly at her.

A servant placed a dish of fruit on a low table at her side. Another servant brought a jug of dark red cordial and three crystal glasses. The King made a small gesture with his fingers, and the servant poured the drink before slipping silently away.

Oberon lifted two glasses, handing one to Gabriel. "To your return, Princess Tania," he said. "And to the blessed Realm of Faerie reborn."

Anita picked up her glass and the three glasses touched rims with a single ringing chime. She sniffed the cordial. It smelled richly of fruit. She sipped. It tasted delicious, and as she swallowed, a warm glow went down through her.

She looked up at the King. "So, what happens now?" she asked.

"The rest of eternity," Oberon replied. He smiled. "Do you remember the song we used to sing?" He began to sing in a deep, sonorous voice:

"Willow pale, willow fair, willow tree
bowed in care,
Dangle your yellow hair, willow, sweet
willow, sad willow.
I come to speak with you, garlands of
morning dew,
Bathing you all anew, willow, sweet
willow, sad willow . . ."

He paused, looking at her as if he expected her to do something.

"I'm sorry," Anita said. "I don't know it."

He frowned. "We sang it many times together," he said, sounding puzzled and even a little bit hurt. "And Zara would play the spinetta." He looked closely at her. "Do you truly not remember?"

She shook her head. "Sorry. I'd love to, but I don't remember a thing." She gave him a regretful smile. It didn't seem like the right time to point out to him that this was all just a dream. "I don't even know what a spinetta is."

The King leaned back, turning his head to look questioningly up at Gabriel.

"She has been lost in the Mortal World for five hundred years, Your Grace," Gabriel said. "All that she once was sleeps now in her mind. But I do not doubt that time will bring back her memories."

Oberon nodded. "Time, and the company of those who love you," he said, smiling again at Anita. "Lord Drake, will you take my daughter to her chamber?"

He rested his hand against Anita's cheek. "There you will find raiment and other such things that may help you to remember who you truly are."

She frowned at him. "Raiment?"

"Clothes," Gabriel explained, coming around from behind the King's chair and holding out a hand to her. She took it and stood up.

"Go now, Tania," the King said. "And tonight there shall be feasting and merrymaking such as this realm has not seen for half a thousand years!" He stood up and kissed her on the forehead. "My blessings upon you, my child," he murmured.

She smiled up at him. "Thanks. And the same to you."

Gabriel helped her back up onto the jetty. She turned and waved. Oberon, still watching her, lifted his hand in reply.

"I like him," she confided to Gabriel as they walked along the jetty. "If I didn't have a really great dad back home, I'd definitely short-list him for the job."

The King's voice rang out. "As soon as the Princess is ready, take her to meet her sisters," he called. "They have longed for her return, and their presence will help her find her true self more swiftly."

"I shall, Your Grace," Gabriel called back.

They began to follow one of the stone paths across the lawns to the palace. "I've got sisters?" Anita asked him. Then something clicked in her head. "That's right; in the story, I'm the *seventh* daughter of Oberon and Titania, aren't I?" she said. She stared at him. "Does that mean I have *six* sisters?"

"Indeed, my lady."

Anita grinned. "It must be a nightmare getting into the bathroom in the morning."

Gabriel smiled and tilted his head. She noticed that he always did that when he didn't understand her.

"It was a joke," she explained. "Don't worry about it. Do I have any brothers?"

"No, my lady."

She gave him a thoughtful look. "Is there any chance of you calling me Anita? All this 'my lady' stuff is a bit formal if we're going to be friends."

Gabriel paused and looked at her. "You have known yourself as Anita for sixteen years," he said. "But for five hundred years, in my memory and in my heart, you have been Princess Tania. Forgive me, but until you remember yourself truly, I beg leave to call you my lady." His voice softened. "But when the Princess Tania returns in mind as well as in body, then perhaps our friendship will deepen, and you will permit me to call you by another, sweeter name."

Anita felt a curious shiver slide down her spine as his deep gray eyes looked into hers. "Uh . . . okay," she said. "I can live with that." She suddenly remembered that in the story, Princess Tania had disappeared on the day she and Gabriel were supposed to get married. Did that mean Gabriel still thought of her as his long-lost fiancée? That would be pretty weird, but Anita decided not to ask him about it just yet.

They carried on walking, under the arched gateway and through into the cobbled courtyard.

"So," she said, feeling uncomfortable with the silence that had grown between them, "where exactly are you taking me?"

"To your chamber," Gabriel said. "In the Royal Apartments. It is not far."

"Royal Apartments, eh?" Anita was looking forward to finding out more about Princess Tania, and her bedroom seemed a good place to start. "Cool!"

Anita stared around the bedchamber in delight. Gabriel had just left to go and tell her sisters that she was back. For the first time since her dream began, she was entirely alone.

She gazed up at the ceiling; a decorative wooden lacework spun like an intricate spider's web against the ivory white plaster. The walls were paneled in dark polished wood and hung with tapestries that glowed with bright, vivid colors. There were rolling green landscapes with distant blue, mist-shrouded mountain peaks, and finely embroidered seascapes with tall ships under full sail, heading toward a far horizon. On another wall, a wide land of golden cornfields seemed to stretch away forever beneath a sapphire sky. And on the fourth there were great cliffs of ice and snow, standing on their own perfect reflections in indigo water.

A hint of remembrance pricked the back of Anita's mind. There was a sense of longing in the tapestries, of a wistful yearning for faraway places, that almost reminded her of something. But no, the more she tried to capture it, the more slippery the memory became. Was she really having faint flashes of a different life, or was it just her dreaming mind playing tricks on her?

The room was dominated by a magnificent four-poster bed hung with crimson curtains that stretched up at least double Anita's height, so that they nearly touched the ceiling. One wall was filled with mullioned windows that looked out over ornate, formal gardens. Another wall held a huge wardrobe. A washstand stood in one corner, with a white porcelain basin and a tall pitcher for water. All the furniture was solid and heavy-looking, the chairs and stools padded with crimson upholstery, the chest of drawers laid out with small personal items.

Anita walked across the polished wood floor to the chest of drawers. Lidded jars and delicate glass bottles stood clustered together. An open wooden box spilled glittering jewelry over the handheld mirror and tortoiseshell brushes that lay next to it.

Anita took a ruby earring out of the box. It was set in white crystal; even the clasp seemed to be made from the same delicate stuff. She held it to the side of her head, looking at her reflection in the hand mirror. She shook her head, putting the earring and the mirror down again. They didn't make the half-glimpsed memories any clearer.

She crossed the room and opened one of the

wardrobe doors. It was filled with beautiful, full-skirted gowns in a dozen different colors.

"Amazing!" she breathed, running her fingers over the scalloped bodices and thick, many-layered skirts. Some of the gowns had fine white lace on them; others were heavily embroidered or sewn with pearls and sequins. They were exactly the kind of clothes she had tried on for her role as Juliet. One thing was for sure, Princess Tania had great taste.

At one end of the wardrobe, Anita found a simple shift of white linen. Quickly shedding her pajamas, she slipped the shift over her head. It came to her knees, and had a low, square-cut neckline and long sleeves. Then she picked out a beautiful aqua-colored gown. She stepped into it and carefully eased it up over her hips, slipping her arms into the sleeves and wriggling until it sat comfortably.

She shook out the floor-length velvet skirts. The heavy, embroidered material felt a little odd, but the gown seemed to fit her perfectly. Anita was beginning to enjoy herself; being a Faerie Princess certainly had its good points.

She had just finished lacing the bodice when her head started to spin. She felt as if she was going to faint. The floor shifted and undulated under her feet, and to her horror, the bed and the furniture and even the walls began to buckle and melt in front of her eyes. Startled, Anita grabbed at the wardrobe door. A roaring wind sang in her ears and bright bursts of colored light flashed in front of her eyes. Wincing, she shut her eyes tightly.

Then, as quickly as it had come, the feeling that the world was becoming molten all around her was gone and she was left shivering and disorientated and sick to her stomach.

She opened her eyes and found herself staring into the wardrobe.

The luxurious dresses had vanished.

She heard the bubble of children's voices close behind her, and then there was a woman's voice, calling for hush.

Anita spun around.

The room was different. The bed was still there, but most of the rest of the furniture had gone. The tapestries still hung from the walls, but the scenes on them had changed. Now they showed men and women in clothing that looked to Anita as if it came from biblical times, and the colors were pale and faded.

A woman stood at the foot of the bed, facing away from Anita and surrounded by a group of girls maybe eight or nine years old. They were dressed in jeans and T-shirts and hooded tops, with brightly colored backpacks slung over their shoulders.

In those few, mad, stomach-churning seconds Anita had been dragged out of her dream and back into the real world. Had she woken up at last?

But she was not in her hospital bed.

V

"This room is known as the Queen's State Bedchamber," the woman announced, completely unaware of Anita standing by the open wardrobe door. "This is the original bed-frame, although the curtains and the bed covers are modern reproductions based on a sixteenth-century design."

Anita stared at the children. Where on earth was she?

It reminded her of somewhere she had been before.

But where, and when?

Hampton Court.

On their school trip, the tour guide had brought them into this very room. Anita recognized the tapestries.

One of the girls at the back of the group turned her head and stared straight at her. The girl's freckled face broke into a wide smile. "I like your dress," she said. "Who are you supposed to be?"

Anita opened her mouth to reply, but before any words could come, she was hit again by the fierce howling wind. She fell to her knees as the storm rushed through her head. The colored lights blinded her, and the floor seethed and rolled under her as if the world had become liquid.

"Stop!" she shouted. "Stop it!"

Everything went still.

She was crouched, panting, on the floor. Behind her the wardrobe was full of gowns, and all around her the tapestries glowed with vibrant color, depicting landscapes and seascapes once more.

Anita used the wardrobe door to help her to her feet. Her legs felt shaky.

"What was *that*?" she breathed. "What just happened to me?"

A dream within a dream?

She took a few deep breaths and the giddiness began to fade. She didn't want to be alone in this room anymore. She didn't want to risk that happening to her again. She walked quickly to the door and pulled it open.

She let out a startled yelp as a young woman appeared right in front of her in the doorway. Anita just had time to see that the girl was wearing a similar type of gown to the one she had on, and the girl had long golden hair and bright blue eyes, before the young woman let out a scream of delight and threw her arms around Anita's neck.

"Tania! It is really you!" she cried, her face buried in Anita's hair. "Gabriel told us that you had been found—after all these endless dark years of waiting and hoping!"

"Hello," Anita said breathlessly. "It's nice to see you too—whoever you are." As gently as she could, she prised the young woman's arms away from her neck and looked into her smiling face. "I'm guessing we should know each other," she said.

"Oh, yes, indeed, my poor darling sister," the young woman said. "Gabriel said you remembered nothing of your real life." She stepped back, looking hopefully into Anita's face. "I am Zara," she said.

Anita stared at her. She was small and slender with a pale, fine-boned face and wide eyes and a wide smile. Her hair curled like spun gold over the shoulders of her yellow gown.

"Hello, Zara," she said.

"Do you remember me?" Zara prompted.

Anita shook her head. "No, not really," she said. "Sorry."

"No matter," Zara said brightly. "Time will heal your wounds. I will take you to meet our sisters." She slipped her hand under Anita's arm and towed her along the corridor. "They will be so glad to see you again," she said. "We have missed you so dreadfully."

Anita smiled at her. "Back home, I'm an only child," she said. "I quite liked being on my own. I don't remember ever wishing for brothers or sisters. So why have I dreamed up six older sisters? It's kind of weird, don't you think? Or is it just because there were seven sisters in the story?"

Zara gave her a confused look and then laughed. "Gabriel told us your words would be strange sometimes," she said.

Anita raised an eyebrow. "What else has he told you?"

"That there is to be a grand ball tonight," Zara said, her voice bubbling with excitement. "A ball to celebrate your return." She broke away from Anita and did an elegant pirouette, spinning so that her gown spread wide and her hair fanned out around her face. "We have not held a ball for five hundred years! Imagine it, Tania. Remember how we used to love dancing, remember the lords who courted us, and the music, and the lights, and the feasting, and the fireworks over the river?"

Anita said nothing. Zara stopped in her tracks, looking at Anita with a sudden devastating pity. "Do you remember nothing of it, Tania?"

"I don't even remember being Tania," Anita said. "I wish I did. It sounds like a lot of fun." She frowned at Zara. "Are you really more than five hundred years old?"

"Nay, I am but seventeen," Zara said. "I have been at my present age ever since time froze. But I will grow toward my maturity now, I am sure."

Anita gulped. "So everyone here is going to get old and die now—and all because I came back?"

"Do you not remember, Tania?" Zara said. "We

people of Faerie do not die."

"Never?"

Zara shook her head. "Never of old age; we die only by mischance or ill fortune."

"So, we're all kind of . . . immortal?"

"Indeed we are!" Zara nodded and ran back to loop her arm around Anita's again. "Come," she said. "We will go to the library. Sancha will be there."

Anita decided to save thinking about being immortal for another time. It was a bit too much to take in right now.

"I'm guessing Sancha is another sister, yes?" she said.

Nodding, Zara pulled Anita along the hallway. "And then, away to the seamstress," she said excitedly. "For we will all need new gowns for the ball."

Smiling, Anita surrendered herself to Zara's enthusiasm.

She followed her sister through high, ornately furnished rooms and along wood-paneled halls and down wide stairways. All around them as they walked, Anita could see the palace coming back to life.

Servants in holly green livery swarmed everywhere, wielding brooms and brushes and cloths for polishing. Windows were being thrown open and gray sheets were being drawn back off the shrouded furniture. The corridors echoed with a buzz of happy, laughing voices.

As the two of them passed, servants and maids bowed and curtsyed with lowered heads. Once, a young servant boy glanced up at Anita, his eyes filled with timid curiosity. Anita grinned at him and went cross-eyed. He looked so startled that Anita laughed out loud.

Zara stopped at a pair of tall, arched doors. She pushed one of the doors and it swung slowly inward. She glanced back at Anita, her eyes sparkling. "Sancha has become even more studious since you have been gone," she said, putting her finger to her lips. "She insists that all be silent upon entering her library."

Anita followed Zara through the part-open doorway.

She found herself in a huge circular hall with a high-domed ceiling. Shafts of sunlight poured in through tall, slender windows, brightening the great well of air. The floor was patterned with spiraling rings of black and white tiles, and tiers of ornate wooden galleries soared upward around them, linked by winding staircases.

Anita stared around in amazement. The curving walls on every level of the hall were clad in shelf after shelf of books. Thousands upon thousands of them. And there was a kind of brooding, scholarly hush in the hall that reminded her of a cathedral and made her walk softly on her bare feet.

A solitary figure sat with its back to them at a round table in the center of the room.

Zara tiptoed forward. Anita followed quietly behind her.

It was another young woman, with long chestnut

brown hair drawn back off her face and tied so that it hung down over the back of her simple black gown. She seemed to be totally absorbed in reading a large book that lay open on the table in front of her.

Zara crept up behind her and leaned in close. "Sancha!"

Sancha almost leaped out of her chair. "Oh! The sun, moon, and stars!" She gasped, her hand to her chest. She turned, frowning at her sister, and Anita saw that she had a long, slender face and deep-set, dark brown, intelligent eyes. "Zara! What naughtiness is this, you foolish child?"

Zara turned and pointed, and Sancha's black eyes came to rest on Anita.

"Oh!" She stood up and walked toward Anita, her eyes wide, reaching out with both hands. "Welcome home, Tania. It has been long, too long."

"Thanks," Anita said, taking Sancha's extended hands. "You'll have to forgive me—I don't remember any of this."

"I doubt it not," Sancha said. "It is wonder enough that you have been brought back to us at all. The long dark waters of Lethe lie between us, but time will surely reveal a boatman to ferry you across."

Anita blinked at her. "Uh . . . yes . . . I'm sure it will."

"Sancha often speaks such nonsense," Zara said, smiling at Anita. "She reads far too much. I gladly admit I do not understand half of what she says."

"That is because you are a flibbertigibbet with the

mind of a mayfly," Sancha replied.

"And you're a little gray mole with inky fingers and melancholy humors," Zara retorted affectionately.

Anita grinned at them. Yes, these two were definitely sisters. No doubt about it.

"I am taking Tania to the Seamstress's Apartments," Zara said. "You must come too, if you can bear to be parted from your books. Father has called for a grand ball, and we must all have new gowns."

"I will come with you," Sancha said. "Although my present gown will serve my needs."

"Black?" Zara said scornfully. "I think not! Come, I shall pick a brighter color for you. Do you have a favorite color, Tania?" While Anita hesitated, thinking, Zara swept on: "No matter. Mistress Mirrlees will find something to delight you." She danced toward the door. "Come, sisters! Time is wasting!"

The seamstress's workroom was a long low chamber filled with sunlight and noise and activity. The walls were lined with shelving that held bales and rolls of colored fabric. From open chests spilled foaming froths of lace, sinuous rivers of silk, and tumbling mounds of cotton dyed in a rainbow of colors. Most of the floor space was filled with long tables where cloth was being measured and cut by women dressed in simple blue gowns.

"Behold! The lost lamb has returned!" Zara called out as the three of them came into the room.

The bustle and the murmur of voices stopped

abruptly as all eyes turned toward them. Moments later, Anita found herself surrounded by an excited crowd of women bobbing and curtsying and staring at her in awe.

She laughed, taken aback by the effect she seemed to have on these people. They were treating her like a movie star at a premiere.

She became aware of three other women approaching her. The green-clad servants parted deferentially to let them pass, and Anita guessed they must be more of her sisters.

"Cordelia," Zara whispered in Anita's ear as the first of them came up to her.

Cordelia was wearing a dark russet dress with a collar of red fur. Her red-gold hair was cut raggedly at her shoulders and her wide, smiling face was full of freckles. She had the same piercing blue eyes as Zara, but there was a wariness in her gaze that made Anita think of wild animals.

Cordelia gave Anita a sudden, fierce hug. "Welcome home," she said.

"Thanks." The fur collar of Cordelia's gown pressed against Anita's cheek. It felt strangely warm. Almost before she had the time to register it, the fur moved and Anita found herself gazing into a pair of bright black beady eyes.

Anita pulled her head back with a gasp.

It was a red squirrel. It swarmed around Cordelia's neck and gathered itself into a watchful russet ball on her shoulder.

"Oh! Hello there," Anita said, reaching out a tentative hand. "You startled me. Aren't you pretty?" The squirrel let out a sharp, high-pitched chirping sound and vanished down Cordelia's back. A split second later, Anita was aware of a red blur racing across the floor, up the shelves, and onto the sill of an open window.

"Have no fear, little one!" Cordelia called to the quivering animal. "It is only our sister!" The squirrel gave another cry and vanished through the window.

Cordelia turned her head back and smiled at Anita. "He will not listen to me," she said with a soft laugh. "I will speak with him later and calm his fears."

Anita stared at her. "I didn't mean to frighten it," she said.

"It is of no matter," Cordelia said. "After dwelling in half-light for so long, the sun has made all the animals uneasy. It will pass."

A second woman approached, very tall and slim, wearing a brown dress embroidered with vines and leaves and dark flowers, and with dark brown hair that hung loose to her waist. She had the same solemn, noble face and intense blue eyes as Oberon.

"Hopie," Zara whispered in Anita's ear. "She is the healer. She has no interest in what clothes she wears. You will see, it will take all my powers to get her out of her brown habit!"

Hopie cupped Anita's face in her hands and gazed levelly at her. "You have been gone too long," she said, and her voice was almost as deep and musical as the King's.

"So people keep telling me," Anita replied. "But I'm back now." She lowered her voice to a whisper. "For however long it lasts."

Hopie frowned.

Anita shook her head and smiled. "Don't worry about it," she said. "I didn't mean anything."

"Rathina?" Zara called to the third woman. "Will you not come to greet your sister?"

"Indeed, I will," the woman said. Anita had been half aware that the third sister had been holding back, but now she stepped forward and gave Anita a hug.

"Welcome, Tania," she said.

Anita gazed at her. She was wearing a scarlet gown trimmed with lace and beaded with ruby jewels. Her hair was long and black and lustrous, and she had the most perfectly beautiful face that Anita had ever seen, heart-shaped with wide hazel-brown eyes, high, slanted cheekbones, and a full red-lipped mouth.

But there was something in Rathina's eyes and in her voice that made Anita feel slightly ill at ease. A kind of wariness or reserve that made her wonder whether they had ever been close friends.

While Anita was still thinking about this, Hopie turned and spoke to a plump woman who stood nearby. "Mistress Mirrlees," she said. "I have much work to do; I cannot waste time over gowns. Pick for me something appropriate—in brown."

"Yes, my lady," the woman said, curtsying.

Hopie rested her hand for a moment against Anita's cheek. "We will speak further anon," she said.

"I'd like that," Anita said. Hopie nodded and strode out of the room.

"I must go and comfort the squirrel," Cordelia said to the woman. "Make me a gown that is the color of spring leaves, and cord it with olive and jade." She smiled at Anita. "We will meet again at the ball."

"I hope so," Anita said.

Zara threw her arms around Mistress Mirrlees's neck. "I want a gown of a blue so striking that all eyes will be on me tonight," she pleaded. "I wish to outshine Rathina, were that ever possible."

"I have the very thing," Mistress Mirrlees said. "A blue sarcanet as bright as the summer sky."

"Show me," Zara ordered, following the seamstress over to one of the tables.

Anita smiled at Rathina. "I don't really know what to choose," she confessed. "I'm not used to these clothes yet."

Rathina gave her a long, slow look. She made a gesture with her hand and one of the servant women approached. "There is a bale of lilac silk," she said, without even turning to look at the woman. "Bring it to Princess Tania. It will make a gown that will become her perfectly."

The woman scuttled off.

"Thanks," Anita said.

Rathina gave a quick, brief smile. "Dorothy, Kat, Martha," she called. "I would examine the crimson taffeta." She swept off, followed by three women.

"All this fuss and bother," Sancha said, frowning

around the room. "I shall wear black, whatever Zara may say." She smiled at Anita. "But I may allow some piping of white and a neck ruff trimmed with pearls."

"That sounds lovely," Anita said distractedly. She was still watching Rathina. "Sancha, is there something the matter with Rathina?" she asked. "I get the impression she doesn't like me very much."

"You are quite wrong," Sancha said. "You and Rathina were always the closest of friends."

"Really? Then why is she being so . . . I don't know . . . so distant?"

"Rathina was with you in your bedchamber on the eve of your wedding," Sancha said.

"Oh. That was when I vanished, right?" She looked over at Rathina. "Yes, you're right, she was there when I disappeared."

"So she was, and the burden of it lies heavy upon her," Sancha replied.

"I suppose it would freak out anyone," Anita said. "Your sister disappearing right in front of your eyes and not turning up again for the next five hundred years."

Zara came running up, draped in electric blue silk. "Tell me honestly," she said, twirling in front of them. "Does it become me? Shall I have Mistress Mirrlees make me a gown of it?"

"It's gorgeous," Anita said.

A serving woman approached, carrying a bale of lilac cloth in her arms. "For you, Princess Tania," she said, curtsying.

"An excellent choice!" Zara exclaimed, fingering the fine silk. "This will be perfect." She smiled at the woman. "Princess Tania's gown should have pinks and slashes in the sleeves and a lining of deep purple shot silk."

The woman bobbed again and scuttled off.

Anita raised her eyebrows. "Is that it? Don't I have to be measured up?"

"Mistress Mirrlees will oversee the work," Zara said. "Have no fear—the gown will fit you perfectly. And now come, let us find something for Sancha."

"Black," Sancha insisted.

"No!" Zara said. "Midnight blue, and sewn with stars and trimmed with comets and moons."

There was a pause, then Sancha smiled. "Yes," she said. "That would be acceptable." She glanced at Anita, her black eyes dancing. "Sobriety must sometimes give way to merriment, especially on such a night as this will be."

"Absolutely!" Anita went with them as they hunted down a swath of material to suit Zara's plans for her scholarly sister.

Rathina was at the far end of the room, standing on a footstool to look at herself in a long mirror that was being supported by two serving women. A third woman held different materials against Rathina for her to choose from.

Six sisters, Anita thought. *Rathina, Zara, Sancha, Hopie, and Cordelia. But that only makes five.*

She looked at Zara. "There's someone missing,"

she said. "There should be seven of us."

Zara and Sancha looked meaningfully at each other.

"Eden will not come here," Sancha confided in a low voice. "She is the eldest of us, but she lives alone and does not seek the company of others."

Zara took Anita's arm and drew her to the far side of the room. She opened a window and pointed over the rooftops. "Do you see yonder?" she said, indicating a square ivy-clad tower with battlements and a steeply pitched slate roof. "Eden's apartments are in that tower. She seldom comes forth these days. She spends her time alone thinking dark thoughts."

Sancha joined them at the window. "She used to go for solitary walks on the battlements when all were abed," she murmured. "But she has not been seen now for many a long day. Her meals are taken to her, and she leaves the empty plates and cups outside her door. That is the only way we know she is still alive."

"Sometimes she is seen as a shadow at that window," Zara added, indicating a small window high in the wall of the gloomy tower. "She watches the world, but will take no part in it."

"Why is she like that?" Anita asked.

"Once she was a great scholar of the Mystic Arts," Sancha told her, "second only in power to our father. But she has forsworn her learning and has not practiced her arts since the Great Twilight came down upon us."

Anita stared at the high, bleak window, thinking of the way Oberon had turned night into day with a sweep of his arms. She assumed that was what Sancha meant by Mystic Arts. "Why did she give it up?"

Sancha rested her hand on Anita's arm. "Eden witnessed the death of our mother," she said. "They were together, boating for pleasure on the river. The boat overturned. Eden swam to shore but our mother was lost."

"They never found her body," Zara whispered. "Our father was already in deep desolation about your disappearance. When he was told of the death of his beloved Queen, his grief plunged all the Realm into darkness."

"He had a mausoleum of white stone built to honor our mother." Sancha sighed. "But it is empty, of course. He never goes there."

Anita sympathized with them, wishing there was something she could say to ease the grief in their voices. She felt relieved that her own mother was safe and well back home, and they'd be meeting again just as soon as this dream came to an end.

. . . as soon as the dream came to an end.

Not yet, Anita thought. *At least not until after the ball. I wouldn't want to miss that.* She smiled to herself. *Especially since it's in my honor.*

Once they had finished their business in Mistress Mirrlees's workrooms, Sancha went back to the library and Zara took Anita up to a cozy room that lay under the eaves of the roof.

"This is our special chamber," Zara told her. "No one else comes here but us sisters." She gave Anita an optimistic look. "Do you remember it at all?"

Anita shook her head. It was a lovely room, like a long gallery, with gable windows set into the sloping ceiling. It was carpeted, and the walls were hung with tapestries; the furnishings were lush and luxurious, with embroidered couches and armchairs deep in velvet cushions. Anita noticed a sewing frame with a half-finished embroidery sampler on it. Next to it was a small table with a chessboard set up and a game in progress. At one end of the room, the floor was raised into a low dais, upon which stood some musical instruments.

Zara caught hold of Anita's hand and pulled her along the room. "Come, come," she urged. "Perhaps music will help you to remember."

Anita stepped onto the platform. Various oddly shaped woodwind instruments stood in a row against the wall, alongside some strange-looking stringed instruments. In the middle of the platform there was something that looked like a kind of early piano, only with a much smaller keyboard and no lid and with the strings running sideways instead of straight ahead.

"That's a spinetta, isn't it?" Anita said. She hadn't been able to picture one when Oberon mentioned the word earlier, but suddenly she knew with absolute certainty that was what this instrument was called.

Zara clapped her hands. "Indeed it is a spinetta,"

she said. "Do you remember the duets we used to play together?" She gathered her skirts under her and sat at the instrument. She ran her fingers over the keys and notes cascaded out like a peal of silver bells as she began to sing.

> *"Come, tarry in the rose garden, while*
> *the summer lasts*
> *For soon the flowers that bloom in June*
> *shall fall to winter's blasts*
> *And you must go, and I must stay, a*
> *martial music calls*
> *Come, tarry in the rose garden, ere the*
> *twilight falls."*

Anita frowned. The words and the melody seemed familiar, but they definitely hadn't appeared in the leather-bound book. Where had she heard them before?

Zara turned on her stool and picked up one of the stringed instruments. "You will remember better if you play along with me," she said, as if she could tell what Anita was thinking. "I have kept your lute in tune ever since last you played it." She smiled. "You see? I always had faith that you would come back to us."

Anita took the heavy instrument. It had a pear-shaped body and a long, fretted neck that bent backward at a sharp angle.

"Sit," Zara said. Anita sat down on the edge of the

platform and rested the body of the lute in her lap. She stared at the strings—there was one thick string, followed by five pairs of more slender strings. Back home she had made some ham-fisted attempts at playing a guitar, but this thing looked a lot more complicated.

She looked up at Zara. "I don't know whether to suck on it or blow into it or hit it with a stick," she said. "I'm no good at this kind of thing."

"Nonsense," Zara said. "I'll play slowly for you, and you will follow."

The threads of silvery notes came cascading out of the spinetta once more.

"This is going to be bad," Anita muttered. She leaned over the lute and put her fingers on the fretboard. Wincing, she strummed the strings with the thumb of her other hand.

A pleasant, musical chord rang out.

Anita laughed, amazed. She strummed again. "Hey, I can do it!"

"Sing with me," Zara instructed. "I will take the part of the descant."

Anita took in a deep breath and opened her mouth. To her astonishment, the words and the melody began to flow from her.

"The twilight deep all love devours, that
gloaming of the soul
And you away to distant fields, the
thunderous drummers' roll

Is louder yet than whispered words, and
   stirs your errant heart
The twilight deep all love devours, for
   you and I must part . . ."

She could hear Zara's high angelic voice swooping and soaring above the melody and for a few wonderful moments, as she sang out the unknowable words and strummed the mysterious chords on the lute, she felt so perfectly at home that tears of joy welled up in her eyes.

But her contentment was short-lived. The roaring wind and the gut-wrenching pain and sickness came at her like an unseen blow. She doubled over in agony, her fingers faltering on the strings, her singing changing to a discordant groan.

The world churned and boiled around her and suddenly everything was different.

The long chamber now looked like some kind of exhibition room. People in light brown shorts and sneakers were peering into glass-fronted display cabinets. Cameras hung around their necks and some of them had headphones on, as if listening to a recorded tour guide.

A man stood by the window with a clipboard.

Anita could still hear the tuneless clang of the fumbled lute, and the man obviously heard it too. His head turned and his face darkened. He took a stride toward her, his mouth opening.

"Hey! You there! What do you think—"

His words were drowned by the howling wind, and his face was lost in glaring explosions of colored light.

The next thing Anita heard was Zara's complaining voice.

"What a dreadful noise!" she exclaimed. "And you started so well. I see you will need to practice." Her voice became concerned. "Tania? Are you unwell? You have become quite pale."

The sickness and disorientation drained away, and Anita turned and gave Zara a weak smile. "Sorry about that," she said. "I'm not sure what happened." She paused. "Did you see anything?"

Zara frowned. "What do you mean? What was there to see?"

"There were people in here," Anita said. "Lots of people."

"In here?" Zara said. "Oh no, there were no people. We are quite alone." She twirled out a run of notes. "Shall we continue?"

"I'd rather not, if you don't mind," Anita apologized. "I feel a bit sick."

"Shall I fetch Hopie?" Zara offered. "She will make you a posset."

"No, don't worry," Anita said, too weak even to wonder what a posset might be. She pointed to a nearby couch. "I'll just lie down for a while. You can carry on playing if you like."

She put down the lute and walked unsteadily over to the couch. She stretched out on it, resting her head on the padded arm.

The shimmering notes of the spinetta filled the air as she lay there with her eyes closed.

That was twice now—once in her bedchamber and once up here. Twice that she had been dragged painfully out of this place and into somewhere else.

Again, it had reminded her of modern-day Hampton Court, and again, the people she had seen were all in modern dress. And again, she had been thrust in and out of that other world in a matter of moments.

It almost seemed as if she was waking up for a few flickering seconds before the dream claimed her again. But surely it couldn't be that? When the dream ended, surely she would wake up in her hospital bed, not in those strange half-familiar places?

Was she in a coma? How badly had she been injured in the accident?

What was happening to her?

VI

Anita spotted her new ball-gown the moment that she and Zara walked into her chamber.

A waterfall of lilac fabric was spread over the bed, shining in the slanting rays of sunlight that poured through the mullioned windows.

Anita carefully lifted the gown off the bed. She was surprised by how light it felt in spite of the wide skirts. It had puffed sleeves, slashed so that the rich purple of the lining showed through. There was a delicate trimming of purple thread around the scalloped neckline, the cuffs of the sleeves, and the deep hem of the skirts. Lavender blue embroidery covered the bodice in a filigree of swirling patterns, and panels of more embroidery ran down the skirts to the hem.

Anita held the gown against herself. "How does it look?"

"It is perfect," Zara declared. "Mistress Mirrlees

has outdone herself!"

"But how did she do all this so quickly?" Anita wondered, gazing down at the intricate embroidered patterns. "It looks like a couple of weeks' work, but we were only there an hour ago."

Zara shook her head. "Poor Tania," she said. "You do not remember anything of this Realm, do you?"

"Apparently not," said Anita. She looked at Zara. "Is it magic, is that how it's done?"

"I do not know that word," Zara said, puzzled. "What does it mean?"

"Magic?" Anita said. "Oh, you know. Hocus-pocus. Open sesame. Rabbits out of hats. All that kind of thing." Zara looked blankly at her. "The way the King brought the daylight back," Anita persisted. "That's what I'm talking about. And the way Gabriel brought me here. That's all magic."

"I do not know what powers Gabriel used to bring you back to us," Zara said. "I have never studied such things. Few of us do. It is hard work! It makes my head spin to think of it." She smiled. "But Mistress Mirrlees has some knowledge of the Mystic Arts, and our father is a great master of them. Come, let us not dwell on such serious things. You are here with us, and the world is bright once more, and tonight we shall dance until dawn!"

Zara helped Anita into her gown, and then the two of them ran along the corridors to Zara's own apartments.

Zara flung open a door and Anita stared into her sister's bedchamber in astonished delight. The walls and ceiling had been painted in banded shades of blue, so that the four-poster bed, with its navy blue covers and curtains, seemed to be sailing in the middle of a vast seascape with a distant horizon at shoulder-height around the walls.

"This is lovely!" Anita said as she stepped over the threshold. She glanced down. The floorboards under her feet had been painted to resemble shingle. There were windows in one wall, draped with deep blue curtains, looking out over the river, but glazed with tinted, rippled glass that gave the light a sapphire sheen.

Anita looked more closely at the walls and gasped. The paintings were alive!

Foam-capped waves washed silently to and fro around her, and tall ships rode the swell, with crisp white sails swelling in the wind. Mermaids and sea serpents rose out of the white foam and then, without a sound, dived beneath the surface again, leaving a plume of creamy spray. Snowy clouds scudded across the azure sky of the upper walls. Seagulls winged their way over the ceiling, their wings casting faint shadows above them.

Anita reached out and tentatively brushed her hand against the wall. It felt cool and solid, like painted stone. A distant ship glided under her fingers—a ship made of colored brushstrokes. It looked like a moving photograph as it sailed noiselessly away in its enchanted world of paint and pigment.

Anita stepped back, looking at Zara. "How?" she breathed, unable to organize her tumbling thoughts enough to make a coherent sentence.

Zara smiled at her. "*Magic*, perhaps?" she said with a laugh. "This is not so extraordinary. We each have bedchambers that give us joy and heart's ease at the day's end. Sancha's walls have endless words flowing across them, telling never-ending stories and tales for her pleasure. Rathina's is a ballroom filled with tireless dancers. Hopie's chamber is a woodland thick with herbs and healing plants. And Cordelia's room teems with the animals that she loves."

"My room isn't like that," Anita said. Her tapestries had shown intricately detailed scenes, but they had been still and two-dimensional, not animated like these painted walls.

Zara looked somber. "Once it was," she said. "Maybe it will come alive for you in time. You must be patient." She turned her head. "But see what Mistress Mirrlees has left for me!" She ran to the bed. An electric blue gown lay there, the bright silk shining out against the dark blue covers. "Come, help me to put it on."

Anita dragged her attention away from the living walls and helped Zara into the gown and laced up the bodice.

The gown was as lovely and as finely detailed as Anita's. The blue fabric seemed to shimmer as Zara moved, with white and pale sapphire jewels that sparkled and glittered in the late afternoon sunlight.

Anita scrambled onto Zara's bed, watching her sister dance against the impossible sea. The steps looked quite complicated.

"I don't know how to dance like that," Anita said.

"You will remember." Zara laughed as she whirled past. "Your fingers remembered the lute; your feet will recall the dance." She paused, gazing at Anita with wide, thrilled eyes. "Do you remember the steps to All in a Garden Green?" she asked. "Or The Chirping of the Nightingale? Or Jenny Pluck Pears? You must remember Fine Companion. That was always your favorite."

Anita shook her head. "Maybe we should practice before the ball?"

At that moment, she heard the distant sound of trumpets ringing out in a fanfare.

Zara's smile widened. "There is no time," she said, leaning across the bed and snatching Anita's hands. "The grand ball awaits!"

Anita slid off the bed. "Oh well," she muttered as Zara hauled her to the door. "What have I got to lose? This is all in my head, anyway. If I make a total idiot of myself, who's going to know?"

Anita had expected to see plenty of people heading for the ball, but the corridors and stairways were quiet and deserted. As they walked the candlelit hallways, she began to feel Zara's infectious excitement welling inside her. But where was everybody?

They came to a lobby lit by only one or two candles. In front of them stood a pair of massive dark wood doors. All was silent.

"Open the doors," said Zara.

Puzzled, Anita turned the handles and thrust open the doors. They swung wide into a thick, velvet darkness.

She looked over her shoulder at Zara, not understanding what was happening, wondering if Zara was playing some kind of trick on her.

"Go in," Zara urged. "You must go in."

With a shrug, Anita stepped over the threshold of the pitch-black room.

She halted, straining her eyes into the darkness.

"Hello?" she called. "Is anyone there?"

She heard a subdued throb of music coming from somewhere above her—a low rumble of cellos and woodwind instruments, and the soft rattle of tambourines. And then, in the pitch darkness far ahead of her, a point of bright yellow light opened up like a flower bud.

"Welcome, my precious daughter." It was Oberon's voice. "A thousand times welcome!" The music swelled in her ears and the flower of light grew until it was a golden radiance that blossomed and spread to fill every corner of the huge room.

She was standing in the Great Hall that she had seen when Gabriel had first brought her into the palace, except this time she had entered through doors that opened beneath the gallery.

The golden light revealed the King standing in front of the two thrones. And as the radiance grew, she saw that a host of brightly clad people filled the hall, every one of them looking straight at her with glad, smiling faces.

A thrilled shiver went through her as she saw the golden glow bloom along the walls, igniting candles in sconces, then rising to bring tongues of white flame to the huge chandeliers that hung from the ceiling.

And while Anita was still trying to take in all of this, the people began to applaud and cheer, and the music swelled to a crescendo.

She stood there trembling, tears pricking her eyes. Was this really just a dream? It felt so *real*.

Oberon came toward her, smiling. Her mouth was dry and her head swimming as he took her hand and rested it in the crook of his arm. He turned, drawing her along with him, and together they walked the length of the hall to the sound of renewed cheering.

"Let the first dance be Greenwood," Oberon called above the tumult. "I shall dance it with my daughter."

There was more applause and the music changed to a lively, tumbling tune. Anita glanced up and saw that musicians filled the gallery.

She looked into the King's face. "I don't know this dance," she said.

"Ah, but you do," the King promised. "Come, take my lead."

The crowd drew back to leave an empty circle in

the floor. Anita let Oberon lead her into the middle of the open space.

The King took a step back from her and gave a low bow.

Anita found herself curtsying to him. He stepped up to her and she instinctively lifted her hands to meet his, palm to palm. He took a backward step, and she stood still as he made a slow gliding movement to the right and danced a ring around her. Then he came to a stop in front of her and she performed the same swirling dance around him, placing her feet as if she had been doing this dance all her life.

The watching courtiers cheered. Oberon laughed, applauding with them.

"See? My daughter has forgotten none of her skills!" he shouted. "Come all you lords and ladies of Faerie! Step forth in a joyous measure! Let the merriment commence!"

Suddenly Anita was surrounded by a whirl of dancing people—and she danced with them. The colored clothes and the music and the candlelight swirled around her until there was no such person as Anita Palmer—there was only Princess Tania of Faerie, come home to her father Oberon and to her royal sisters.

As the night wore on, Anita danced until her head was spinning. She knew the steps to every dance! There was the stately Saraband, in which the lords and ladies formed long lines facing each other across the Great

Hall. The men bowed, the ladies curtsied. Moving in perfect harmony to the music, Anita and the other ladies approached their partners, clasping hands with them, gracefully circling them—and then, lord and lady linked arms to weave in and out of the other couples with wonderful elegance and precision.

Then there were the ring dances such as Rose Is White and Rose Is Red, where the dancers separated into circles—sometimes of four, sometimes of eight, and sometimes forming themselves into great rings that revolved clockwise and counterclockwise, one inside the other as the jaunty music urged them ever onward.

Anita's feet never faltered. Sometimes she would find herself facing Gabriel for a while, at other times Oberon or one of the other Faerie lords would be her partner, but she had little time to catch her breath, and no time for conversation.

She had no idea how much time had passed when she finally made her way from the dance floor and sought out a corner where she could sit and catch her breath. Lords and ladies who were not dancing sat or stood in small groups around the walls, talking and laughing and watching the dancers twirl and spin across the floor as the music rang out to the beat of drums and the clatter of tambourines.

Sancha and Cordelia came to sit with her and they watched as Zara took the lead in a particularly strenuous dance called The Voltaira.

"She never stops, does she?" Anita remarked after

a move in the energetic dance that involved the men grasping the women by the waists and launching them into the air. "Where does she get the energy from?"

"From five hundred years of yearning," Sancha said solemnly.

"That's a long time to wait for a good night out," Anita murmured. She gazed across the hall. Oberon was seated on his throne, speaking with some nobles. *The King of Faerie.* It gave her a curious feeling of pride as she watched the lords and ladies of the Court bow to him, almost as if he really was her father and she really was Princess Tania.

"Idiot!" she told herself. "This isn't real. Don't forget that!"

Hopie and a tall, dark-haired and -bearded man were standing arm in arm by the throne, speaking with the King.

"Who's that with Hopie?" she asked.

"That is her husband, the Lord Brython of Cantus," Sancha said. "He is a wise and learned man, high in the King's Council."

Anita looked at Sancha. "Are you married?"

Sancha laughed softly. "No, indeed," she said. "My time is all taken up by my studies. I do not need distractions such as that."

Anita turned to Cordelia. "How about you? Anyone special?"

Cordelia frowned and shook her head. "I find little of delight in the company of men," she said.

"Nor in that of women, truth be told," Sancha

added. "Cordelia lives only for her animals."

Cordelia lifted an eyebrow. "They are not *my* animals," she said. "They each belong to themselves." She looked at Anita. "You are welcome to visit the menagerie, if you wish."

"A menagerie?" Anita said. "That sounds great. I love animals." She smiled, remembering the incident in Mistress Mirrlees's workroom. "Even squirrels that I scare half witless."

"Don't worry, he no longer fears you," Cordelia said. "I have spoken with him. He now knows that you are a friend."

"Uh . . . that's good," Anita said, wondering exactly what Cordelia meant by "spoken with him."

She looked over to where Rathina stood surrounded by an attentive group of handsome young lords. So far that evening, Rathina was the only one of her sisters who had not spoken to her, but then the beautiful Faerie princess did seem to be permanently occupied with her competing admirers.

"So, do I have any other brothers-in-law I should know about?" Anita asked.

"Eden has a husband," said Sancha. "The Earl Valentyne, but he quit the Court a long time ago, soon after the darkness fell, and Eden locked herself in her tower. We do not know where he went. Perhaps back to his own people in Mynwy Clun, a hundred leagues from here in the mountainous west." She followed the line of Anita's eyes. "As you can see, Rathina does not lack for suitors, but none yet has claimed her heart.

And as for Zara, I pity indeed the man who seeks to capture *her* heart, which is as light and as blithe as a butterfly on the wing!"

Anita spotted Gabriel on the far side of the hall. He was in conversation with Edric. She had not noticed Edric in the hall before, and the sight of that familiar but now achingly unknown face gave her quite a jolt.

She pushed away her feelings of betrayal. Why did Edric's treachery hurt her so much? This was only a *dream*; why did seeing him make her feel so bad?

"And then there's Gabriel," she murmured under her breath. She turned to Sancha and said more loudly, "Back then, before I disappeared . . . had Gabriel captured my heart? He must have, if I was going to marry him, but I can't remember it at all."

Sancha looked thoughtful. "You seemed content to marry him," she said at last. "But I know not whether you truly loved him."

Anita stared at her in surprise. "Really? Why do you say that?"

"The marriage would have brought together two great houses of Faerie," Sancha explained. "Our own house and the House of Weir. You knew our father longed for an alliance with the powerful Dukedom of the North. When Gabriel proposed to you, I think you may have agreed to the marriage partly to please our father."

"It seemed to me that you were dazzled by the glamour and the excitement of it all," Cordelia added, overhearing. "But you liked Gabriel well enough, I believe." She watched him across the room. "He is a handsome man, I dare say, for those who admire such things."

Suddenly Zara appeared in front of them. "What's this!" she exclaimed, snatching at Anita's hands. "Weary already? Fie! The night is young; come, I have called for your favorite dance—Fine Companion. It will blow away all the cobwebs! On your feet, lazy-bones; there is many a measure to tread before dawn!"

Anita gave Sancha and Cordelia a helpless grin as she was towed onto the dance floor by her tireless sister.

It was not until three more dances had passed that Anita was able to escape Zara's attentions. Slightly dizzy from being spun around and around, she made her way through the courtiers, looking for a place to sit and rest for a while.

Suddenly a hand grasped her wrist and a familiar voice hissed close to her ear. "We must talk."

She turned her head and saw Edric's face at her shoulder.

For a split second she was vividly reminded of another time when a boy she knew as Evan Thomas had taken hold of her wrist.

A concert, a few months ago in North London. Loud rock music, battering at her ears, electric guitars screaming through her head, the bass rumbling in the pit of her stomach. The dance floor heaving with sweating bodies. Strobe lights raking the darkened walls. And her in the middle of the crush, enjoying every frenzied moment of it, until she was caught by a fierce press of bodies as the crowd surged toward the stage. She was trapped in the stampede, gasping for breath, unable to get out. In real danger of falling and being trampled underfoot.

And then—rescue! Evan's hand, grabbing hold of her wrist, yanking her out of the suffocating pack, towing her to safety.

Relieved. Throwing her arms around his neck. Laughing above the noise. Yelling in his ear. "I think you just saved my life!" And in that moment, awakening to the awesome notion that she just might be in love with him.

The memory only lasted for a moment. Then she was back in the Great Hall of the Royal Palace and the face she was staring at was no longer that of her boyfriend, Evan; it was the face of Edric Chanticleer, the deceitful servant of Gabriel Drake.

"Let go of me," she snapped. "I have nothing to say to you." She wrenched her arm free and pushed her way through the crowd, desperate to get as far away from him as possible. The thought of the cruel way he had manipulated her emotions filled her with raw pain, gnawing at her, making her feet stumble. Why did she feel that way? She knew this was only a dream, so why did the sight of him hurt so much?

"Well met, my lady!" She was brought up sharp by Gabriel's voice. He was standing right in front of her. She had been so intent on putting distance between herself and Edric that she had almost walked straight into him.

"Oh! Sorry." She gasped, grateful for a friendly face to banish her dark thoughts. She smiled at him. "Are you having a good time?"

"It is a joy indeed," he said, looking deep into her eyes. "But to step another measure with my lady would put all other pleasures to shame."

Anita raised one eyebrow. "You're asking me for a dance, right?"

Gabriel bowed. "If my lady pleases."

"Okay," she said. "I'm up for it. But nothing too energetic, please."

"Trust me," he said. "I shall lead you in a dance like no other!"

That sounded intriguing. She allowed him to usher her onto the dance floor.

They stood facing each other. He bowed and reached out his arms. She took both his hands and they danced in a slowly spinning circle.

His gaze was constantly on her face, but his silvery eyes had a faraway look in them.

"What are you thinking about?" she asked.

"I was remembering the last time we danced together."

"That was some time ago, I suppose," she said.

"Indeed, a long, long time ago."

She shook her head. "I don't remember it at all."

"Your true self will return in time," Gabriel promised.

She looked pensively at him. Had she loved him— "a long, long time ago?" She could see how it would be possible to fall for him. He was very appealing—charming and kind and extremely attractive. She smiled to herself. And rich and powerful, she assumed, although she wasn't sure whether that ought to matter to a princess.

He gazed back at her, and now his eyes were focused intently on her, as if she was the only point of interest in the whole whirling world.

They were such strange eyes. Silver-gray. Like moonlight shimmering on the surface of a deep, dark lake. Like a white flame reflecting on burnished steel. Like sparks flying as the hammer strikes the anvil. The room spun and she found she could not look away.

The intimacy of their eye contact began to make her feel uneasy, as if she needed to break loose from him before something momentous happened. She tried to pull her hands out of his.

"Do not let go of my hands, my lady," he said softly.

His eyes seemed to expand until all she could see was the silver of his irises and the black of his pupils. The silver shone like moonlight and the black sparked with points of white light, like a whole sky full of stars. Silver and black. Drawing her in. Holding her fast.

"No," she whispered. "I won't."

"Look down," he said. "And have no fear."

Anita looked down. The floor, the Great Hall, and the dancing courtiers had vanished. Instead, the night sky surrounded them—star-strewn and lit by a crescent moon that hung low in a thin veil of lacy mist. There was nothing under her feet; Gabriel was holding her suspended in the rushing air, and the night-washed land lay far below them.

Overwhelmed by a sudden panic, she let out a moan of fear and clutched at his hands.

"You will not fall," he said. "Trust me."

She swallowed hard. This time she had no wings, no control. She had only Gabriel to save her from falling. She had to believe in him.

They were moving very fast through the sky. The wind was on her face and in her eyes, cool and refreshing after the heat of the Great Hall. Her ears were full of its soft voice as it whispered and sang to her. It rustled and hissed in her dress. It plucked at her hair until she felt it streaming out into the night.

Far away, and far below, she could see a ribbon of tiny bright lights, sparkling like scattered diamonds. It was the Faerie Palace speeding away from them, the lights winking out one by one until the night swallowed them all.

Vast stretches of empty heath slipped beneath them, deep purple hills rising and falling like a swollen sea of petrified shadows. At the edge of the moorland, a vast forest stretched out to the edge of sight, dark and dense in the glancing moonlight.

"Where are you taking me?" Anita asked.

"Over the hills and far away," Gabriel said lightly. He dropped his right hand and lifted his left and she gave a breathless scream as they plunged earthward.

"No! Don't!" she shouted as the trees hurtled toward them. "Please!"

Her feet were brushing the leaf-laden upper branches when Gabriel lifted his right hand again and their precipitous fall ended in a smooth curving ascent. The stars swam above her head, the moon rocked on the black horizon. The air hummed in her ears.

She gasped. "You did that on purpose, didn't you?"

"For your delight, my lady," Gabriel said, smiling.

A little uncertain about his definition of *delight*, she forced herself to relax and gazed down between her feet. There was a clearing in the forest immediately below them. Anita saw dark, angular shapes and tiny squares of yellow and rose-tinted light. Thatched roofs. Gray tracks leading in and out of the trees.

Gone in an instant.

Hills, forest-cloaked at first then rising steeply out of the trees and swelling into rounded green slopes. A wide valley. A long lake so black and still that every star in the sky shone up from it, as if there was another world down there, another night, another Realm of Faerie.

Another stretch of moorland rushed between her hanging feet. A circle of standing stones, white under the moon. Gray meadows fled by, dotted with sheep. A shining waterfall. Rivers like dark snakes gliding through farmlands and woodland. Another village with fleeting lights, and another.

On and on they flew, the wind chiming like bells across the ever-changing landscape of Faerie.

The land became more rugged. Angled fists of

rock jutted out of the earth. Gnarled fingers of stone clawed at the moon. Sharp valleys clove the mountains, drowned in darkness, harsh and sinister. Planes of cracked and riven rock dimly reflected the moonlight. They were in a land of sultry shadows and of cold light now—a harsh land, cloven and torn open so that the raw bones of the world showed through.

Gabriel dipped his hand again and suddenly they were flying between the jagged peaks. Anita was aware of movement in the valley beneath them. She looked more intently. It was just a gray blur at first, but as they drew nearer she saw that it was a herd of animals with silvery hides running wildly along the narrow valley floor. Their manes and tails rippled as they ran. Their hooves sparked on the stones.

Horses? No! Not horses. Anita saw slender threads of light at their fast-nodding heads, moonlight reflecting off a single spiraling horn.

"Unicorns!" She gasped.

"Indeed," Gabriel said. "The wild unicorns of Caer Liel. A dangerous breed and untameable." He began to sing softly, a slow, sonorous melody that made Anita shiver.

> *"Ride swift for home and hearth, my*
> *child, for the unicorns are at your heel,*
> *The ravens hang on the freckled cliffs,*
> *watchful as the day ends,*
> *The gale-torn roadway shudders, my*
> *child, the castle gates slam at your back,*

The horses are sweating, hard-ridden and
steaming in the courtyard,
You are safe now, my child—for the present,
you are safe."

"What is that?" Anita asked. "It sounds so sad."

"It is but a song I learned as an infant," he replied. He turned his head and stared into the distance. "Behold, my lady," he said, his voice thrilling with a strange excitement. "The lights of Caer Liel, of Castle Weir, the mountain home of my family, the cradle of my childhood!"

Anita stared into the cracked mountains and saw, perched high on a bleak cliff, a great dark castle with massive stone walls and time-gnawed battlements. Within the walls were rows of sharp, pointed towers and turrets and keeps. A narrow road zigzagged its way up the mountain face to a fortified gatehouse where red-and-black banners fluttered. Crimson flames pranced high on the walls, watch fires troubled by the shrieking wind. Yellow and white lights shone out from lofty windows.

The castle looked ancient and strong, but it made her feel lonesome and mournful to see it clinging there to its high pinnacle, so deep in the heart of these unfriendly mountains.

Anita looked at Gabriel. "Is this what you wanted to show me? The place where you were born?"

Gabriel smiled. "It is a sight worth seeing, I believe. The Castle of Weir may seem an ominous and forbidding place, my lady, but there is always good cheer and a warm welcome within."

"Are we going inside, then? Will I get to meet your family?"

Gabriel shook his head. "Nay, my lady, that is a feat beyond my meager powers."

"I'm sorry? What do you mean?"

"Only this," Gabriel said, and suddenly the floor of the Great Hall was pressing against her feet again and there was candlelight in her eyes and music in her ears and the swirl of Faerie dancers all around her.

"Oh!" She stumbled and almost fell; Gabriel's hands in hers were the only thing that prevented her from ending up sprawled on the dance floor.

She gazed dizzily into his eyes. Silver and black. Letting her go. Releasing her from his enchantment.

He led her to the side of the room.

She smiled at him, her brain gradually unscrambling. "Thank you," she said. "That was some enchantment. It was amazing!"

He bowed and kissed her hand. "My greatest pleasure is in pleasing my lady," he said. "And now I must beg your leave. I would not overstay my welcome, and there are many others who wish to dance with you." He straightened up, and with a final smiling glance, he stepped away into the crowd.

Anita gazed after him, her eyes still full of starlight and her ears still ringing with the night wind.

"Amazing . . ." she breathed. "Totally amazing."

VII

Anita and Zara were sitting on the bed in Anita's chamber. The ball had ended, but although they were both exhausted, they were far too excited to sleep. They had been laughing and talking excitedly together for some time, but Anita hadn't told Zara about her marvelous night flight over Faerie. She wanted to keep it special and private for a little while.

"I saw you dancing with Gabriel," Zara teased. "He seemed to please you. How you stared into his eyes!" She looked mischievously at Anita. "Are the wedding bells to ring out after all?"

"I don't think that's very likely," Anita replied evasively. "I hardly know him."

"But once you did," Zara argued. "Once you loved him."

"Well, I don't now," Anita said.

"Ah, poor Tania." Zara sighed. "To have lost yourself

and your true love at a stroke. It is sad, indeed."

"But I don't feel sad," Anita insisted. "I don't remember any of it."

"That is a blessing, I suppose," Zara said, stifling a yawn. "And it is a delight to have you home once more, even if your mind is addled!" She yawned again. "Oh, mercy!" she said. "I must sleep." She slumped back on the bed.

"Hey!" Anita protested, shaking her. "In your own bed, please!"

"Oh, very well." Zara clambered off the bed and headed for the door. "Did you notice how handsome the Earl of Anvis was looking tonight?" she mused as she opened the door. "Now there is a man to sweep a lady off on a white steed!"

"I don't even know which one he was," Anita said. "Go to bed!" She laughed as the door closed behind her sister.

Alone in her silent chamber, her ears ringing from the music, she got into her nightgown and slipped between the bedcovers. She lay in bed, propped up on pillows, gazing through the window into a night sky that teemed with stars, remembering how she and Gabriel had seemed to soar together, hand in hand over the drowsy land of Faerie.

Although that had been the highlight of the ball for her, she had joined in with many more dances afterward. She could still see a whirl of rainbow-colored gowns and doublets in front of her eyes. She thought of that first dance with the King, saw his happy face smiling proudly down at her.

Her father the King.

She grinned. Amazing.

And then she pictured her real father's gentle, round face, his expression concerned as he leaned over her hospital bed. His voice echoed in her mind. *"How are you doing, my little girl?"*

Anita stared into the distance, shocked. For a moment she had nearly forgotten that this was just a dream. This had to stop.

She blew out the candle. The darkened room filled with the mellow shimmer of starlight. The stars seemed bigger here than back home. Brighter. More mysterious.

She pressed back into her pillows, drawing the covers up to her chin.

"Okay," she said aloud, sternly. "Listen very carefully. You are going to sleep now. And when you wake up in the morning, you will *wake up properly* back in the real world. Do you hear me? All this Faerie stuff has been lovely, but enough is enough."

She closed her eyes, concentrating on what the hospital ward looked like, remembering the faces of her mother and father. Refusing to let in Faerie.

She had to get out of this dreamworld.

"Wake up now." It was a woman's voice. Anita felt a hand on her shoulder, gently shaking her.

She opened bleary eyes. The room was very bright.

"Nurse?" she mumbled. "What time is it?"

"Half the morning has passed, Tania, and yet I find you slumbering still." The voice had laughter in it. "Come, it is a beautiful day, and you yet abed, sister! Fie! You should be ashamed!"

Anita forced herself to focus.

She was still in her bedchamber in Faerie. An ocean of flower-scented sunlight was pouring in through her thrown-open windows.

Rathina was sitting by her side, leaning over her, smiling anxiously

"Dearest sister," Rathina said. "I have not been a friend to you since you returned, and for that I am sorry. I thought you would blame me for what happened to you. But there cannot be coldness between us, Tania. We were always such good friends. Can it be so again? Will you forgive me?"

Anita sat up, rubbing the sleep out of her eyes.

"Forgive you for what?" she asked.

Rathina hung her head. "If I had not encouraged you to test the powers spoken of in the ancient verse, you would never have been lost to us."

Still groggy from sleep, Anita blinked at her. "Can you run that past me again?" she said. "I mean, I don't understand what you're talking about."

Rathina leaned forward and took hold of one of Anita's hands. "On the eve of your wedding, we were together in this chamber," she said. "We talked about the rhyme we had grown up with, the rhyme we had known since childhood: *One alone will walk both worlds,*

Daughter last of daughters seven.'"

Anita nodded. It was the poem from the book.

"The lore-masters said that if *you* were the seventh daughter spoken of in the verse, then your powers would come to you on your sixteenth birthday." Rathina stared into Anita's eyes. "And from that moment on, you would have the power to walk both in Faerie and in the Mortal World." Her fingers tightened around her hand. "You were to be wed to Gabriel Drake on your sixteenth birthday. We waited until the midnight bell had struck, and then I urged you to try to step out of our world and into . . . into that other place." She shook her head. "It was but a game, Tania. I meant no harm. My heart near broke with fear when you . . . when you . . ." Her voice trailed away.

Anita felt a stab of sympathy. Five hundred years was a long time to think you had helped your sister to disappear!

"It wasn't your fault," she said. "I don't remember anything about it. In fact, I don't remember anything about this place at all, except for a few weird things that don't make sense to me. But I'm sure you didn't do anything to make me disappear. I was the one who walked between the worlds when I didn't know what would happen." She smiled. "Of course we can be friends. I'd really like that."

Rathina let out a relieved breath and jumped off the bed. "The very best of friends!"

Anita nodded. "Sounds good to me."

"Then get up, sleepyhead!" Rathina said, yanking the bedclothes away from Anita. "There is much for you to see and do today. You say you remember nothing? Then I shall be your guide. We shall tour the palace together, and by evening, you will have remembered everything!"

Anita clambered out of bed. "Okay," she said. "It's a deal. But do I get breakfast first? I'm starved."

"Breakfast first, indeed," Rathina said. She ran to the window, spreading her arms wide. "And then, away into the world!"

Rathina took her first to a small dining room where servants brought them chunks of fresh-baked bread with butter and cheese, and pieces of fresh fruit, all washed down by a tall glass of milk.

Anita had hoped to find Zara or one of the other sisters there, but it seemed that Zara was still in bed, and that the others had breakfasted and gone about their business some hours earlier. The servants told them that the King and various other important lords and ladies of the Court were "closeted together in conclave," whatever that meant, and weren't expected to emerge until noon. Anita assumed they were having some kind of high-powered meeting. Perhaps this was the Council she had heard Oberon mention. She wondered if they used magic—the Mystic Arts—to govern the kingdom.

After breakfast, the tour of the palace began.

Rathina led Anita up a long winding stairway in a

narrow tower. They squeezed through a small door-way and emerged onto a flat, walled rooftop. The warm breeze whipped their hair around their faces as they looked down on the palace grounds.

Anita leaned over the battlements and gasped. The palace was even larger than she had imagined. She had seen it briefly before, during her flight, but it had been dark then and she hadn't been able to grasp the scale of the place.

The red-brick buildings and courtyards immediately below her were laid out exactly like Hampton Court Palace, with long lawns that sloped gently down to the river. Yet the Faerie Palace was far more expansive than the historic house Anita had seen on her school trip; here, they stretched way beyond the confines of Hampton Court in twenty-first-century London. The great red-brick buildings with their cream-colored stone ornamentations and their arched windows and slotted battlements extended eastward along the river into a hazy blue distance, tower beyond tower, wall after wall, bastions, turrets, and gatehouses, spreading out alongside the winding river as far as she could see. On the very edge of sight, the river became wider, and she could just make out large wharves and jetties and great sailing ships with tall masts and rigging like cobwebs under the blazing sun.

To the south, across the river, the land seemed to be one great green forest that went on forever. A few bridges spanned the flowing blue water, including the one with the white towers that she already knew.

Where the bridges met the far bank, there were always a few clustered houses and mooring places, and Anita got the impression of roads pushing their way in under the trees.

"What do you call the river?" she asked, gazing down at the crystal water as it glinted and sparkled in the sunlight.

"The Tamesis," Rathina replied, leaning over her shoulder.

"Tamesis?" Anita echoed. "That's quite like Thames." She looked into Rathina's inquiring face. "That's the name of the river that runs through London," she said.

"London?"

Anita shook her head. "It doesn't matter."

She made her way over to the other side of the tower. To the north, the land was more open. Close under the wall of the palace, she saw wide, ornate gardens with yellow pathways and colorful flower beds. Farther away there were scattered clumps of woodland, but there were also wide-open stretches of grass, like a vast park. There was a lake of clear blue water, encircled by reeds and willows. In a ring of tall trees, she glimpsed the slender white spires of a solitary building. And beyond that the land rose into rolling hills of purple heather.

Anita leaned farther over the parapet wall and stared down at something that had caught her eye, close under the tower where she was standing. It was a triangular clump of greenery. As she looked more carefully she saw that it was a tight network of neatly tended hedges.

"Is that a maze?"

"It is," Rathina said. "Do you remember it?"

"Well, yes," Anita said. "But not from here." She looked at her sister. "I remember it from back home. From Hampton Court."

Rathina smiled uncertainly. "I have never heard of that place. Is it far from here?"

"That's the whole point," Anita said. "It's not *here* at all. Or at least, it is, but it's different. It's back in the world I come from—the real . . . I mean, the Mortal World." It felt odd to use that phrase.

"Ah yes, I have heard of such things," Rathina said, to Anita's surprise. "Sancha would be able to explain it more clearly."

"Explain what?"

Rathina held her hands up, palm to palm but not quite touching. "The Realm of Faerie and the Mortal World lie close together," she said. "But there are places where the veil between the two worlds is very thin, where Faerie and the Mortal World almost touch." She brought her hands together, linking her fingers. "Maybe this is such a place."

"I suppose that would explain how I ended up here," Anita said. *And keep slipping back*, she thought. She smiled at Rathina. "So, where to now?"

"To the Queen's Apartments," Rathina said.

They went back down the winding stairway and walked arm in arm through a seemingly endless succession of function rooms and gorgeous sun-filled courtyards and shady ivied cloisters and enclosed formal gardens. Anita recognized some of it as being part of Hampton Court, but there was far more that she didn't know and had never seen. They came into a wide, grassy courtyard, and for the first time, Anita found herself in the presence of Faerie children.

Two young women in sky blue gowns were watching over them as they played. The children ranged from babies to a few that Anita guessed must be about nine or ten years old. But what struck her with a jolt was the sight of long slender gossamer wings sprouting through slots in the backs of the children's clothing.

Wings!

They looked exactly the same as the ones she had grown and lost that night in the hospital.

A toddler of about eighteen months was sitting in the lap of one of the women, playing with a straw doll. Every now and then, he would toss it away, and then clap his hands and rise up out of the woman's lap and fly awkwardly on straining wings to fetch it back. Once his little wings failed him and he plopped down into the grass and cried so that he had to be gathered up and comforted.

A group of older children was playing with a ball, throwing it high into the air so that each in turn had to spring up and fly to retrieve it. Others were playing tag, chasing one another around the courtyard, flying into the air to escape being caught, their fine wings iridescent in the sunlight.

Anita felt a pang of loss that her wings had with-ered so quickly. It would be wonderful to fly again.

Then she noticed that the eldest children were playing games that did not involve flying, and one or two of them were even wearing clothing that covered their wings, creating lumps in the backs of their clothes.

She looked curiously at Rathina. "You haven't got wings, have you?" she asked.

Rathina gave her a shocked, slightly offended look. "Indeed not," she said. "Fie, Tania! Do you think me a child?"

Anita tapped her forehead with one finger. "No memory," she said. "Remember?"

Rathina laughed. "Then you are forgiven, but to suggest that a grown person still has their wings is to call them childish."

"Why is that?"

"We are born winged, and for the first ten or twelve years of our lives the wings grow with us, but as we near adulthood, the wings wither and fail until at last they are quite gone." She squeezed Anita's arms. "I remember you as a child, flitting through the corri-dors like an errant damselfly, full of mischief and way-wardness. You told me once that you never wanted to lose your wings, that you wanted to be able to fly for-ever." She smiled. "But on your tenth birthday, you ordered a gown without the back slashes and you never flew again." She nodded. "And that was as it should be. We cast off such childishness when we are grown."

Anita looked at her without saying anything. She had been intending to tell Rathina about that marvelous flight of hers, of how breathtakingly wonderful it had been to soar and swoop through the night air. But now she decided not to. She didn't want Rathina to think she was childish. Maybe later, when they knew each other better, she could make the confession. Or perhaps Zara was a better person to confide in; fun-loving Zara might understand.

They watched the Faerie children for a little while longer. Anita was saddened a little that their joy in flying wouldn't last.

At last, Rathina led Anita out of the courtyard and on through the boundless expanse of the Royal Palace.

At the top of a wide flight of white marble stairs, they came to a high-domed lobby with pure white walls. A pair of tall white doors stood closed ahead of them. Rathina had been quiet for several minutes, and now she stood in front of the doors with her head bowed.

"Our mother's apartments," she murmured. "We come here seldom. It is too sad. But you should see them, I think."

She touched the doors with her fingertips and they swung silently open.

Anita stepped over the threshold and gazed around. The room was very large, with a high ceiling of intricately decorated plaster. The rugs and furniture were all either white or ivory-colored—the wood as pale as cream, the upholstered chairs and couches as white as snow. Several doors opened from the room, and at the far end were tall windows that stretched from floor to ceiling, draped with white lace. Anita saw that one of the long windows was partly open. A gentle breeze wafted into the room, scented with lilies, making the drapes shiver like falling water.

Scattered around the room were personal items: a sewing frame with white linen stretched over it, the embroidered pattern half finished. In one corner stood a harp. A book lay open on a low table.

Rathina walked over to a glass dome set on a small circular table. Under the clear glass lay a white crystal crown inlaid with black jewels. Rathina touched the glass with gentle fingers.

Anita stood at her side. She had seen that delicate crown once before, on the head of the Queen when she had first arrived in Faerie and Gabriel's enchantment had given her a glimpse of the palace before five hundred years of twilight descended.

Rathina sighed and turned away.

It felt to Anita as if the room had only been left empty for a few seconds, as though the Faerie Queen might walk in there at any moment. It was almost impossible to believe that all this hushed beauty had been frozen in time for five hundred years and that its owner was long-dead.

"Do you remember our mother at all?" Rathina

asked her in a subdued voice.

Anita frowned. There was certainly something about this room that stirred up feeling in her—sorrow and loss and a kind of regret, almost. But she could not see Titania in her mind's eye, and she had no real sense of connection with the Queen who had once lived in these apartments.

Then she remembered her own mother and felt a pang of homesickness. She wondered how long it would be before she woke up and found herself back with her real family.

She shook her head. "No, not at all," she said. "Let's go."

The melancholy of the Queen's apartments seemed to linger as they retraced their steps through the palace, and it was a while before Anita felt like speaking.

"Where to now?"

"Would you like to see Cordelia's menagerie?" Rathina suggested.

"That would be great." A menagerie sounded fascinating, and maybe spending time with some animals would help to lighten her mood.

The interiors of the palace were far too complex for Anita to be able to tell where she was, with narrow winding corridors and rooms that led into other rooms, and twisty staircases where the dazzling sunlight shone through curiously shaped windows. But she knew Rathina was leading her back more or less the way they had come. Walking along a high gallery with windows to one side, Anita was startled when hands slapped at the outside of the glass near her and a small impish face looked in and grimaced at her for a second.

The face dropped away and Anita looked down through the window and saw that they were above the courtyard with the children in it. The child who had surprised her at the glass was flying back down to the grass in long, lazy circles while one of the women called up to her.

Anita recognized something as they walked across a long cobbled courtyard with a stone fountain in the middle. At the far end of the courtyard was a square tower with a pointed roof, its walls overgrown with a dense blanket of ivy. "Isn't that where Eden lives?"

"Indeed it is," Rathina said. "But we do not go that way. Our path lies through this gateway here." She indicated an exit that led off in the opposite direction.

But Anita stopped and gazed up at the gloomy tower with its leaf-mantled walls and small, dark windows. She tried to imagine what it must be like for Eden to have locked herself away in that place for such a long time.

She couldn't understand why Eden hadn't come out of her tower when she had arrived in Faerie. Everyone else was delighted to see her; why not Eden? Maybe she didn't even know her long-lost sister was back. Well, she could soon change that.

She walked toward the tower.

"Tania—come away," Rathina called.

Anita lifted a hand without looking around. "I'll only be a minute," she called back.

At the base of the tower she saw three gray stone steps that led up to a square black door, over which the ivy hung in long tendrils. There were no windows at ground level. She walked around a corner of the tower. Now she saw a large circular window. It was half overrun with ivy, and the glass was dark and grimy. She could make out that it was divided into some kind of pattern, and that the glass was colored, like stained glass windows she had seen in churches. She stood under the window; the curve of the lower sill was at shoulder height. The daylight reflected gray off the glass so that she could not see through it very clearly.

She rubbed the glass with the heel of her hand and peered more closely. She let out a breath. She thought she could see something now: a dark figure standing in the room beyond, shrouded in some kind of dark habit or hooded cloak.

"Eden?" Anita breathed. Such an air of despair and grief came from the vague shape that she felt a coldness fingering its way up her spine and a darkness seeping into her mind.

Suddenly a hand snatched at her wrist and she was dragged away from the glass.

"We must not linger here, Tania," Rathina scolded as Anita stood blinking at her, astonished to find that it was still bright daylight in the courtyard. "Come away."

"I saw something," she said as Rathina drew her across the courtyard. "Through the round window. I'm not sure what it was."

"The room was our sister's sanctum," Rathina said. "It was there that she practiced the Mystic Arts long ago." Her voice was insistent. "We do not go there, Tania. The place is shunned."

"Yes. I understand. Sorry." She looked back at the tower. For a moment she thought she saw a face at the upper window, but it was gone in an instant and she couldn't be sure that it was anything more than a trick of the sunlight.

They walked along a corridor and through a large airy room with doors that opened onto the sunlit palace gardens. A network of yellow paths was divided by clipped lawns and teeming flower beds, flanked by statues and fountains and rows of slender, neatly trimmed trees.

Rathina led the way along a path that ran under the palace walls. It wound through an aisle of tall rhododendron bushes, and at the far end, it opened out in front of the maze.

It looked eerily similar to the one Anita had seen at Hampton Court—an exact copy, in fact, except that here there were no signs and no black metal turnstiles barricading the entrance. She walked closer and peered through the towering, rustling hedges.

"We were on a school trip," she said. "I just walked in and found my way to the middle as if I'd done it a hundred times before." She looked at Rathina. "Weird, huh?"

"We used to play hide-and-seek in the maze," Rathina said. "Zara and Cordelia and you and me, when we were children."

"Not the others?"

"Sancha sometimes, when we could tear her away from her books," Rathina said. "But Hopie and Eden were too solemn for such pastimes." She smiled. "You were always the best at such games, although you would often cheat by flying above the hedges."

"I was a bit headstrong, then?" Anita said.

"Indeed you were."

As she gazed down the leaf-lined walkway, she had a fleeting memory of herself zipping along between the bushes on fast-beating wings, her feet skimming the ground, her arms outstretched, her body lying flat in the air, yelling with laughter as her shouting sisters chased after her.

She shook her head. Not real. *Not real!*

She heard children's voices calling out from inside the maze.

"They are playing, as we once did," Rathina said. "Do you wish to enter?"

Anita shook her head. Seeing the maze had brought the school trip back to her more vividly than ever. It had been immediately after that trip that she had first met Evan. In this dreamworld Evan didn't love her— he had betrayed her, lied to her, made her look like a fool—and she didn't want to think about that.

They walked on through a grove of fruit trees and came to a cluster of low wooden buildings with thatched roofs. The buildings stood at the edge of a network of paddocks and small ponds divided by rows of trees or by low fences of wickerwork panels.

Anita saw roe deer grazing alongside goats and sheep and small, long-horned cows with shaggy coats of brown and white. There were beavers and otters in the pools, and squirrels and martens and long-limbed monkeys in the trees. Round eyes peered and long tails whisked as Anita and Rathina walked past. Swans glided on the ponds and geese and ducks waddled to and fro beside the water. Ravens and kestrels and kites perched watchfully on the fences, and gray doves fluttered prettily in and out of a large dovecote.

A small brown goat came and nuzzled Anita's hand, gazing up at her with gentle, questioning animal eyes. She stopped for a moment to fondle the long soft ears.

"Tania, do not dawdle," Rathina said, walking on. "By my troth, you were ever thus."

"I like animals," Anita defended herself as she ran to catch up with her sister.

She heard a scampering sound and saw a large brown crested lizardlike creature darting through the tall grass. Including the whipping tail, she guessed that it must be almost four feet long.

"It's a salamander," Rathina told her. "Beware, it has fiery breath. It will burn you if you venture too close."

"Really?" Anita stared in amazement as the animal flicked out of sight.

A few moments later, she noticed a thatched hutch with a closed and barred door. As she approached it, a glittering red eye regarded her from a small window about four feet from the ground.

"What's in there?" Anita asked.

"A basilisk," Rathina said. "It is sick. Cordelia believes she can nurse it to health, and then it will be taken into the mountains and released."

"What's a basilisk?" Anita asked, drawing closer to the window.

Rathina didn't reply. Anita glanced over her shoulder and saw that she had moved a little way off and was leaning over a low fence, watching otters playing on the muddy bank of a pond.

"Hello there," Anita whispered, crouching down to look through the window. "Who are you then?" She lightly tapped the glass. The red eye had drawn away into the darkness, but she still had the feeling of being watched with wary intensity. "Don't be frightened," she said. "I won't hurt you."

There was a sudden flurry of movement inside the hutch as the creature lurched toward the window. A fierce curved beak snapped at the glass and a malevolent eye stared out at her, red as blood and as cold as stone.

Anita fell back, gasping as the dreadful, glittering eye held her gaze. A dizziness swam in her head and her limbs felt heavy and clumsy. She tried to get to her feet, but she had no strength. She stared into the eye, the blood throbbing in her temples, her vision rimmed with red fire.

There was a pain in her chest, like a fist squeezing her heart. The booming of the blood in her head began to slow. An evil red darkness bled down over her eyes. A coldness seeped through her.

"My lady!" The voice came to her from a vast distance, filled with urgency. "My lady, look at me!" A face emerged from the darkness.

"Gabriel?" She felt as if a suffocating weight had been lifted off her. She blinked, amazed by the bright daylight. She was sprawling on the ground and Gabriel was crouching over her, shaking her shoulders, his anxious eyes looking into hers.

"What happened?" She gasped.

"Can you stand?"

"Yes, I think so." He drew her to her feet. Pins and needles swarmed in her legs as he walked her back to the path.

Rathina was standing there, her hands over her mouth. "I did not think that she would go so close to the beast," she said. "Tania, has it done you harm?"

Anita shook her head to clear the fiery shadows out of her brain. "I'm fine," she said. She looked back fearfully at the hutch. "What *is* that thing?"

"A basilisk of Fidach Ren," Gabriel said. "It is a dangerous creature—an evil blend of cockerel and serpent. Its gaze is deadly." He looked at Rathina. "My lady, you should not have left Princess Tania alone. She knows not the dangers that lurk in this Realm."

Rathina lifted her head and gave him a cold look. "I do not need to be schooled in my duties to my sister," she said. "You may leave us, my lord."

Gabriel gave a shallow bow. "Forgive me, my lady," he said. He looked at Anita. "I will depart, with your leave," he said. "I have been summoned to the King's Council."

Anita smiled at him, the terror of the basilisk's gaze already fading away in the glorious Faerie afternoon. "Thanks for saving me," she said.

"Always your devoted servant," Gabriel said, bowing low again and then turning and walking quickly away toward the palace.

Anita looked at Rathina with a raised eyebrow. "That was a bit harsh," she said. "He did rescue me from that thing."

Rathina linked her arm with Anita's and led her along the path. "I am a princess of the Royal House of Faerie," she said. "I will not be scolded by the likes of Gabriel Drake."

"Even if he was right?"

Rathina's face broke into a smile. "Most especially if he was right," she said. She squeezed Anita's arm. "I should have warned you about the basilisk," she continued. "Had I been the one to discover the monster, I should have cut its head off without a moment's thought. But Cordelia has a soft heart and will aid any animal in distress. Why, once she even found a griffin in the woods, wounded by a huntsman's arrow. She tried to nurse it back to health, but it proved too wild even for her patience, so she released it into the forest." She looked at Anita. "Not all is beauty and grace in this land, Tania," she said. "You would be wise to remember that."

"I will," Anita replied fervently. "I certainly will."

They walked onward, arm in arm through the menagerie. A reclining leopard regarded them lazily with luminous yellow eyes from the shade of a tree. A fox dozed in a patch of sunlight. A stag walked unconcernedly across their path, turning its splendidly antlered head to look at them for a moment.

Anita wandered through the menagerie in absolute delight, twisting her head at each new movement, at each new pair of fearless, curious eyes.

A small, delicate creature ran past, its hooves making the softest tapping sound on the path. It was like a slender white horse, with a pale blue mane and tail, and large violet eyes. But it was no bigger than a fallow deer; its head only came to Anita's waist. As it tossed its head, the sunlight sparkled on its single horn.

Anita gaped at it. "I thought unicorns were dangerous."

"The great ones that dwell in the far north are deadly," Rathina said. "But their southern brethren are small and gentle and easily tamed. You used to have one as a pet. It's name was Percival. Do you not remember?"

Anita shook her head. At times it was very frustrating that the dream would not allow her to recall her past in this world. Princess Tania seemed to have had a fabulous childhood.

They came to where a servant girl stood scattering grain to a graceful assembly of peacocks. The beautiful birds were bobbing their heads and pecking up the grain, their long tails furled up. But as Anita and Rathina approached, one bird lifted its head and its great fan-shaped tail spread out in a magnificent display.

"Where is Princess Cordelia?" Rathina asked the servant girl.

"At the kennels, my lady," she replied with a curtsy.

"Belladonna, one of her favorite bitches, whelped a few weeks ago," Rathina explained to Anita. "No doubt we shall find Cordelia festooned with pups."

They headed toward the kennel buildings. Anita stopped as a white duck led a long trail of fluffy yellow ducklings across their path. She watched, smiling, as the mother urged her children into a nearby pond.

Rathina clicked her tongue with mock impatience. "Give me a good mettlesome steed," she said, "and all the rest may take care of themselves. Come, now. Belladonna's pups await!"

Anita could hear the puppies yapping as they approached the kennels. Rathina opened the wicker gate to let them in.

Cordelia was sitting on the ground covered with leaping and crawling puppies. They were all light brown with yellow eyes; from a quick count Anita calculated there were eight or nine of them.

A fully grown dog lay nearby, panting in the heat, watching her pups with her ears half-pricked.

"Cordelia, is this any way to behave?" Rathina chided. "These are meant to be working animals, not silly lapdogs. What would Father say to see you treat them so?"

Cordelia laughed, fending off the madcap puppies with both hands. "There is time enough for them to learn their duties," she said. "Tania! Come and help me, please. I am overthrown!" And she gave a shout of laughter as the weight of puppies sent her rolling onto her back in the grass.

Anita ran over to the puppies and dropped down to her knees. Within moments there was a wriggling puppy in her lap and a wide wet tongue was licking her face. "They're totally adorable!" She gasped as another puppy attacked her from the side.

"Fie! What children you are," Rathina said with a laugh. "I have sterner pleasures to attend! I shall away to the stables and have Maddalena saddled. Then we shall try a few jumps together out on Puck's Heath." She looked down at Anita. "I shall leave you to your newfound friends," she said. "Mind you wash and change before luncheon. I'll not sit a-table with a sister who stinks of hounds." And with a last shake of her head she strode away.

Cordelia pushed herself upright and smiled at Anita. "The other hounds need to be exercised," she said. "Would you like to come with me?"

"Of course," Anita said, carefully putting the puppies onto the grass and scrambling to her feet.

A few of the more adventurous puppies followed them until Cordelia gave them a sharp command and they all went scuttling back to their mother.

They went through another gate into a fenced-off area filled with long-legged dogs who clamored to be let out as soon as they caught sight of Cordelia.

She opened the gate and for a few moments she and Anita were knee-deep in a racing tide of dogs. The hounds had deep chests; tightly muscled, powerful flanks; and thin, whiplike tails. Their heads were small, with long, narrow snouts and large intelligent eyes. Bright pink tongues lolled between sharp teeth as they panted.

At a word from Cordelia, the pack headed across the fields in a fluid stream, baying and barking as they ran.

Anita and Cordelia chased after them, Cordelia calling out instructions that sent the pack veering to the left or to the right or brought them to a panting, eager halt while the two of them caught up.

One hound left the pack and went racing away toward a clump of trees.

"Pyewhacket!" Cordelia called. "Come back!"

The dog came to a tumbling halt and trotted slowly toward her with his head down. He sat at her feet, staring up at her with great amber eyes.

"You must learn to obey my commands," Cordelia

said to the hound. "Do you not wish to become one of the King's pack when you are old enough?"

The dog made some whimpering sounds and then barked.

"I have heard that story before from you," Cordelia said sternly. "But you are grown too old for such puppy-dog tales! Away with you, go, wait with the others."

The dog got up and ambled over to the rest of the pack, looking back at her every now and then with remorseful eyes.

"I'm sorry if this sounds like a stupid question," Anita said. "But did you just understand what that dog said to you?"

"Indeed I did," Cordelia said. "He told me that he was urged on by Will-o'-the-wisp and Fletch. He always blames others for his misdeeds." She smiled. "The ability to understand the speech of all animals is my special gift," she added.

Anita stared at her, unable to think of anything to say in reply but wondering what other surprises awaited her in this astounding dreamworld.

They continued to walk as the tree-scattered parkland rose in a long gentle slope. It wasn't long before they had left the menagerie and the buildings some way behind. Anita turned, shielding her eyes against the sun, and gazed back at the palace. And for a moment, as she stood there with the wind in her hair, the smell of the hounds and the grass in her nostrils, and the wide-open lands of Faerie at her back, she was overwhelmed by such a sensation of contentment—of *belonging*—that she felt as if she could almost have reached out and touched it.

She turned to Cordelia, who was a short distance away, running up the slope in a sea of hounds.

"I'm meant to be here!" she shouted after her sister. "Gabriel was right! This is my home—"

The ground seethed under her feet. The world rippled—grass, trees, hill, and sky all dissolving in front of her eyes. A roaring wind burned through her head. She stumbled, dizzy and filled with sickness.

"No!"

All of Faerie had ripped open around her.

She heard the blare of traffic. The feel of hard tarmac under her feet.

She was standing in the middle of a busy street, surrounded by traffic that swerved to avoid her. Horns blasted in her ears and the driver of a white van shouted angrily at her from his open window.

Anita stared wildly around, reeling from shock—disorientated and nauseous and utterly terrified. The deafening blast of a horn rang out behind her and she spun around. A bus was bearing down on her, the driver staring at her in horror and wrenching frantically at the wheel. But it was too late. The bus was moving too fast. There was no way for it to avoid her.

Instinctively, she threw her arms up over her face.

The dream had ended. Somehow she had wandered out of her hospital bed in a blacked-out state, and she had come to her senses just in time to be run down and killed.

VIII

Anita felt the bus hit her. It was like a rushing wall, a crashing wave, a thundering avalanche slamming into her body. The pain seemed to tear her apart, to blast her to atoms. She screamed, her mind consumed by a darkness that was lashed with red flame and filled with a scorching, searing heat.

She felt herself tumbling over and over. But as she plummeted, she saw a pale light flickering below her. It sped toward her, a clear blue light, and there was a face in the light, an anxious face.

"Tania? What is it?"

Anita came slamming back into Faerie with a force that left her gasping. She was back on the grassy hillside with a river of hounds moving around her legs and Cordelia staring worriedly into her face.

Waves of heat and cold coursed through her. She collapsed to her knees, doubling up.

Cordelia crouched beside her. "Shall I fetch Hopie?"

"No," Anita managed to croak. "It's okay. I'll be

fine." She looked into Cordelia's face. "Did I disappear?"

"Disappear? I do not know." Cordelia laid her hand on Anita's forehead. "I was busy with the hounds. I turned when I heard you scream. You looked moonstruck, as if you were seeing demons. What happened?"

Anita wiped the back of her hand across her mouth and knelt back on her heels.

"It's difficult to explain," she said. The feverishness was leaving her, but there was still a buzzing in her ears and a tingling in her hands and feet. She smiled weakly although her head was throbbing. "Help me up."

Cordelia gave her a hand and Anita got to her feet. She took a long, deep breath.

"I would like to know what ails you," Cordelia said, her voice serious.

"You wouldn't believe me if I told you," she warned.

Cordelia frowned. "If you speak honestly, then I will certainly believe you." She pointed to a grassy hillock shaded by a huge oak tree. "Come, let us sit, and you shall tell me these truths that cannot be believed."

Anita smiled grimly. "Okay," she said. "You asked for it."

They sat with their backs to the trunk of the oak tree. The hounds snuffled the grass around them. Anita was comforted by the sound, although she had her eyes closed as she spoke.

"The thing is," she began, "this place, this whole world, is a dream. The fact is, I'm lying in a hospital bed right now. I might even be in some kind of a coma. Or maybe they've given me some kind of drugs that are making me dream all this crazy stuff." She paused, expecting some kind of response from Cordelia. "You think I'm crazy, don't you?" she said into the silence. She opened her eyes and looked at her sister. "You think I'm crazy."

Cordelia shook her head. "I do not think that, Tania," she said. "But part of you is surely lost still."

Anita sighed. "Well, of course *you're* not going to believe me," she said. "You're part of the dream. And I love this place, Cordelia, I really do. But I can't spend the rest of my life in a dream. I have to wake up, and when I wake up, all this," she spread her arms, "all this will disappear." She swallowed hard. "I'll be back in the real world where my boyfriend has gone missing." She frowned. "Except in this dream, he's not missing at all. He's here, but I'm dreaming him all *wrong*. He doesn't love me here . . . and . . ." Her voice cracked as her emotions threatened to overwhelm her. ". . . and I just want it to end. I want to go home!"

Cordelia didn't reply for a while. "This is not a dream," she said at last. "The Realm of Faerie is as real as the Mortal World."

"No, it isn't," Anita insisted. "I was just back in the

real world. That's what happened to me. I'd woken up!"

Cordelia looked calmly at her. "You did not wake up, Tania. You moved from our Realm into the Mortal World, because you alone have the power to do so."

Anita shook her head. "I woke up," she insisted. "You won't ever believe me, but that's what happened."

"And how did you fare in the Mortal World?" Cordelia asked.

"Not very well," Anita said with a shudder, remembering that careering bus. "I was hit by . . ." Her voice faded away. She was hit by a bus. She had been standing in the middle of the road and a speeding bus had run her down. "I should be dead," she breathed. "That bus should have killed me."

It was impossible that she could have survived the impact, and yet here she was.

She curled over, her face in her hands. "This is totally insane," she murmured. "What's happening to me?"

This had to be a dream. *It had to be!* Otherwise everything she remembered about herself—her mum and dad, Evan, Jade, and her other friends—everything she had ever done or said or felt or experienced was gone forever.

"You belong in the Realm of Faerie," Cordelia said gently. "You are Princess Tania, my beloved sister, returned to us at last." She touched Anita's arm. "The fact that you moved between the worlds a few moments ago only goes to prove that I am right. You may not yet be able to control the power, but it is yours by birthright, and yours alone."

"No!" Anita shouted. "No! No! No!" She scrambled to her feet. "Just shut up!" she shouted. "You're not real!"

She ran wildly along the hillside, tears flooding from her eyes so that she was half blinded. She heard Cordelia calling after her, but soon the voice faded, and still she ran, not caring where she was going. She blundered through copses of rustling trees and over stretches of long grass, running and running till her legs ached and her lungs burned and a terrible pain stabbed deep into her side.

The ground leveled out and she plunged into a great expanse of waving, shoulder-high reeds. She ploughed onward, sweeping the reeds aside with her arms, crushing them under her feet.

But no matter how fast she ran, no matter how far she went, she couldn't outdistance her dream, and the whole vivid world of Faerie kept pace with her until at last she tripped and fell sprawling onto her face.

The shock cleared her mind a little—that, and the fact that her hands had splashed into water. She pulled herself up onto her hands and knees and drew the curtain of reeds aside. She found herself staring out over a wide lake. Swifts swooped and darted over the still water. All around her she heard the chirrup of grasshoppers. Insects hovered above the burnished surface.

On the far side of the lake she saw thin white spires rising out of tall trees.

It was the building she had seen from the tower earlier that day; the lonely white building with the slender spires.

She got up and made her way back through the trampled reeds, coming out into the open and walking around the lake toward the building. She felt strangely calm, as if the effort of all that running had drained the confusion and anxiety out of her. All she could think of was reaching that solitary building.

She walked in under the trees and the white structure appeared ahead of her, surrounded by slender silver birch trees. It stood on a plinth of shining white marble. Polished stone steps led up to a massive covered entrance with a roof supported by white pillars. Above the trees, the spires pierced the sky like needles.

Anita's heart began to beat fast as she mounted the steps. The mausoleum towered forty or fifty feet into the sky, dwarfing her. She walked toward an immense open doorway four times her own height. She paused, staring up at the lintel. Words were carved into the white stone.

TITANIA. BELOVED WIFE.
BELOVED MOTHER. BELOVED QUEEN.

Now she knew what this lonely building was—it was the mausoleum that Sancha and Zara had told her about in Mistress Mirrlees's workroom. The great mausoleum that the King had built in memory of his drowned wife.

It was the empty tomb of the woman who, in this dream world, was Anita's dead mother.

Trembling, Anita made her way into the silent building. The statue of a woman stood directly in front of her—life-size and painted in colors that made it seem almost alive.

The woman was wearing a long, light blue gown picked out with white patterns. She was smiling, standing with her arms outstretched in welcome. She had a heart-shaped face with a wide red-lipped mouth and high slanted cheekbones. In her long, flowing red hair, she wore a crystal coronet set with jewels. Her eyes were a smoky green.

Anita came closer, staring up into that familiar face—staring into those eyes.

Her heart missed a beat.

Time stopped.

The green eyes had golden flecks in them.

"No!"

Anita backed away.

She remembered the words that Oberon had said to her that first day, on the barge: *You are as I remembered—the very image and reflection of your mother.*

The face of the statue could have been her own face.

"This is *insane!*" Anita shouted, and her voice came echoing back to her. *Insane. Insane. Insane.* "I'm not your daughter!" *Daughter. Daughter. Daughter.*

She stumbled away from the statue, unable to tear her eyes from that gentle face, but desperate to get out of there.

She was suddenly aware of empty air under her foot. She snatched her head around, realizing too late that she had come to the top of the long stone stairway. She clawed at the air as she plunged backward and fell helplessly down the marble steps.

Her head throbbed. She could feel an intense pain in her shoulder and her ribs, and more pain driving up her right leg and into her hip.

There was light beyond her closed eyelids.

She groaned. The pain was real, there was no doubt about it—as real as the pain she had felt when she had first woken up after the accident on the Thames.

"At last!" She forced open her eyes, convinced that she would find herself in her hospital bed.

A cloudless blue sky stretched above her. She felt grass under her fingers.

"Oh, please, no!"

"Hush, my sister," came a mellow, soothing voice. A face swam into sight. It was Hopie, her brown hair falling across her cheeks as she bent over Anita. Her hand felt cool as she rested it on Anita's forehead.

Anita brought her hands up to cover her face. "I'm still here," she breathed. "How can I still be here?"

"Is she badly hurt?" It was Cordelia's voice.

"There are no broken bones," Hopie said. "It was a long fall, but it could have been much worse. What was she doing here?"

"I do not know," Cordelia said. "She ran from me. I followed, but she was like a wild thing. The hounds found her as you see her, at the foot of the steps. I could not make her wake. I left the hounds to protect her and ran to fetch you."

"Tania? Can you stand?"

"Leave me alone." Anita moaned.

"Sister!" Hopie's voice took a hard edge. "Come now! You are not seriously hurt. Cordelia and I will support you. We must take you to my chamber. There are herbs and potions in my workroom that will give you ease."

"Go away," Anita breathed, but she felt strong hands on her, lifting her from the grass. She tested her feet under her. The pain still throbbed in her shoulder, ribs, and leg, but she could stand, as long as Hopie's hand was at her elbow.

"Now, then," Hopie said. "Lean on us as you walk. Be brave now, Tania. All will be well."

It seemed an age before Anita was finally able to stretch out on cool sheets in Hopie's bedchamber. A warm hand stroked her forehead.

"Hopie will be here in a moment," Cordelia said. "She has medicaments and unguents that will take away the pain."

Anita lay with one arm thrown over her eyes. She

was too exhausted and in too much pain to reply.

She was vaguely aware of someone coming into the room, but she didn't open her eyes.

"How does she fare?" Hopie's voice.

"As you see," Cordelia replied.

"Hmm. Help her to sit up. She must drink this."

"Get off me!" Anita groaned as she was hoisted up into a sitting position. "I don't want anything."

Hopie's voice was stern. "Drink!"

Anita felt the wooden rim of a dish pressed against her lower lip. She opened her mouth and something was spooned in. It tasted bitter. She tried to spit it out. "Swallow!" Hopie ordered. Anita swallowed the nasty, slimy stuff. She opened her eyes. The thick mixture in the bowl was green-gray, like pond scum.

"What *is* that?" she croaked, gagging at the smell.

"White willow and elder to ease the pain," Hopie said. "Gentian root and witch hazel to ward off infection. And sprigs of meadowsweet and myrtle steeped in bergamot oil to lessen the bruising."

"It tastes foul!"

"It is *medicine*," Hopie said. "I did not mix it to taste pleasant. You will feel the benefit shortly."

"I should go and tend the hounds," Cordelia said.

"Yes," Hopie said. "Go. There is nothing more that you can do here."

Cordelia leaned over and touched Anita's cheek with her fingers. "My poor sister," she said. "I wish you well."

"Thanks," Anita mumbled.

Cordelia left the room.

Hopie sat on the edge of the bed, her hand resting on Anita's forehead. "How is the pain?"

"*Painful*," Anita growled. She glared at Hopie. "I don't want to be here anymore," she said. "I want to go home."

Hopie looked at her, her sky-colored eyes sympathetic though her voice was firm. "You are a daughter of the Royal House of Faerie," she said. "You have a duty to your family and to this Realm. This is your home, Tania, not the Mortal World. We have already suffered five hundred years of darkness because of your foolishness."

"No!" Anita said angrily. "That wasn't my fault. That was because Titania drowned. You can't blame me for that."

"Indeed not?" Hopie raised her eyebrows. "Had our father not already been stricken to the heart by your disappearance, then his despair at the death of our mother would not have been so deep." She raised a warning finger. "Be assured, sister, it is only your presence here that makes the sun turn in the sky once more. And you wish to return to the Mortal World and plunge us once more into eternal twilight? How can you be so selfish?"

Anita opened her mouth to reply, but she couldn't think of anything to say.

Hopie stood up. "How is the pain now?"

"Better," she admitted.

"Good. I will leave the potion at the bedside. Take

more if needs be." She frowned. "I have other duties to perform. Call for me if the pain is not gone by cockshut time."

Anita stared after her as she left the room, too bewildered to ask what "cockshut time" might be. She felt her shoulder, surprised by how quickly the pain was receding.

That stuff might taste and smell like something that had been scooped out of a drain, but it certainly did the trick.

She looked around. The walls and ceiling of Hopie's bedchamber were paneled in rich, dark wood, carved to resemble trees and ferns and tall brittle grasses. Polished wood vines climbed the posts of the bed and spread out under the canopy, hanging with bunches of wooden grapes and large flowers carved in the shape of stars.

As Anita stared up, a small movement caught her eye. A bumblebee was busy at one of the flowers. It was the same deep brown color as the carved wood, but it was *moving*. As she gazed at it, the wooden bee took to the air and hovered for a moment before flying ponderously along under the canopy of vines to another wooden flower.

She remembered what Zara had told her yesterday when she had asked about the living paintings in her bedchamber: *"Hopie's chamber is a dark woodland."*

She sat up, her pain almost forgotten. All around her, the paneled walls rippled with subtle movement. The carved trees swayed in a breeze that she could neither hear nor feel. Blades of grass moved as small creatures passed by in the undergrowth. A deer peered out from behind a brown trunk for an instant and then was gone without a sound, its short tail flicking away into the carved shades.

Enthralled by the gentle charm of the room, she looked at a chest-of-drawers carved so that it resembled the stump of a great, felled tree. She noticed a hand mirror lying on the polished surface of tightly coiled tree rings.

She remembered how eerie it had been to look into the face of the statue of Titania in the mausoleum.

Were they really so very similar?

She swung off the bed and limped across to the chest-of-drawers. She was brought up with a gasp as a wooden dragonfly emerged from the forested wall, startling her, hanging for a moment in front of her, then darting back into the trees.

She picked up the hand mirror and went back to sit on the bed.

She stared into the glass.

"If this is a dream and the pain was just part of the dream, then why did it hurt so much?" she said aloud to her reflection. "And if the pain was *real*, why didn't it wake me up?"

Her face gazed back at her.

Queen Titania's face.

Her face.

They were one and the same.

Anita brought the mirror closer so that only her eyes were reflected.

Smoky green, flecked with gold; widening with a sudden, overwhelming understanding.

This wasn't a dream.

She was the daughter of Queen Titania and King Oberon. She was a Princess of the eternal Realm of Faerie.

Stunned, she made herself say the words aloud:

"I am not Anita . . . I am *Tania*!"

Part Two: Tania

IX

Tania awoke with a start. She remembered returning to her own chamber, exhausted and bewildered, throwing herself fully-clothed onto the bedcovers and falling immediately into a deep, dreamless sleep.

She felt strangely refreshed and alert, although at first she couldn't think why. Then she realized that the pain of her fall was all but gone. There was a vague, faraway thunder in her head and a twinge or two in her shoulder and leg, but otherwise she felt fine.

She sat up. Golden sunlight raked across her room from left to right, making the wood paneling glow and lighting up the colors of the tapestries. Beams of sunlight picked out the deep red of the bed curtains and made the glass bottles on the chest-of-drawers glint and sparkle.

She got off the bed, gingerly testing her leg on the floor. No pain. She slipped out of her gown and, dressed only in her shift, went over to the washstand. She picked up the jug and splashed water into the basin. Holding her hair back, she plunged her face into the cool water.

Toweling her face, she gazed at the tapestry that hung in front of her eyes.

She let out a low gasp. The embroidered panel showed distant mountains just as it had always done, high and wild and achingly beautiful. But now Tania was aware of a tiny slender shape picked out in the very finest black stitch work, and the shape was moving, flying across the blue needlework sky. She watched in wonder as the thin shape glided toward her in a long, lazy curve.

"An eagle!" she breathed. Now she could make out the wide span of the up-curved wings, the ragged feather-ends spread out like black fingers. She could see the white head and the magnificent curved beak. As the bird came closer and closer, she found herself gazing into its bright black eye. The beak opened as though the bird was calling. Tania stepped back, alarmed that the eagle was going to fly right out of the tapestry. But at the last second, it wheeled to one side and soared away, making slow circles as it descended into a purple valley.

Her heart thumping, Tania ran from tapestry to tapestry. The perfect mirrored image of the icebergs rippled in the cobalt sea. A polar bear lumbered across an ice floe and dived ponderously into the water. In another of the tapestries, a thunderstorm was raging over the bowed heads of granite gray hills. A jagged strand of sewn lightning snapped at the hills, the needlework hills flaring for a moment into a frenzied blaze of white thread. The black and swollen clouds rolled. Stitches of slanting white rain fell onto a small horse-drawn wagon that fought its way along a narrow path.

Thrilled, she ran to another tapestry, a seascape of serene blue water. She gave a laugh of pure joy as she saw flying fish break the calm surface, their sleek scales catching the sunlight and mirroring it back in turquoise and emerald and sapphire thread before they slipped back again under the smooth skin of the embroidered sea.

Her room had come alive.

She ran to the window and threw the casement wide open. The light of the fading day was rich and heavy, casting long rich shadows and bathing the gardens in warm golden air. She leaned out of a window. The western horizon was banded with sun-drenched yellows and purples and reds. The scents of buddleia and honeysuckle drifted up to her. She breathed deeply, filling her head with the flowery perfume.

"I'm Tania!" she called into the air. "I really am a princess!"

She felt as if she had awoken after a long illness to find herself miraculously cured. And while she had slept, the enchantments of Faerie had come flooding back into her room, awakening her tapestries and filling them with life and movement.

But why *now*? Why had they been so still and life-less before?

She knew the answer without having to think about it.

Because she had finally accepted that the Realm of Faerie was real.

For a long time, she wandered around the room, drinking in the wonder and the beauty of her living tapestries, trying to come to terms with what it all meant. From schoolgirl to princess. From London to a Faerie Palace. From Anita to Tania.

It dawned on her that she was still dressed only in her shift. She walked over to her wardrobe and opened the door. She chose a simple white gown; she was still lacing the bodice when there was a gentle tapping at her door.

"Come in."

A servant girl entered. "By your leave, my lady, the King awaits you in the Privy Dining Room."

"I'm afraid I don't know where that is," Tania admitted.

"I will guide you, my lady."

Tania finished lacing her gown and smoothed down the skirts. "Lead on, then," she said. "I haven't had a thing since breakfast. I could eat a horse." Eyeing her with alarm, the puzzled-looking maid led her out of the room.

One of the problems with being a princess, Tania realized as they walked down a wide flight of stairs, was that ordinary people were kind of scared of you. She had tried to engage the maid in conversation, but the nervous girl answered only in monosyllables with "my lady" added on, and soon Tania gave up.

The Privy Dining Room was relatively small and inviting, although it had the same kind of high, ornate ceiling as all the other royal chambers, and rich, wood-paneled walls. Tall windows had been thrown open to give a view over the ornamental gardens. Dusk was coming and torches had been lit along the paths, casting a warm, soft glow over the stones. The room was dominated by a long dark wood table to which servants were ferrying dishes and platters and bowls. Tania sniffed appreciatively at the delicious smells of the waiting food.

The aromas that filled her head were of roast meat and fresh-baked pies and of steaming vegetables glazed with yellow butter, and of loaves of bread that still smelled of the oven.

The King sat at one end of the table. Ranged around him were most of Tania's sisters and a couple of lords and ladies that she half recognized. Gabriel was sitting at his right-hand side.

Oberon and the other men rose as Tania entered.

"Come, sit by me, Tania," said the King. "Are you recovered from your fall?"

"Yes, I'm much better now, thank you," Tania said, making her way around the table. Zara looked up at her anxiously and reached out a hand as she passed. Tania squeezed her fingers. "I'm all right, really," she said. She leaned in close to her sister's head. "My tapestries have come to life," she whispered.

Zara's eyes brightened. "That is joyous news," she said. "I am so very glad."

"Yes. Me too." Tania looked across the table to where Hopie sat. *Thanks,* she mouthed. Hopie gave her a grave nod.

Rathina leaned toward her. "I rode Maddalena over hurdles as high as my shoulder this afternoon and never once came near to falling," she said. "I am glad you did yourself no harm, but you must take better care of yourself."

"I think the fall did me some good, actually," Tania said, spreading a heavy linen napkin on her lap.

She saw Gabriel looking at her with concerned eyes. She smiled at him and his face cleared.

The King's voice rang out across the table. "I crave your attention, my friends." Everyone turned to look at him. "Honored guests and wise counselors, my beloved daughters, we are gathered here for a parting feast. Tomorrow I shall ride out to meet with the lords of the far-flung Earldoms of my Realm."

"You're leaving?" Tania asked in surprise. She had been hoping for the chance to get to know him better . . . especially if he really was her father.

His hand cupped her cheek. "It must be so, dearest daughter. Far too long have I neglected my duties. I must see to my Realm. I go to meet the lords of Talebolion and of Dinsel, and of far-flung Prydein and of mountainous Minith Bannawg. I have summoned them to meet me at Castle Ravensare in two days' time, and it is a long ride and a hard road for man and horse. I shall take with me a retinue of fifty courtiers. And as is the custom and tradition of this Court, I leave my eldest daughter, Eden, as Regent in my absence." He frowned and his voice lowered. "But she rules in name only, for she has refused to yield her long solitude, so it is to the noble Lord Drake that I bestow the duties of the Court." He nodded to Gabriel. "Full well has he served me, and I hold him in high regard."

Tania looked at Gabriel. Nothing showed on his face except for a gleam of excitement that she caught in his silver eyes.

"And now, good folk, to the feast!" the King declared. "I ride in the morn!"

Tania gazed around the table. It was laden with many different dishes—roast fowl and meat on the bone, savory pies and puddings, and tureens of soup and stew, as well as dishes of vegetables and loaves of warm bread.

Looking down, she noticed that her knife was made of a bone handle onto which a finely worked sliver of sharp gray stone had been fixed. Her fork was also made of bone. She looked around the table— all the plates and bowls and serving dishes were made of wood or china.

"Why don't you use metal?" she whispered to Sancha, who was beside her.

Sancha gave her a puzzled look. "I do not know

that word," she said. "What is *metal*?"

"Iron and steel," Tania told her. "Gold. Silver. Lead. Tin. There are lots of different types. We use it all the time back home." She stopped. "In the Mortal World, I mean. We make knives and forks out of it, for instance. And jewelry and cars and airplanes and bridges and watches and computers. All kinds of things."

Sancha gave her an uneasy look. "I think I know the substance of which you speak," she said, leaning close and speaking in a low voice. "Here it is called *Isenmort*. It is a dire and deadly bane, as virulent as poison." She shuddered. "The folk of the Mortal World must wind themselves about with powerful incantations to protect themselves from its blight."

"It's not really like that back there," Tania told her. "Metal is completely harmless. We wouldn't be able to do without it." Her eyes widened. "Oh! I've just remembered something. Just before the accident, before I came here, every time I touched something made of metal it gave off sparks. Dad just told me it was static electricity, but I knew there was more to it than that." She looked at Sancha. "So, why is metal such nasty stuff here?"

"Because it is not natural to this world," said Sancha. "Its touch withers the skin and gnaws at the very vitals of the body."

"No wonder I was getting sparks from it," Tania breathed. "I suppose I should be grateful it didn't kill me on the spot." She frowned. "But if I belong in this world, and if I'm allergic to metal, then why did it only start affecting me a few weeks ago?"

"Mayhap you were growing into your Faerie self?" Sancha suggested.

Tania nodded. Maybe.

She ate for a while in thoughtful silence.

And as she ate, the full reality of her situation began gradually to fill her mind; her life as she had known it for the past sixteen years was gone forever.

Gone forever . . .

A single tear ran down her cheek.

A single huge tear for her mother and her father, for Jade and for all the other friends that she would never see again, for the life that she always assumed would be hers. Playing Juliet. Finishing school. A long summer touring Europe. And then? A brilliant career? A family? A big house on the coast?

Evan Thomas?

Gone. All gone.

Taken away from her in an instant when Gabriel had appeared in front of her and she had got up out of her hospital bed and followed him.

She imagined that empty bed, the tousled covers thrown back. Nurses scouring the hospital for her. Finding nothing.

She imagined the faces of her mother and father, gray and drawn with anxiety and loss. They could have no idea what had happened to her. How could they? They would be frantic with worry.

"Mum . . ." Tania whispered. "Dad . . ."

"Tania, will you play a duet with me? I can have your lute brought down." It was Zara's voice.

Dragged from her mournful thoughts, Tania blinked at her.

"Our father would like us to play for him," Zara explained.

Tania stood up. "No," she said, pushing her chair away from the table. "I'm sorry, I can't." She stumbled to the door and shoved her way out into the corridor. She needed fresh air, she needed to be alone, she needed time to *think*.

She was halfway to her chamber when she came to a halt. Daylight was fading rapidly, and candles were already flickering in wall sconces along the corridor.

"I have to get back home," she said. "I have to see Mum and Dad again."

But how?

She knew she had the power to walk between the worlds, but so far her trips to the Mortal World had been uncontrolled and very alarming. Was there any way she could go back on purpose and use her powers to her advantage?

"Maybe," she murmured. "If I go back to the first place I remember seeing, maybe I'll be able to work out what to do. It has to be worth a try." She turned on her heel, casting back through her memories of the vast palace, trying to recall the route by which Gabriel had first brought her here.

"The bridge," she muttered under her breath as

she ran. "The white bridge."

She ran to a window, but it faced north over the gardens. Wrong. She ran through various rooms and along several corridors until she found a window that looked out over the river.

Yes. That was the way. She made her way down to ground level and out through a doorway that led into a wide courtyard. The river was to her left, and ahead of her she saw the white towers of the bridge rising into the darkening sky.

She ran across the courtyard, already breathless, but determined to find her way back to the Mortal World, to the hospital, to her parents. Even if she was destined to stay in Faerie, she had to see her mum and dad at least once more—to explain, to try and help them make sense of what had happened to her.

Mum, Dad, guess what? I'm a Faerie princess!

It was so absurd that she could have laughed if it hadn't also been so very awful.

She raced along the bridge, the wind whipping her hair, her skirts heavy around her legs. The night air was cool on her burning face.

She came to the far end of the bridge. She made her way down to the jetty where she had been standing when she had first arrived.

She stood in the same spot, her feet firmly planted, her arms stretched out, her head tilted back, and her face to the sky. "I want to go back!" she shouted.

The trees rustled. The river flowed softly by.

The white stars gazed impassively down at her.

She shook her head. It wasn't going to work, not like this. Then how?

Behind her, a rough, stony track led from the bridge into the forest. Was that the direction from which Gabriel had brought her? Was that her path back?

She jumped down off the jetty and ran under the arch of branches.

The wind rushed in her ears. The blood pounded in her temples.

She gasped for breath, her feet hammering on the packed earth. The trees seemed to tighten around her like a closing fist. The pathway dwindled in the distance to a black pinpoint.

The wind began to roar and bellow in her ears. The world spun like a pinwheel in front of her. She was running on tree trunks, in the branches, upside down with the leaves crunching under her feet. Spinning out of control.

And then the trees were gone and she was running along a white corridor.

She smelled disinfectant. Electric strip-lighting flickered above her head. She saw a sign.

MERCY WARD.

She was back in the hospital.

X

For a few moments, Tania just stood in the corridor, bent over, one hand to her side, sucking in air; recovering from the insanity of that long race between the worlds.

She heard voices and glanced around. There was a large metal-framed cart parked against the wall, filled with laundry. It was nighttime; if she was seen, she would be asked what she was doing there, and probably why she was wearing an old-fashioned dress. She didn't want to waste time with that kind of thing right now.

She slipped behind the cart and pressed herself against the wall, holding her breath as two doctors walked toward her.

"I already do longer hours than any other surgeon in this hospital," one of them was saying. "They don't seem to appreciate that I have a family at home that's being neglected because of this place."

The two doctors didn't notice Tania standing in the shadows.

She breathed out shakily as they turned off the corridor.

She glanced at the chrome rails of the laundry cart. Should she try it? Yes, she had to make sure. Very gingerly, she reached out a forefinger toward the metal. A blue spark arced from the rail, biting at her fingertip, sharp as a wasp sting.

She pulled back her hand, sucking her tingling finger. If anything, the shock was even fiercer than before. *Isenmort*, she thought with a shudder.

She listened for more voices. There didn't seem to be anyone around. She walked quickly along the corridor, heading for Mercy Ward, the same ward she had been in a couple of days ago before her life had been turned inside out.

Was it really only a couple of days? As she walked through the lobby that led to the ward, she felt as if she was revisiting a place she had known years and years before, like returning to a childhood haunt and finding it quite different from the way she remembered it. Not because the place had changed, but because *she* had.

The ward was dimly lit and very quiet. She saw the night-nurse's station with its small pool of light. But no one was sitting at the desk. She walked softly to the end of the room that had held her bed.

She felt an odd, disturbing chill when she saw

there was someone in the bed. What if it was *her*?

But it was a middle-aged man. And he was snoring.

She heard approaching footsteps sharp as the cracking of broken glass in the stillness.

She slid out of sight behind the folded-back curtains.

She could see two nurses approaching. She recognized one as the dark-haired nurse who had picked her up off the bathroom floor the other night; the other one she didn't know.

". . . monitoring bed nine," the dark-haired nurse was saying. "But apart from that you should have a quiet time. You missed all the fun while you were on leave."

"Why, what happened?"

"Only that we had two patients go missing off this ward in one day," the dark-haired nurse told the newcomer. "Unbelievable. And there are supposed to be security people on all the doors down there. Management hit the roof. They've had us on high alert ever since, although what good that's supposed to do is anyone's guess."

"How do you mean, they went missing?" the new nurse asked.

"Well, there was a young man who'd been in a speedboat accident. There wasn't anything seriously wrong with him except that he hadn't regained consciousness. He was the first to do a vanishing act, just disappeared overnight. And then the next morning, in broad daylight, the girl he was brought in with vanished as well. Can you believe that? If you want my opinion, the boy came back and fetched her away and they're halfway to Gretna Green to get married. She's only sixteen, the little fool. And not a thought for her parents, poor things. Isn't that just typical?"

"Didn't anyone see her leave?" said the other nurse.

"A couple of people said they saw her go through the TV room and out onto the balcony. They don't remember her coming back in again, but there's no way she could have made it down to street level off that balcony, it's far too high up. Not unless she flew down." The dark-haired nurse paused to unhook a clipboard from the end of a patient's bed. She checked the notes, then looked up at her colleague. "Mind you, she was a bit odd—odd in the head, I mean."

"In what way?"

"Well, the night before she vanished," the dark-haired nurse began, "I found her on the floor in . . . Oh, good lord, look at the time. I'll miss my bus. I'll tell you all about it tomorrow. Have a nice quiet shift. Oh, speaking of that girl, her belongings have been packed in a box and left in the family room. Her parents are meant to be picking them up in the morning. I just thought I'd mention it in case they come in early and you're still around."

She hooked the clipboard back onto the bed, walked briskly over to the nurse's station to retrieve her coat, and vanished down the corridor.

A bit odd, am I? Tania mused. *And I've run off with my boyfriend? Well, it makes more sense than the truth.*

She waited behind the curtain until the new nurse had taken her seat behind the desk and was busy with some documents. Then she slipped quietly back the way she had come, heading for the family room.

She felt a tight pain in her chest when she thought of her mum and dad. What was worse? Imagining your daughter has been abducted against her will, or assuming that she'd run off with some boy without bothering to say a word about it?

Now that she was back here, her first priority was to make contact with them, to let them know she was all right. But how to explain what had happened?

Tania wasn't concerned that her parents would think she was lying when she told them about Faerie. They'd probably accept that *she* believed it all, but they'd also probably think she was delusional because of the bang on the head. *Off her rocker*, as her dad would say.

She needed some way of proving to them that she wasn't out of her mind.

She thought of the leather-bound book. It would be among her belongings. It had been blank when she had first received it, but now it told the story of her Faerie childhood, right up to the point when she stepped out of Faerie on the eve of her wedding. She had no idea why the writing had been invisible or missing when she had first opened it, but the important thing was that the story was there now. She would be able to show it to her mum and dad. Proof that she wasn't out of her mind.

Tania still had no idea who could have sent the book. Gabriel had never mentioned it, so it was unlikely to be part of his plans. But whoever was responsible, she was in no doubt that it was a Faerie book. At first, when she had believed that her Faerie life was all in her head, she had assumed that the dream had been inspired by the book. But now she knew that wasn't the case at all. The book was the chronicle of her life, all the way from her birth to her disappearance.

But who had sent it to her? Evan? If so, why? To help her come to terms with the truth? To learn about who she really was? Possibly, but why would he send it to her through the mail? Why not just give it to her on the boat trip?

She peered along the corridor, watching for any movement. There was no one around. She opened the door to the family room and slipped inside. The walls were covered in cheerful paintings and posters. The cardboard box stood on a cabinet under the window. She walked over to it and lifted the lid.

She saw her neatly folded jacket on top. She drew it out and stood for a few moments just looking at it. There was a long ragged tear down one sleeve and signs of scuffing on the shoulder and back. But it was clean and dry, not rumpled and drenched and smelling of the river as it must have been when she arrived at the hospital.

She put down the jacket and looked into the box

again. Her shoulder bag lay on the top. Tania reached out and ran her finger over the faded canvas. She knew that it held all the normal, everyday things that proved who she was. Who *Anita Palmer* was. Her school ID card. Her bus pass. Old movie tickets. Lip balm. Elastic hair bands. Her address book. House keys. Her cell phone.

Her cell phone!

If there was any power left in the battery, she could call her mum and dad right now to tell them she was okay, tell them she was on her way home. She could even get them to drive over and pick her up.

Her heart leaped. She picked up the bag. Lying under it was the leather-bound book.

Tania reached down into the cardboard box to pick it up.

The moment her fingers touched the ancient brown leather a howling tornado ripped upward from the box, almost lifting her off her feet.

"No!"

The colored walls began to revolve around her. She tried to pull her fingers away from the book, but it was too late. The room spun, the colors stretching and blurring until she was surrounded by whirling bands of painted light. Red. Green. Blue. Yellow. Red. Green. Blue. Yellow. Faster and faster. And then the lights began to swivel around her, making a nonsense of up and down and left and right, and she lost her balance and fell, screaming, into the terrifying mael-strom.

XI

She was crouched on the ground with her arms folded against her chest, her body bent double so that her head was almost on her knees. From somewhere close by she heard the liquid call of a nightingale. A warm breeze rustled the leaves above her head. She could smell the pungent scents of earth and trees.

"Oh, great!" she groaned, lifting her head. "Perfect!"

She was back in the forest.

The only difference from her previous world slips was that there was no feeling of nausea this time. Maybe she was just too plain angry for that.

She knelt up, sitting on her heels. She was still clutching the leather-bound book. In a fit of rage, she flung it away. It thudded onto the path, falling open in a flurry of thick ivory-colored pages.

"Why can't I control it?" she shouted. "What's the use of having this power if I can't *control* it?"

The canopy of branches deadened her voice.

She gave a snarl of frustration. Ahead of her, the forest trail opened up and she could see part of the white bridge. She looked over her shoulder, staring deeper into the forest. Was it worth trying to get back again?

She shook her head. She was too tired. Her legs felt like lead. She just wanted to get back to her room.

She glared at the book lying open in front of her.

"This is all your fault," she snarled at it. "Stupid, stupid book!"

She crawled over to it.

It had fallen open on the page with the poem.

> *One alone will walk both worlds*
> *Daughter last of daughters seven*
> *With her true love by her side*
> *Honest hand in true love given*

The book was only a record of her life. Of Princess Tania's life. It wasn't the book's fault she couldn't control her power.

Tania picked it up and got to her feet. She gently closed it and smoothed the leather cover, as if trying to make up for her burst of anger.

She began the weary hike back to the palace.

She paused in the middle of the bridge and leaned over the sliding star-speckled water, remembering how Gabriel had given her his cloak when he had first brought her into Faerie, how he had been so gentle and kind, as if he understood how confused she must have been.

There was a small stone lying on the parapet of the bridge. She picked it up and reached out over the water to drop it. It was swallowed up by the river with a soft *clop*. The field of mirrored stars wavered and ripples rimmed with tiny points of light spread out below her.

"The thing is," she said quietly, "if I'm really Princess Tania, then *everything* here is real." A cold shiver ran down her spine. "Everything!"

Including the dreadful truth that Edric really was Gabriel's servant and that he . . . that Evan . . . had *never* loved her. That the boy she loved more than she had ever loved anyone in her life had never really existed. That it had all been pretense.

She turned around and slid forlornly down the wall of the bridge. She sat there, huddled up, clutching the book against her chest and staring up into the sky.

Tears began to flow down her cheeks, and for an endless, desolate time, she surrendered herself to a misery more profound than anything she had ever known before.

She had lost all track of time. Gradually, the tears had stopped. Gradually she had pulled herself to her feet to continue the long walk back to her chamber.

She was glad that she met no one on the way.

She opened the door to her chamber and went

inside. Candles had been lit and placed inside red glass flutes; they bathed the room in a warm ruby glow. She glanced at the tapestries. Night brooded in sultry colors on every embroidered panel, and she could see from the movement of clouds, the rippling of leaves, the wash of the sea, that they were still alive. But they gave her no comfort now. She walked across to the bed and slipped the book under her pillow. Then she crossed to open a window.

She heard a sound behind her, the sharp creak of a floorboard.

There was someone in the room. She spun around.

It was Edric. He must have been standing behind the door. But now he was in full view, blocking her way out.

He was dressed in a dark gray doublet and hose, his blond hair swept back off his face. The face she loved. The face of the man who had betrayed her.

A surge of fury rose in Tania.

"What do you want?" she demanded.

He took a step toward her. "I need to talk to you."

She backed away. "Well, I don't need to talk to you, Evan," she said between gritted teeth. "Oh, sorry, it isn't Evan, is it? What was your real name again? Edric? Yes, that's it. Edric." She glared at him. "Do you know what I hate most about you right now, Edric? It's not that you were hired to drag me here whether I liked it or not. It's the fact that you tricked me into believing you loved me. You must have thought I was such a fool!" She choked, and it was a second or two before she could continue. "That's why I am never, ever going to forgive you. And that's why I want you out of my room." Her voice rose to a shout. "Now!"

Edric strode toward her. She took another step backward, feeling the paneled wall against her back. His hands came down on her shoulders, holding her there.

"You must listen to me!" he said fiercely.

She brought one arm up to knock his hand away. Her other hand rammed into his chest and sent him staggering backward.

"Get your hands off me!"

"I'm sorry." he gasped. "But you have to know the truth."

"What would you know about the truth? You lied to me from the moment we met!" she screamed. "Get out! Get out! Get *out*!" She lunged at him, flailing with her fists.

He fell back, holding his hands up to defend himself.

"What coil is this?" A new voice cut across the room.

Tania saw Gabriel standing in the open doorway, his eyes shining like moons.

"Gabriel!" She gasped, relief flooding through her.

Gabriel swept into the room. He glowered at his servant. "Edric? What mischief do you make in Princess Tania's bedchamber?"

Edric fell onto one knee, his head bowed low. "My lord," he said. "I only came here to beg the princess's pardon for my pretenses of affection in the Mortal World. I wanted to explain that everything that I did was for her own sake." He glanced up at Tania. "I wish only for her most gracious forgiveness."

Tania stared down at him, filled with contempt and loathing. "Fat chance!" she hissed.

Her fingers moved up to the warm amber teardrop that hung from her throat, the pendant she had believed had been a gift from the boy who loved her. Her fist closed around it; she intended to rip it from around her neck and throw it in Edric's face.

Gabriel raised his hand to stop her. "Do not, my lady," he said. She stared at him—it was almost as if he had read her mind. "The Amber Stone was never a gift from this man. It was my gift to you. I had meant to give it to you on our wedding eve."

Tania blinked. "Oh."

"It was because of the Amber Stone that I was able to come to you in the Mortal World and bring you back home," Gabriel said. "While you wear it, I will always be able to find you, both in this world and in the other."

The teardrop glowed in her hand as she clutched it.

Gabriel turned back to the kneeling servant.

"Get you hence from here," he growled, all the velvet gone from his voice. "If you force your company upon Princess Tania again, it will be the worse for you." He pointed a warning finger at him. "Beware the Amber Prison, Master Chanticleer! Beware!"

Edric slunk from the room like a beaten dog. Tania was glad to see him go; he deserved worse than a reprimand, in her opinion. As the door closed behind him, Gabriel took hold of Tania's hands.

"I apologize for my servant's actions," he said. "I would not have you distressed by such things." He smiled at her. "All this world must be a confusion and a bitter torment to you. Memories of your mortal life must flock like ravens in your mind. I wish that I could find a way to ease your suffering."

"It is kind of freaky," Tania agreed. "But I suppose I'll find some way to get over it . . . eventually."

"I pray that it be so."

She looked into his face. "This is all really happening, isn't it?" she said quietly.

"It is." His eyes were warm and comforting as he gazed back at her.

She frowned. "Back . . . back where I came from," she began hesitantly, "Edric was a real person. But you were, kind of, not quite there. I could see through you. Why was that?"

"I sent Edric to you as a real man," he said. "He was protected by black amber, a rare stone that holds back the poison of Isenmort."

"His wristband," Tania said. "That's why he always wore it."

"Indeed," Gabriel said. "It would have been perilous indeed for him to have taken it off. But I, my lady, I was but an image in your mind."

"But I touched you, on the balcony; I had hold of your hand."

Gabriel smiled. "That was not I, my lady—that was done by your own powers—reaching to me across the worlds."

Tania looked thoughtfully into his face.

"I was about to marry you when I disappeared, wasn't I?"

He closed his eyes for a moment before replying. "You need not speak of that, my lady," he said. "As earth covers earth, so let the past bury the past."

"I'm not exactly sure what you mean by that," Tania said. "But I'd like to talk about it now, if that's okay with you." She gave a half-smile. "I suppose we must have been . . . well, *fond* of each other."

"There was great affection," he said quietly. "For my part, at the very least."

"So you must have been upset when I just vanished like that," she said.

"Truly," he said, his voice only just above a whisper. "I searched for you down all the long ages until at last I found you."

"How did you find me?" Tania asked. "Was it something to do with that school trip to Hampton Court? I felt weird all the time I was there, as if I knew the place without ever having been there. And parts of this palace are just like it."

"Indeed, my lady. There are places where Faerie and the Mortal World come close to each other."

"Yes, Rathina told me about that," Tania said. "And Hampton Court and this palace are one of them. Did you *see* me when I was on the school trip?"

"I did not see you with my eyes," Gabriel said. "But I felt your presence." He touched his fingers to his head and to his chest. "In my mind and in my heart. For a long time, I worked with the Mystic Arts to find a way of sending an emissary into the Mortal World. I chose Edric, believing him faithful and keen of wit, and I sent him through the portal in pursuit of you." He smiled. "And he performed his duties well, my lady."

"Yes," Tania said dryly. "A bit too well, in some cases." She looked at him. "I'm sorry if this is a difficult question for you," she said. "But are you still hoping that we'll get married?"

It was a few moments before Gabriel replied. "I brought you here for the good of the King and for the Realm of Faerie," he said. "I had no thought for myself. You have no memory of our bond of affection, and I would never ask you to fulfill a promise made five centuries ago by a woman you do not even remember being." He gazed over her shoulder and out of the window. "To see the sun rise each morn over Faerie, and to watch the stars revolve in their ancient nighttime dance is blessing enough, my lady. I desire nothing more."

"Call me Tania," she said. "And tell me about a Faerie Wedding. I'd like to know what happens when a duke and a princess get married."

Gabriel let out a gentle laugh. "Surely, I will," he

said. "Have you a mirror, Tania?"

"Yes, over there."

"Come, then, and I shall show you great wonders."

She led him to the chest-of-drawers and picked up the hand mirror.

"Sit you down," he said. She pulled a chair from against the wall and sat on it. Gabriel stood behind her, one hand resting on the back of the chair. He leaned over her and passed his hand across the mirror, whispering words she didn't catch.

"A royal wedding lasts for three days and three nights." His soft voice came from close behind her. "It begins with the Ritual of Hand-Fasting, which takes place in the Hall of Light."

As he spoke, the mirror clouded over; when the mist had gone, Tania found herself staring into a huge, bright hall. But moments later, with no sensation of movement at all, she was no longer holding the mirror and seeing the hall through it; she was actually in the huge room.

It had a high-vaulted ceiling and walls pierced by many tall stained glass windows burning with sunlight so that the whole hall was filled with rainbows of color. Choral music filled the air, and the hall was crowded with people in gorgeous, glittering clothes.

A narrow aisle ran the length of the hall, ending at a platform where a cauldron stood on four stout feet. The air above the cauldron shimmered as if there was something hot inside. Gabriel was standing beside the cauldron, looking every inch the Duke of Faerie.

Oberon and Titania were seated on thrones behind the cauldron. They wore slender crystal crowns, and great white cloaks of silk and ermine, fur-lined and sparkling with star white jewels, were draped over their shoulders.

Tania looked down at herself and realized she was dressed in a white wedding gown. As she walked along the aisle, she felt the weight of a long train dragging behind her. White rose petals fluttered down from the ceiling until the air was sweet and heavy with their scent.

She heard light steps at her back, and, turning her head, she saw her sisters walking behind her, their arms filled with white flowers.

When she came to the end of the aisle, Gabriel reached down to help her onto the dais. The touch of his fingers made her tremble with anticipation. Now she could see that the cauldron was full of a restless amber liquid that seethed and fumed and shone like trapped sunlight.

Gabriel took a small glass jug from a table beside the cauldron. He dipped it into the swirling liquid and lifted it out. Glistening amber drops ran down the sides of the jug and fell back into the cauldron. Tania held her hand out over the liquid, feeling the rising warmth on her skin. Gabriel clasped her hand. He tipped the jug and a flood of thick fluid amber poured down over their hands. Tania winced, expecting it to burn, but it was only warm and as heavy as honey, coating their joined hands and running off in big golden drops.

She gave a gasp of surprise as her hand, her arm, and her whole body began to tingle. She turned her head to look at Gabriel as the intense sensation burned through her. He was gazing at her and his eyes were filled with love and joy.

She felt as if she was going to faint. She gasped for breath, her head swimming, only his brilliant silver eyes remaining constant in the heady swirl of her senses.

"Gabriel . . . I . . . ." But before she could say any more, the Hall of Light dissolved around her and she was back in her bedchamber, gazing into the clouded mirror.

"Oh, wow!" she breathed as the clouds faded and she found herself staring at her own face again. "That was *unbelievable!*" She put down the mirror, her hand shaking. "And the night before all that, I just disappeared," Tania said, gazing out of the window at the starry sky. "But why didn't I come back to you?"

"Only you know the answer to that question, Tania," Gabriel said. "*One alone shall walk both worlds.* I think perhaps you did not mean to walk that path at that time and in that way."

"Rathina said the same thing," Tania admitted. "She said we were just messing about."

"You walked between the worlds again this night, did you not?" Gabriel asked her.

"Yes, how did you know that?"

"The Amber Stone calls to me," Gabriel said. "While you wear it, you can never again be lost. You entered the Mortal World to speak with those whom you knew as your parents, but Faerie drew you back."

There was a sadness in his voice that gave Tania an unexpected pang of guilt. Gabriel was obviously hurt and upset that she had gone back into the Mortal World.

"I beg you not to go there again, Tania," he said softly. "It is perilous indeed. This is your true home; this is where you belong."

"I know that now," she said. "But I have to let my mum and dad know that I'm all right."

Gabriel's voice was little more than a whisper. "I would not lose you again, Tania. I would not have harm befall you."

Tania was lost in silent thought for a few moments. She felt a rush of sympathy and understanding for him, or was it more than that? "It must have been really bad for you," she said. "Losing the person you loved on the night before you were meant to be married."

He didn't reply.

"I'm really sorry." She reached back over her shoulder, holding her open hand out to him.

He didn't take it.

"Gabriel?" She turned her head.

He was gone—but a single, long-stemmed red rose lay on her bed, and her room was suddenly full of its sweet scent.

XII

Tania opened a window and leaned out into the warm, aromatic night. Edric wouldn't be paying her any more unannounced visits, she was sure of that. She wondered what the Amber Prison was. Judging by the look on Edric's face when Gabriel mentioned it, she guessed it wasn't exactly a theme park.

"Who am I?" she asked aloud into the star-filled sky. "I know I'm Princess Tania—at least, I'm pretty sure I am—but I still don't *feel* much like her. I feel like Anita Palmer." She frowned and said the name again aloud. "Anita Palmer of nineteen Eddison Terrace, London, the United Kingdom, Europe, Earth, the Solar System, the Milky Way, the Universe." She smiled, remembering that she had written her address out like that for a few weeks after a visit to the planetarium on her eighth birthday.

And now?

Princess Tania of the Royal Palace, Faerie. What had Princess Tania done on her eighth birthday? She didn't have a clue.

But she knew where she could probably find out.

She went over to her bed and pulled the book out from under her pillow. She sat cross-legged on the covers and rested the book in her lap.

She made her way through her early years, skimming the text for points of interest in the endless details of her infancy.

She had spent her early years entirely in the palace grounds, playing with her sisters or being taught to read and write in a nursery filled with marvelous toys. When she was older, she went for long walks with her mother, Queen Titania, and she was also taught to ride, to play the lute, to dance, to shoot a bow, and to fence with a sword, along with all the other things that a princess had to know about.

In summer, the royal family would travel to Veraglad Palace, a castle built on a high cliff overlooking the sea. Tania read of her pet unicorn, Percival, and of blissful days and weeks spent combing the beaches with him, and of them returning to the palace with necklaces of periwinkle shells strung around their necks. She read of picnics on the beach by the light of roaring bonfires, and of swimming with dolphins and playing catch-as-catch-can with her sisters around the rocks and tide pools that lay in the shadow of the white cliffs.

It seemed to have been a wonderful childhood. A

lump grew in Tania's throat as she turned those heavy pages of lost memories.

When she was ten, she had accompanied her father in the Royal Galleon on a voyage to the outlying islands of his Realm, to Chalcedony and Urm and to the rocky headlands of Highmost Voltar, where the seabirds swarmed as thick as smoke.

On her twelfth birthday the entire palace was given over to her coming-of-age festival. It lasted for five whole days, and there were masques and balls and feasts and entertainments by sunlight and by moonlight. There was music and laughter and fireworks at midnight.

Tania blinked away tears. It was so sad that she remembered nothing about all of this. She couldn't have realized how dangerous it would be to try out her powers that night five hundred years ago. She couldn't have realized that she might *lose* herself.

She leaned back against the padded head of her bed and closed her eyes, desperately searching her mind for any hint that the things she had been reading about had actually happened to her. But it was useless. She remembered nothing.

She couldn't even remember having any feelings for Gabriel, although she was sure she must have, despite what Sancha and Cordelia had said at the ball. And were those feelings stirring again? She frowned, unsure of herself. She liked him, and she was drawn to him, but love? No, not that, not yet; it would be a long time before she would ever let herself be vulnerable in that way again—not after what Edric had put her through.

But Gabriel had loved her, she felt certain of that. And he loved her still.

She opened her eyes and stared across the room.

"I have to let Mum and Dad know I'm okay," she said, closing the book. "After that . . . well, we'll see." She knew that she could probably get into the Mortal World again, but she had no idea how to prevent herself from being whipped straight out of there against her will and without any warning.

What she needed was someone who could show her how to walk safely between the worlds, to explain to her how to get her power under control. But who?

Oberon would know. He had Mystic Powers. She remembered the way he had brought the sky to life with the spreading of his hands, and how he had lit all those candles at the ball with just a gesture. Gabriel had power too. And Eden, her strange, reclusive sister. What was it that Sancha had said? That Eden had been second only to Oberon in the Mystic Arts before she had given it all up and retreated to her lonely, ivy-covered tower. Not that Tania had any real idea of what those Mystic Arts might be.

She knew she couldn't ask Gabriel. He had made it quite clear that he didn't want her to go back into the Mortal World. And Oberon would definitely feel the same.

But what about Eden? Could she be able to help?

If she could, there might even be the possibility of having the control to step in and out of both worlds at will. Tania smiled at the thought. Morning in London, evening in Faerie. Summer in the Mortal World, winter in the Immortal Realm. Not bad!

She undressed and pulled on her nightgown. Then she went around the room, blowing out the candles until the only light remaining was the glimmer of stars.

She laid Gabriel's red rose on the nightstand and got into bed, pulling the covers up over her shoulders.

First thing in the morning, she was going to Eden's apartments to ask for her help. She just hoped that her sister would understand how important it was for her to be able to go into the Mortal World and let her parents know she was all right. If she promised to return to Faerie, she didn't see how Eden could refuse.

The sun hadn't even shown itself over the eastern towers and battlements when Tania slipped out of her room and went in search of her eldest sister.

The cool of morning had dampened her spirits a little, but not enough to make her give up without trying. She knew that Zara and all the others were wary of their older sister but Tania wanted to meet Eden and make up her own mind. She couldn't think of any reason why Eden would be less pleased to see her than the others, and she certainly had no reason to be afraid of her.

She managed to lose herself twice in the tangle of rooms and corridors before she finally stepped into the long cobbled courtyard with the stone fountain in its center. The bleak, ivy-shrouded tower rose up ahead, looking even darker and more grim in the stark, predawn light.

Tania shivered. There was something about the tower that made the hairs stand up on the back of her neck.

Squaring her shoulders, she walked across the ringing cobbles and mounted the three stone steps to the wide black door. She looked around for some kind of knocker, but there wasn't one. She made a fist and hammered on the door panels. The sound was dull and flat.

Then she noticed something else. There was no door handle—in fact there was no obvious way of getting the door open at all. If Eden came out, how did she get back in? Did that mean she *never* left the tower? She banged her knuckles on the black wood again, harder this time.

She waited, sucking her knuckles. She pressed her ear to the door, hoping for some sound of approaching footsteps.

Nothing.

Now what?

"Rats!" She thumped the door with both hands, and gave a start of surprise. She was certain that the huge door had given a fraction under her hands. She put her shoulder to the door and pushed.

The door swung silently open.

"Eden?" she called. Her voice sounded thin and weak. "Eden?"

The silence seemed to grow heavier and deeper as she stepped into the small, bare hallway. To her right a narrow arch led to a flight of worn stone steps that spiraled up out of sight. To the left was a simple door of rough gray wood.

Tania ducked under the arch of the stairway and peered up into the darkness. She didn't like the idea of climbing the winding staircase without even a candle to light her way.

"E-e-e-den!" Her voice was suffocated by the gloom.

Rubbing her hands together for warmth, she walked over to the door. A wooden latch held it closed. She lifted the latch and pushed. The door opened.

The room beyond was very long and thin, with a low ceiling and a single circular window in the far wall.

"Of course!" Tania remembered seeing through this window from the other side, when she had stood outside and tried to sneak a look through the grimy glass. This was the room in which she had glimpsed that miserable, solitary figure.

She walked down the room, her footsteps echoing on the bare boards. The walls and ceiling were smoke gray, but as she moved across the floor, she thought she glimpsed shapes in the grayness. She paused, staring at a section of the wall where she could have sworn she had seen a grotesque face staring out at her. There was nothing there, but again, from the corner of her eye, she saw another leering face with wild eyes.

The twisted mouth moved and a thin, piercing voice spoke. "The fool who enters this room shall die; the crows will pluck out your putrid eyes."

She spun around, but the face dissolved into the wall with a hiss.

Another face grimaced on the edge of sight. A shrill voice called out. "Leave this place, while you can, for if you stay the blood will surely rot in your veins."

Alarmed now, she turned again.

Nothing.

She paused, gathering her courage. "I'm not scared of you!" she said, hoping she sounded braver than she felt. "Either show yourselves or shut up and leave me alone!"

There was a sibilant hiss of ghostly laughter, but still the hideous faces melted away from her direct gaze.

Taking a deep breath, she carried on walking toward the round window.

Malevolent eyes stared at her from the walls and ceiling; faces scowled and sneered. Forked tongues flickered and teeth gnashed as the hissing voices continued to make their chilling threats.

Her spirits began to rise as she approached the window unharmed. She was sure that the contorted faces that glowered all around her and spat out those cruel threats weren't capable of doing her any real damage.

She guessed they must be some kind of mystic protection, intended to scare people away. Well, Oberon's seventh daughter didn't scare that easily.

At last she stood directly in front of the round window. It was as wide as her outstretched arms and its lower rim was at waist height. She tried to make sense of the pattern of grimy lead lights, an intricate design of many-sided glass panels. She could even see the clearer patch in the pane that she had rubbed with her sleeve yesterday.

As she stood there, a faint glow began to light up the window. It seemed to blossom outward from a small heart of brightness near the center, spreading golden petals like a flower unfurling. Tania stepped back in surprise. Then she realized what the light must be: The sun had climbed above the palace rooftops, high enough to shine down into the courtyard. The heart of brightness that was lighting up the window was the sun!

She smiled. As the sunlight grew stronger, it seemed as if the grime and dirt were bleached away, leaving the glass panels to shine out in sheets of pure, radiant color.

And suddenly she saw what the pattern was: It was a multicolored maze of glass that burned with a brightness so intense she could hardly look at it.

Suddenly she could hear voices. Chattering voices from beyond the window.

"Hey, Christina! Take my picture like this!"

"According to the map, this is the Fountain Court, which means the Tudor Kitchens must be this way."

"The trains leave from Hampton Wick Station every half hour, so we've got plenty of time."

"What a great day! We've been really lucky with the weather so far, knock on wood."

Tania stepped closer to the window again. Those were not Faerie voices.

Shielding her eyes from the dazzling light, she stared through the window. The courtyard had changed. The cobbles were now a long manicured lawn, and the fountain was a wide stone pool spouting thin jets of water. Where the walls of the Faerie Palace had stood, there were decorated cloisters and flat-fronted buildings with tall windows and carved white wreaths set into the brickwork.

And walking around this transformed scene were modern-day people with jeans and backpacks and cameras and baseball caps.

The window was showing her the Mortal World.

Her heart leaping, Tania put her fingers to the glass. It was warm and yielding, like a standing pool of liquid light. It melted beneath her touch and allowed her hand to flow right through. The images beyond rippled and swayed and the voices slipped in and out of focus.

Could she simply step right through the window into that other world?

"Stand away from the window. If you value your life, stand back!"

Tania spun around in shock.

A tall woman in a hooded black cloak was standing at the open doorway, her dark eyes blazing. She lifted her arm and made a sweeping, sideways gesture.

Tania gave a stifled cry as invisible hands plucked her off her feet and sent her spinning across the room. She crashed into the wall and fell gasping to the floor as the woman strode toward her with deadly anger in her face.

XIII

Tania scrambled to her feet. Even though the woman's features were twisted with rage, Tania could see the resemblance to Oberon in her pale, drawn face.

Panting, she held her hands up. "Eden, stop!"

"You fool!" Eden spat. "What are you doing here? The Oriole Glass is a dark and murderous thing."

"What do you mean?"

"It is a portal into the Mortal World." Eden turned toward the window and gave a high, passing move with her hand. The rainbow of lights dimmed and the room became bleak and gray again.

"It is closed now," she said. "The peril is gone."

"But I'm supposed to be able to get into the Mortal World, and get back again," Tania said. "It's in the poem. I'm the seventh daughter, aren't I?" She watched her sister closely. "That's why I came here to see you. I need to know how to control the power. I want you to help me learn how to walk between the worlds."

Eden turned to look at her. She was close enough now for Tania to see the pain in her deep brown eyes and in the tense lines around her mouth.

"That I shall never do," Eden said.

Tania stepped forward but Eden moved back quickly, as if to avoid being touched.

"I have to let my parents know that I'm all right," Tania pleaded. "They'll be crazy with worry." She gave Eden a determined look. "You have to help me," she said. "I'm not leaving here till you do."

Eden's eyes flashed.

Uh-oh, Tania thought. *Wrong thing to say.*

Eden thrust out an arm toward Tania. She was beyond Eden's reach, but a force hit her like an invisible wall crashing against her chest. It curled around her, wrapping her in a fierce embrace that pinned her arms to her sides. She couldn't move; she could barely breathe.

She felt herself being lifted from the floor.

"Eden," she managed to gasp. "Don't—"

Eden gave a flick of her wrist and suddenly Tania was speeding through the air, still held immobile by the clenched fist of Eden's power. She was whisked helplessly through the gray door, across the lobby, and out into the courtyard.

She heard the hollow boom as the black door slammed at her back. She was held for a moment, her feet dangling above the cobbles. Then, as if released by an opening hand, she dropped to the ground. The impact sent her crashing onto her hands and knees, gulping for air like a stranded fish.

She scrambled to her feet and ran back to the door.

"Eden!" she shouted, hammering on the wood with both fists. "You have to let me back in!"

But this time the door didn't open, and no matter how hard she threw herself against the black panels, it stayed closed.

She slid down the door and sat heavily on the top step. She gave the door a final despairing thump with the side of her fist and then slumped down, her face in her hands. Without Eden's help she might never learn how to control her power. She might never see her mortal parents again.

She only let herself lose hope for a few moments before she got to her feet and ran around to the window. She stared in through the glass—but the room was empty. Eden was gone.

"Oh, nice going, Tania," she muttered. "You really messed up that one."

She turned and walked back across the courtyard.

Someone was standing under the archway that led to the gardens. He stepped into the light, his black cloak billowing around him.

"Gabriel!" Tania gasped. "You startled me."

"You should not have come to this sad place," Gabriel said gently. "There is nothing here for you."

Tania gave a shrug of her shoulders. "I thought

Eden might help me to contact my parents," she explained. "My *mortal* parents, I mean."

"Come, let us be away from here," Gabriel said.

Tania allowed herself to be shepherded out of the courtyard.

"I understand your desire to ease the suffering of those whom you have left behind," Gabriel went on. "But it is a dangerous thing that you are attempting."

"You mean you know why I want to see my parents, but you don't think it's a great idea, right?"

Gabriel frowned. "No, it is not a *great idea*," he echoed carefully. He hesitated before going on. "You know that I am your friend."

She touched his arm. "Of course."

"Then listen to me. You should not go to Princess Eden for help. Her spirit is cracked and twisted. I do not know why. Perhaps her heart was broken by the death of the Queen. But I fear it was by studying the Mystic Arts too deeply that she was driven out of her mind."

Tania looked sharply at him. "Can that happen? Can the Mystic Arts make you crazy?"

"There is a saying," Gabriel said. "Go not so deep into the dragon's cave that you cannot see the light at your back."

"Um," Tania said, biting her lower lip. "And you think Eden went too deep into the dragon's cave and kind of got . . . *eaten* by the dragon, is that it?"

"Princess Eden has wandered far from the light," Gabriel said. "I would not have you follow her along that dreadful path."

"I understand." Tania sighed. "I don't know what to do, Gabriel," she said. "I'm so mixed up right now that I feel like I've spent the last few days in a blender. My life made some kind of sense back home, but *here*?" She shook her head. "I haven't got a clue who I am or what I'm supposed to do with the rest of my life." She frowned. "The only thing I know for sure is that I have to see my parents, even if it's only for one last time." She looked pleadingly at him. "I have to!"

"I know it is hard," he said, his voice full of sympathy. "But you are Princess Tania of Faerie; that is the undying truth. The person you were in the Mortal World is gone forever. Trust me, Tania, I wish only to bring you comfort. Do not grieve for that which is gone. Forget the Mortal World." His intense eyes burned into her face. "There are those here that love you, that have always loved you. Turn from the past, Tania, and accept that you have purposes and duties here in your father's Realm."

"What kind of duties?" she asked. "And what *purpose*? I don't feel like I have either of those things."

"Then learn more of your inheritance," he said. "Discover who you are and seek to know the Realm of Faerie better."

"How?"

"Your sister Princess Sancha may hold the answers," he said. "She spends her days steeped in the ancient texts, and she has much wisdom. Go to the library and speak with her." He stopped walking and turned, resting his hands on her shoulders and looking deep into her eyes. Tania realized that without her even noticing, he had brought her all the way to the door of her bedchamber.

"I must leave you, Tania," he said. "But heed my words: Do not go again to Princess Eden for aid. She can give you none, and I would not have you poisoned by the serpent of her unreason."

He bowed low, lifting her hand and kissing it lingeringly and softly before turning on his heel and striding away. She gazed after him, suppressing an urge to run after him.

At last, she went into her room and closed the door, deep in thought. Maybe Gabriel was right; maybe Eden wasn't the right person to go to for help.

"I'm not going to give up on getting to see my parents, though," she said aloud. "I don't care what anyone says." She walked over to the bed and picked up the book. She would go and talk to Sancha. And she'd show her the leather-bound book; maybe someone with Sancha's knowledge would be able to shed some light on where the book came from, and who may have sent it to her.

She found Sancha alone in the great library, sitting at her desk with a large open book in front of her. The pages were framed with narrow, intricately intertwined ribbons of bright colors—green and red and yellow. The beautiful, scrolling script looked handwritten, a pale powder blue against the ivory pages, and at the start of each new paragraph, the first letter was decorated with finely drawn illustrations of vines and leaves and flowers.

She read a few words over Sancha's shoulder.

We are all still here—no one has gone away . . .

"Hello," Tania said. "Are you busy?"

Sancha smiled up at her. "No, I am at my leisure," she said. "I am reading Earl Marshal Cornelius's diary of the Wars of Lyonesse. But are you well, Tania? I was concerned when you fled the dining table last eve. We wished to follow you and give you comfort, but Gabriel said we were wiser to let you be. What was the matter?"

"Oh, you know." Tania shrugged. "Just stuff."

Sancha looked puzzled. "Stuff . . . ?"

Tania placed the book in front of her sister on the desk. "I thought you might be able to tell me something about this," she said.

Sancha stared at the book in amazement. "By the sun, moon, and stars!" She gasped. "Whence came this? How is it that you have it?"

"Good question," Tania said. "I was kind of hoping you'd be able to tell me." She smiled. "I take it you know what it is, then?"

"It is your Soul Book," Sancha said, reaching out one long-fingered hand but drawing it back again without actually touching the book. "It has been missing for centuries." She looked up at Tania. "It was in your keeping all the time?"

"No way. The first I saw of it was a couple of days

back," Tania explained. "It was sent to me on my birthday. No return address, no note inside, nothing." She frowned. "What's a Soul Book?"

"Come," Sancha said. "Bring the book. I will show you where it belongs." She stood up. She made a liquid gesture with her hand over the book that she had been reading. Tania watched in astonishment as the book closed itself and lifted off the table. It floated for a moment, then glided across the library, turning slowly until it stood upright in the air, before slipping into a gap on one of the shelves.

Sancha was halfway across the floor. She turned. "Will you come?" she asked.

Tania let out a breath. "Is that your *gift*?" she asked. "Being able to move things without touching them?"

Sancha smiled. "Indeed," she said. "And most useful, is it not, for one whose life is spent among all these weighty tomes."

"Do we all have gifts?" Tania asked, hefting her book in her arms and walking over to where Sancha was standing. "I know Cordelia can understand animals, but what about Zara and the others?"

"Zara's gift is in her music," Sancha said. "She can weave enchantments in song that would make the stars weep and the sun roar with laughter!" She smiled. "Hopie's gift is healing," she continued, but now her voice fell. "And Eden had a great aptitude for the Mystic Arts."

"What about Rathina?"

"Her gift has not yet revealed itself," Sancha said. "But she is only seventeen—the gifts usually make themselves known during our sixteenth year, but sometimes they come later, so there is time yet for Rathina to discover her own unique blessing."

Sancha led Tania across the black-and-white floor to a winding wooden staircase. They climbed to the first book-lined gallery, then circled the room until they came to a second stairway.

Sancha led her all the way up to the fourth gallery, high above the floor. Tania's head was filled with the smell of leather and of ancient paper. Particles of dust circled in the golden sunlight that poured in through the long windows. There was a kind of stillness up here near the domed ceiling that made Tania want to hold her breath and move on tiptoe so that it would not be disturbed.

She looked down over the polished wood banister. The spiral pattern of the floor seemed to start revolving. She quickly looked away.

Sancha stepped into a small alcove with padded leather benches. At the far end, under a sunlit window, stood a reading lectern carved into the shape of an eagle with its wings spread wide. The shelves were filled with books. Sancha pointed to a dark gap between two of them.

"Here is where your Soul Book should rest," she said. "Between the Soul Book of Zara and that of Earl Marshal Cornelius of Talebolion." She looked at Tania. "He is our uncle, the younger brother of our beloved father. Do you see? The books are in order of rank; all the high-born of Faerie have Soul Books. They tell the tale of our lives. Yours went missing soon after you disappeared. Some thought you had taken it away with you, but Rathina said it was not so." She frowned. "Did the book come to you while you were still in the Mortal World?"

Tania nodded.

"But you know not from whom?"

"I don't have a clue," Tania admitted. "I've read some of it, but the story stops when I did my vanishing act, and there's nothing in there to explain exactly what happened."

"Now that the book has been returned, the story of your life will begin to spin out onto the pages once more," Sancha said.

"Sorry?" Tania said. "Run that past me again."

Sancha blinked at her. "The book belongs here," she explained. "Now that it has been returned, more words will come."

"Will they?" Tania said. "How? Who's going to write it?"

"The book will write itself."

Tania grinned. "Get out of here!"

"Mercy, Tania!" Sancha looked shocked. "You cannot order me from my own library!"

"No, sorry, I didn't mean . . ." Tania began. "Oh, never mind. But you mean the story will just carry on now that the book's back here? That's amazing. Am I allowed to take a look?"

Sancha nodded, gesturing toward the lectern. "Let it rest there, and you will see."

Tania opened the book on the lectern, turning the pages until she came to the place where the story of her life had just stopped dead.

"Oh, wow!" Sancha was right. There was already more writing than she had seen before.

She followed the new gothic script with one finger, reading aloud.

"*Full joyous was King Oberon and all of his Realm upon the return of Princess Tania after five hundred years of sadness,*" she recited. "*Grim night turned into glorious day and all the people made merry, returning to the palace to give thanks and to gladden their eyes with the sight of the one who had been lost to us for so long.*"

Tania turned the page, desperate to find out what had happened to her between leaving Faerie and being born as Anita Palmer sixteen years ago. There was plenty more writing, but all it did was detail the things than had been going on over the past few days.

Disappointed, she turned back to the original ending. "There's nothing about what happened to me after I disappeared," she said. "There's a five hundred year gap!"

"It could be that the power that dwells in the books cannot see into the Mortal World," Sancha said.

"Which means it can only tell me what happens when I'm here, in Faerie," Tania said. "Well, that's just great!" She looked at Sancha. "How am I ever going to make sense of who I am without knowing what happened to me over the past five hundred years?" She felt a catch in her voice. "Sancha, I'm only sixteen. I've got a birth certificate and everything. That leaves four hundred and eighty-four years that I don't know anything about. Isn't there any way of finding out?"

Sancha looked nervously at her. "There is a way, possibly."

"What way?"

"If your spirit is strong enough, then it may be that I can learn what befell you," Sancha said. "But it is perilous."

"I'll risk it," Tania said.

"The strength of spirit must be yours," Sancha said. "But the peril will be mine."

"Oh." Tania frowned. "Is it really dangerous?"

"It is, indeed," Sancha said. Her dark eyes were very somber. "The Soul Book belongs to Faerie, but your spirit is split between this Realm and the Mortal World. I may be able to use the power of the book to bring the two halves of your spirit together, and then you may learn the lost secrets of your mortal past."

"Couldn't I do it on my own?" Tania asked.

Sancha shook her head. "You do not have the power within you while your spirit is divided," she said. "But I will help you, Tania. Come, take my hand, and we shall see what we shall see."

Sancha clasped Tania's hand. Then, without looking directly at the book, she reached out and rested her other hand on the open pages.

"No matter what happens, you must not break the

bond," Sancha said, closing her eyes.

It was a long time before anything happened. Tania watched her sister's face closely for a sign that she could see into Tania's past mortal lives. There was nothing, except that Sancha's breathing got more and more shallow.

She was about to suggest they give up when Sancha began to speak in the softest of whispers.

"Swans fly o'er the coral roofs," she murmured. "Entwined with lace and ribbons of powder blue . . . low, below the slow hello, the eyes upturned, the faces pale . . ."

"Sancha?"

". . . the majestic sweep of the ice blue sea . . . and white-eyed cliffs a'towering . . ." Sancha's voice had a low, melodic lilt, but Tania couldn't make any sense of what she was saying. ". . . enticed by distant murky mouthings, to wander in the baleful depths . . ." Then Sancha's body stiffened and her fingers dug into Tania's hand.

"Ahh! This is a perilous place, indeed," she muttered, and her eyelids flickered restlessly. "There is disease and death and malice and wickedness here." She grimaced. Her voice grew louder; she sounded frightened. Beneath Sancha's hand, Tania saw that the pages of the book were glowing with a grisly dark red light, as if the paper was smouldering and about to burst into flames. Thin wisps of smoke began to rise between her fingers. Tania got ready to pull her sister away from the book, prepared to stop this, no matter what Sancha had said.

"This is a horrible place," Sancha said, her voice cracked and weak now, as if from long suffering. "I am not Tania. I am Tania. I am not. I am. Oh, angels of mercy defend me! I am in a small dark room, in a hovel, lying in a bed with filthy sheets over me. Oh, the stench, the stench of it. There is dirty straw on the floor. I am sick, so sick, and there is such pain, terrible pain." Sancha's head rolled from side to side. "People loom over me, but their faces are clouded with resignation and despair. I am dying. It is such a strange, dreadful feeling as the life drains from me. I have some terrible, terrible disease, a deadly sickness, I am mortal." Her voice rose to a wild scream. "I am *dying!*"

XIV

Tania wrenched her sister's hand away from the smouldering book and the two of them went tumbling to the floor. Sancha's screams stopped abruptly, but Tania was afraid that she had broken the link too late.

Her sister lay on the boards for a few moments, panting and trembling, her face shocked and ash white.

"I'm so sorry." Tania gasped, crouching over her. "Are you all right?"

"The book burned so," Sancha said. She lifted her hand and gave it a puzzled look. "But the pain is gone, and there is no hurt," she said, displaying her flawless palm to Tania. "I believed the danger would be far greater." Her face clouded. "Mercy! The book!"

They scrambled up. The open book lay unharmed on the lectern. There was no sign of charring or burning on the ivory pages.

"Weird," Tania breathed.

Sancha straightened her clothes. "'Twas a curious and fearful experience, indeed," she said. "And not one that I ever shall repeat."

"But did it work?" Tania asked. "Did you find out what happened to me when I first went into the Mortal World?"

Sancha frowned. "Do you remember nothing?"

Tania shook her head.

"Then your spirit is too deeply divided," Sancha said with a sigh. "I am sorry, but I fear that you may never be able to remember your mortal past." She shuddered. "It is a monstrous place, the Mortal World. I know not how you endured it for so long."

Tania looked at her. "Please tell me what the Soul Book showed you," she begged.

"I must rest," said Sancha, putting a hand to her chest. "I am very weary." She walked unsteadily to one of the benches and sat down.

Tania sat beside her and rested her arm across Sancha's bent shoulders. "I'm so sorry you had to go through that," she murmured. "It sounded terrible."

Sancha lifted her head to look at Tania. "I believe I know how you fared when you first entered the Mortal World. You fell victim to some deadly plague almost at once."

"I died?" Tania asked with a shudder.

"Indeed, for once you were there, you became subject to all the illnesses and misfortunes of that awful place." Her eyes filled with tears. "My poor sister, all alone and in pain, such pain!"

Tania squeezed Sancha's shoulders. "It's all right, I'm fine now," she said. "But if I died, how come I'm still here?"

Sancha straightened up and took her hand. "Your spirit was released by the death of your mortal body," she said. "Light and helpless as thistledown in the wind, your spirit waited to be born anew—babe after babe, down all the long mortal years. And as your mortal form succumbed to sickness or mishap, your spirit drifted free to be born again and again."

Tania leaned back against the wall. "That's a lot to take in," she breathed. "Basically, I've been alive one way or another since the *sixteenth century*." She gave a breathless laugh. "I could probably work out how many people I've been if I thought about it." She shook her head. "Actually, I don't want to think about it. My head would probably explode."

"I wish that you could remember those lives," Sancha said. "I would very much like to know more of the Mortal World, despite its horrors."

"It's not so bad these days," Tania told her. "Whatever I died of the first time around is probably totally curable now." She looked at her sister. "I'd go back, just for a while, if I knew how to control my power," she confessed. "I want to see my parents—my mortal parents, I mean."

Sancha's eyes were soft with sympathy. "I cannot help you," she said gently. "Nor would I, even if I could. You belong here now. None of us would risk losing you again."

Tania knew there was nothing more to say. She couldn't expect anyone here to understand why she wanted to go back to the Mortal World. But that wouldn't stop her from trying. She couldn't let her parents suffer not knowing where she had gone or if she was even still alive. She would have to find a way of walking between the worlds, and if she had to do it alone, perhaps that was for the best.

Later that morning, Tania, Zara, and Rathina watched from the battlements above the Great Northern Gateway as Oberon and fifty lords and ladies of Faerie rode out with pennants and banners fluttering to begin the long journey to Castle Ravensare. Riding behind the King and the nobles of the Court were squires and attendants, some leading heavily laden pack ponies. And at the end of the procession, two mule-drawn wagons rumbled along, filled with supplies for the journey and gifts for the earls and dukes who would attend the gathering.

"It is two days' ride," Zara told Tania, leaning over the battlements and waving at the colorful horseback figures as they followed the path that led through the parklands and up into the purple-heathered downs. "I wish Father had taken me with them. It will be such a grand procession, and there will be feasting and merrymaking at journey's end." Her eyes shone.

"Uncle Cornelius will be there with his wife's sons, Titus and Corin. They are so handsome. Indeed, I do not know who I like the better." She grinned at Tania. "But there would be much sport in the choosing!"

"Fie, Zara!" Rathina scolded. "Do you never think beyond such frivolities?"

"Never!" Zara laughed. "The Counsel at Ravensare will last for three days, and when Father returns, I pray that he brings the beautiful sons of the Marchioness with him!" She danced a few quick steps. "I will need a new gown. Tania, will you come with me to Mistress Mirrlees and help me to choose?"

"Actually, I was thinking of taking a walk in the gardens," Tania said. She wanted to be alone with her thoughts.

After Zara had gone, Tania stood next to Rathina for a while, and they watched in silence as the King's procession dwindled away into the distance.

"I shall go saddle Maddalena," Rathina said at last. She looked closely at Tania and frowned. "You are not at ease," she said, touching Tania's arm. "What ails you?"

"I guess I'm just having trouble coming to terms with being two people," Tania admitted. "I'm afraid that my brain is going to fall out!"

"A brisk ride over break and spinney with the reins in your hands and the wind in your face would blow away all doubts and fears," Rathina declared. "I will find a fine, even-tempered steed for you if you wish."

"No, thanks," Tania said. She liked horses, but she

had never ridden one, not that she could remember, anyway. And a wild gallop with an experienced and fearless rider like Rathina didn't sound like a particularly safe way to start.

"I haven't told anyone else about this," she went on hesitantly, "but the night before I came here, I grew a pair of wings, and I flew."

Rathina's dark eyes were unreadable. "In your dreams or in the real world?"

"I'm not sure, not any more," Tania said. "It felt very real. And it was totally amazing. I mean, it felt so good, as if I should always have been able to fly. But then the wings shriveled up and fell away, and I was just me again." She looked sideways at Rathina. "I know flying is supposed to be really childish, but I loved it, Rathina, I really loved it. And I miss it!"

Rathina rested her arm across Tania's shoulders and drew her close. "When I am riding upon Maddalena, and the wind is high and the moors stretch out forever ahead of me, why, there are times when I can almost believe that I am flying again," she said in a faraway voice. "You are not alone with such desires, Tania. I too wish at times for the continued gift of wings."

Tania felt a surge of affection for her sister. "I'm glad it's not just me."

"There are tales," Rathina went on. "Old tales that speak of a time when we were winged for all of our lives."

"Really?" Tania stared at her. "So what happened?"

"Alas," Rathina said. "I know not, and mayhap they are but stories for children." She shook her head like a dog shaking its pelt after a swim. "But we are grown up and we are wingless. Fie! How do you put such silly thoughts into my head, Tania?" She gave her a quick kiss on the cheek. "Maddalena awaits," she said. "Let this conversation be a secret between us!"

Tania nodded, smiling. It felt good to have confided in Rathina, and it helped to know that she had such a loyal and true friend. With her sisters around her, and supported also by Gabriel's unwavering friendship, maybe she really could be happy here . . . eventually.

The Privy Gardens were quiet in the sun-drenched afternoon. Tania wandered the gravel paths between the long manicured lawns, delighting in the bright bursts of color that teemed in the well-tended flower beds. Trees lined the paths, cut into neat, rounded shapes with not a leaf out of place. There were also hedges of boxwood, trimmed into the shapes of horses and birds and chess pieces. And where the networks of paths met one another, there were statues and leaping fountains.

The only people Tania encountered were a few gardeners, busy with their work. She approached one woman who was kneeling with a trowel, waist-deep in an ocean of dark red blooms and surrounded by a snowstorm of white butterflies.

"What flowers are these?" Tania asked her.

"They are gaillardias, my lady," the woman replied.

"The butterflies seem to like them."

"Indeed, my lady. They smell sweet, do they not?"

Tania smiled. "They smell lovely."

The woman looked cautiously at her. "My lady? May I speak?"

"Of course," Tania said.

"I do not heed rumor and gossip," the woman began. "But I have heard it said that you are determined to quit this land and return to that Other Place." She shuddered and made a face as if she had tasted something bitter. "My lady, it is not for me to ask, I know, but I beg you not to leave us. The King would not be able to bear it." She touched one of the red blooms. "I would not have these blossoms fade and wither under another five hundred years of twilight. Indeed, I would not."

Tania looked at the woman without speaking for a few moments. "I never intended to go away permanently," she said at last. "I just want to see my parents again, that's all."

The woman stared at her in surprise. "Your father dwells in this Realm, my lady," she said. "And your mother is dead. For what reason would you return to the creatures that held you prisoner in that Other Place?" Her mouth twisted with distaste. "Surely you do not feel kinship with those foul demons?"

"They're not demons!" Tania exclaimed. "It's not like that at all."

The woman's mouth tightened in disapproval but she lowered her head and didn't speak again.

Tania swallowed through a lump that filled her throat. No one here understood how hard this was for her! They all acted like she had been broken out of prison, as if she should be grateful for having been dragged out of her real life and dumped in this crazy place!

She turned and walked rapidly away from the kneeling woman. It felt as if everyone in Faerie was making demands of her, forcing her to do what *they* wanted. She didn't want this; she had never asked to be a princess!

She wanted to be an ordinary sixteen-year-old. She wanted to chill out in her bedroom with a can of Coke and a family-sized bag of barbecue-style crisps and watch DVDs with her friends. She wanted to jump down the stairs in one go and crash into the living room and groan at her dad's feeble jokes. She wanted to raid the fridge and drink milk from the carton and stuff her face with leftover pizza. She wanted to go shopping for new shoes. She wanted to talk to Jade for half the night on her cell phone and spend an afternoon in the mall trying on outrageous clothes that she'd never buy in a million years.

She stormed along the gravel pathways for a long time, blazing with resentment, not paying attention to where she was going.

She saw a small group of figures in the distance. Men, gathered by a fountain, talking together. Coming closer, she realized that one of them was Gabriel. She thought it would probably be best to avoid him for the moment, at least until her mood had improved, so she turned and walked back the way she had come.

She heard quick footsteps behind her. Resignedly, she stopped.

"Tania?" Gabriel's voice was full of concern. "Why would you not approach? What is the matter?"

She looked into his eyes, seeing only affection and kindness in them. "It's nothing," she said.

He frowned, coming closer and resting his hand gently on her shoulder. "It is clearly not nothing, Tania," he said. "Can I not help? Can I not be your friend?"

"You *are* my friend," Tania said fervently. "You *are*! But I have to think, and you can't help me do that." She gazed into his face. "I already know what you'll say. I know what you think I should do. But it's too hard; it's just so unfair."

His hand came up to cup her cheek. "I would not have you in such distress for the whole Realm!" he whispered.

"I know." She felt a sudden need to be held and comforted. She stepped awkwardly forward, putting her arms around him and holding him tightly.

"Tania . . ." His breath was in her hair, his arms close around her.

She pulled away after a few moments. "I'm fine," she said, not meeting his eyes. "Please don't follow me." She rested her hand for a second on his chest then turned and walked away quickly.

She tried to push thoughts of him out of her mind. Her brain was filled with enough turmoil without potential feelings for Gabriel being added to the mix.

She walked the gardens alone for a long time, and still she couldn't find a way through her confusion, still she couldn't make sense of who she really was.

At last she came to a low stone bridge that crossed a stream of water all grown over with green weeds. There was a wooden gate in a tall hedge at the far end of the bridge. Beyond the gate, she saw the rising parklands, and away in the distance, she spotted a solitary figure surrounded by hounds.

"Cordelia," she breathed, suddenly desperate not to be alone with her thoughts anymore.

She ran across the bridge and pushed through the gate, racing up the gentle hillside with her hair flying and her skirts tangling around her legs.

The two sisters walked through the high northern parklands in a constantly moving river of hounds. To Tania's relief, Cordelia asked her no questions and seemed happy to be silent or simply to talk about her beloved animals.

They came to an area where the trees grew more thickly. Finally feeling her mood lighten, Tania ran through the trees and the hounds flowed after her, their hides dappled with leaf green light.

Cordelia whistled and the hounds swooped away to join her. Laughing breathlessly, Tania watched as the hounds flooded down the hill and swarmed around their mistress.

She came to the edge of the knot of trees and waved. Cordelia waved back. Tania was about to run down to join her when a soft voice brought her up short.

She stared back into the trees.

"Tania, it's me." Edric stepped out from behind a tree trunk.

Tania frowned, her mood immediately darkening again.

"Please," he begged, taking a step toward her. "Hear me out."

Tania stalked up to him and slapped him hard across the face. She had a moment to see his expression of shock and pain before she turned on her heel and ran down the grassy slope toward her sister and the dogs.

Cordelia was staring at her in amazement. "What trespass did Master Chanticleer commit that you should strike him so?"

"Him?" Tania looked back the way she had come. There was no sign of Edric now. "Oh, he's just a pig. Don't ask!"

"I already have asked," Cordelia said.

"Well, I'm not telling you. He deserved it that's all you need to know." Tania scooped up a stick and threw it, running with the hounds as they chased it down the hill.

With any luck, that would be the last she'd see of

Edric. He had tricked her and lied to her and he'd made her fall in love with him, all on his master's orders. And now he wanted to try and make it up with her! Why? So he'd feel better about himself? Not a chance! And if he did come slithering back trying to smooth-talk her again, he'd just get more of the same!

XV

I'll tarry not where the darling buds of
   Spring adorn the land,
Nor will I stray where the country feels
   the grip of Winter's hand,
And when the Summer high blazes from
   the meadow sky,
I'll be far from here and by your side.

It was late afternoon of the same day; Tania and Zara were in the Princesses' Gallery, singing together to the accompaniment of the spinetta and the lute. Zara's voice lifted in descant while Tania sang the melody, her fingers unhesitatingly picking out the notes on the lute. The instrument felt so natural in her hands, its pear-shaped belly resting in her lap, the fret-board held firmly in the crook of thumb and forefinger, and her fingers dancing over the strings.

Cordelia and Sancha were also in the long attic room that stretched out under the roof of the Royal Apartments. Sancha had a book open in her lap, but she had looked up from the page. Cordelia's fingers held a fine bone needle threaded with green silk. She was working on some embroidery, but had paused to pay better attention to her sisters' duet.

The song came to an end. Zara gave a final trill on the spinetta, which Tania echoed on her lute. Cordelia and Sancha clapped.

"I have sorely missed your music-making," Sancha said. "And that is a lovely melody indeed."

"And a most charming lyric," Cordelia added. "*I'll be far from here and by your side.*" She smiled. "Not, I think, a sentiment that Master Chanticleer will ever hear from Tania's lips!"

Tania turned to her. "We weren't going to talk about that, remember?" She had asked Cordelia not to mention her encounter with Edric.

Zara looked up with interest. "Tell on," she prompted. "What of Gabriel's servant?"

Cordelia grinned. "I can say no more," she declared. "I am sworn to silence."

"Oh, thanks," said Tania with a roll of her eyes. "Way to keep a secret, Cordie!"

Zara slid off her stool and came to sit beside Tania. "I offer you two choices," she said, putting her arm around Tania's neck. "You may tell all this instant, or you may endure the pricks and thorns of my curiosity from now until doomsday. The choice is yours."

Tania looked at Cordelia. "See what you've done?"

"You would best confess all," Sancha said with a laugh. "Zara is remorseless in pursuit of such gossip."

Tania shook her head in resignation. Sisters! It was worse than being at school. A person couldn't keep anything private.

"Is it a great scandal?" Zara asked gleefully. "Has he made improper advances to you? A kiss, mayhap, in a cloistered arbor? Words of love whispered at a midnight tryst?"

"No! Nothing like that!" Tania retorted. "Look, if you absolutely have to know, I don't like the way he helped Gabriel bring me here."

Sancha closed her book and leaned forward. "Of what methods do you speak?"

"He lied to me," Tania said. "He told me . . . Well, never mind what he told me. I don't think much of it, that's all."

"He lied?" Sancha echoed, puzzled. "I do not understand. What falsehoods could he have spoken?"

Zara's eyes widened in sudden understanding. "He professed love, did he not?" she breathed. "He gulled you with passionate words in order to draw you away from the Mortal World. By my troth, what a rogue!"

Tania felt her cheeks go scarlet. "Well, yes," she mumbled. "Something like that." She shook off Zara's arm and stood up. "Can we talk about something else, please?"

"Indeed we cannot!" Zara exclaimed. "I must be

told every detail of Master Chanticleer's perfidy, or I shall not be able to sleep for thinking on it!"

Tania looked at her. She wasn't upset by her sister's guileless curiosity, but her history with Edric was still too painful for light-hearted conversation. "Then I'm afraid you'll just have to lie awake nights," she said with a half-smile. "I'm going to find Rathina; at least she won't make fun of me."

Cordelia looked up at her. "Do not be angry," she said. "Zara meant it only in jest."

Tania smiled. "Yes, I know that," she said. "I'm not annoyed." She headed for the door. "I'll see you guys later."

She ran down the long twisting stairway, suddenly eager to be with Rathina, maybe even to confide in her once more—to pour out all her fears and troubles and pain, to rekindle the loving friendship of her forgotten childhood.

She knocked on the door of Rathina's chamber. There was no answer from within. Disappointed, she turned the handle. The door opened silently into a room of dark red shadows.

"Rathina?" Tania called. Still no reply. She stepped over the threshold and looked around. Red silk drapes stretched in swaths across the ceiling and hung from the high walls, moving constantly in billows and ripples as though troubled by a breeze. If there were any windows in the room, they were shuttered. The only light came from a large chandelier that hung from the ceiling, the thick yellow candles giving off a sultry, brooding glow.

Where the candlelight struck the blousing drapes, the silk glowed scarlet, but in the folds and creases, the sumptuous shadows were a deep wine red.

The bed was also swathed in dark red silk, the curtains gathered at the head and spilling down so that the bed seemed to flow with dark blood. Swags and swaths of silk hung from the furniture, collecting in a scarlet froth on the maroon floorboards.

Tania became aware that dark shades were moving across the swelling curtains of silk, human figures gliding in a slow dance, their dark and ghostly images somehow imprinted on the flowing silk.

She shivered, the hairs on the back of her neck prickling. The atmosphere of the room was weird and disturbing. Uneasily, she approached the rippling drapes. The slow-moving dancers slid silently over the silk, holding hands, their heads bowed, their eyes hidden. Suddenly, as she came closer, a head lifted and a face looked briefly into hers—a gaunt white face with hollowed-out featureless eyes. A hand reached toward her and skeleton-thin fingers beckoned.

Tania stepped back with a gasp.

She heard a sound behind her.

"Tania!" Rathina swept into the room. She pulled curtains aside and threw open a shuttered window. Warm evening sunlight poured into the room, driving away the shadows.

Tania gasped, blinking in the sudden burst of

light. "I was looking for you."

"And I for you, my dear sister," Rathina said with a smile. "Did my dancers unsettle you? Do not fear; they are always sad when I am absent. See how they dance now!"

Tania gazed at the flowing silken drapes. The mournful tempo of the dance had changed completely. Now the brightly dressed figures were circling the room with swift-moving feet and merry faces.

"What did you want me for?" Tania asked.

"It is time for you to meet with Maddalena," Rathina said, linking her arm with Tania's and leading her from the room. "And maybe in the morn, your riding lessons can begin."

"I'd like that," Tania said. "I'd like that a lot." She looked fondly at her sister. "And there are some things I'd like to talk to you about, if that's okay."

"It is most definitely . . . *okay*," Rathina said slowly, then she smiled. "You see? I have been practicing. Soon I shall have learned all your strange new words."

Tania laughed, squeezing Rathina's arm. "Good for you!"

Rathina led Tania out across the twilight gardens for her first visit to the royal stables, a huge complex of wooden buildings that lay west of the maze. Several pairs of intelligent equine eyes watched the princesses from behind half-doors. The cobbled courtyards were filled with warm pools of evening shade; stable boys and girls ran about their duties, bedding the horses down for the night and lighting the lanterns that swung from the gables.

Having spent the last sixteen years of her life living in a city, Tania felt a little intimidated about being up close to such big animals, and she was wary and watchful as Rathina led her into the stall of her favorite horse.

"This is my bold beauty, Maddalena," Rathina told her, giving the neck of the glossy bay mare a firm pat with the flat of her hand. "She is beautiful, is she not? Do not be afraid to touch her. She will do you no harm."

Tania reached out tentatively and stroked the horse's long nose. She was certainly a handsome animal, with a flowing black mane and large, clever dark eyes. Maddalena snorted and nodded, one forehoof thumping the ground.

"She's wonderful," Tania said, breathing in the strong scent of horse and straw.

"I shall show you my finest saddle and bridle and trappings," Rathina said. "They were a gift from our father on my sixteenth birthday. Made by the finest leather-workers in all of Dinsel. Come." She opened the gate to the stall and Tania followed her out into the walkway.

"Fare you well, my darling," Rathina called to Maddalena as she closed the gate behind them. "I shall see you anon." The horse whinnied.

"Did I ride much . . . uh . . . *before*?" Tania asked, sniffing her hand and quite liking the horsey smell that lingered there.

"You did, indeed," Rathina said as they walked along. "But you sat in the saddle like a sack of wheat and spent much of the time clinging onto your steed like a leaf in an autumn gale."

"Oh! That's a shame." She had hoped that she might have been a good rider.

"I shall tutor you in better ways, if you would have me do so," Rathina offered. "Give me six weeks, and I shall make a centaur of you!"

"I'd like that," Tania said, meaning it.

They walked across another cobbled courtyard, and Rathina led Tania through a small door in a low thatched building of white plaster and black timbers.

The walls were hung with bridles and reins and girths and halters and bits. There were saddles on wooden stands, and folded blankets and sacks of feed and wooden boxes that held various pieces of equipment that Tania didn't recognize. The room smelled powerfully of leather and grain.

Tania paused in the middle of the room, suddenly aware that Rathina had stopped in the doorway. She turned. There was a strange expression on Rathina's face. Tania couldn't quite make it out. It was like a mixture of determination and unease, as though Rathina was about to do something that she knew Tania wouldn't like.

"What's wrong?" Tania asked.

Then Rathina's eyes slid off her face and Tania saw that she was looking at something beyond her shoulder. She turned to follow the line of her sister's gaze.

Edric had appeared from behind a wooden partition.

Tania froze. "What's going on?"

"He begged me to bring you here," Rathina explained. "You must stay and listen to his words." She backed out, drawing the door closed behind her. "Forgive me, Tania; it is meant for the good."

The door banged shut and the latch clicked down.

For the space of maybe three heartbeats, Tania stared at the closed door, before she slowly turned and faced Edric.

"Well?"

She saw him swallow. "I want you to know the truth," he said. "You have to listen to me. If you don't believe what I tell you, I promise I won't bother you again." He gave a weak smile, his hand coming up to his cheek. "You can even hit me again if it makes you feel any better, but please just listen to me first."

"If I remember correctly, I did a whole lot of listening to you back home," she said in an icy voice. "I don't want to hear any more of your lies." It annoyed her that her voice sounded so choked up. All she wanted to do was to get out of there before she burst into tears.

She spun on her heel and headed for the door, already stretching one hand toward the latch.

"You're still my sun!" She turned at his voice, trembling, and looked at him again. "Remember?" he said. "Romeo and Juliet. *But soft! What light through yonder window breaks. It is the east, and Juliet is my sun!*"

"Don't!" Tania spat. "Don't say that." Against her will, all her old feelings for him were being stirred up again. "Don't talk to me like that. It was all lies!"

"No, it wasn't," Edric said, taking a step forward.

"Get away from me!" she said, backing toward the door.

He stopped. "I love you." He shook his head, his eyes pleading. "It wasn't supposed to happen like that. I was sent into your world to bring you back here. And yes, I made friends with you at first in order to do what Drake wanted. But then, when I got to know you better, I realized I didn't care about his plans anymore. I just wanted to be with you."

She stared at him, unable to speak. Her blood was pounding in her ears, beating out *Liar! Liar! Liar!*

"You destroyed my life. . . ."

"I know you think that," he said. "And I know I hurt you. But that day on the river, I was going to tell you the truth. The whole truth about who I was and about who you really were."

Tania remembered him saying he had something important to tell her. She had been so nervous that he might be going to tell her he loved her! That would have been a whole lot easier to deal with than the truth.

"And then," Edric was still speaking, "then I was going to tell you the truth about Drake."

"What do you mean? What about Gabriel?"

"He never loved you," Edric said, gazing steadily

at her with the eyes she knew so very well. "Not now, and not before you disappeared all those years ago. He only ever wanted to marry you because he wanted your power to walk both worlds. That's *all* he wants from you, a way into the Mortal World." He moved toward her again, and this time she didn't back away. "That day on the river, do you remember what happened?"

She nodded.

"Just before we crashed," he urged. "Did you see anything on the water? Anything strange?"

She forced her mind back to those panic-filled moments. She heard Evan's voice, rising above the growl of the engine and the smash of water on the hull. "*There's something important I have to tell you.*"

And then she remembered how a cold shadow had suddenly come down over them out of nowhere. Evan had gasped. His head had turned suddenly. He had looked scared.

She had stared ahead along the river and she had seen . . . *something*.

"A boat," she whispered, seeing it again in her mind's eye. "A big boat on the river. No, not a boat—a barge. I only saw it for a moment. It was very low in the water." Her eyes widened. "It was just like Oberon's barge."

And then she remembered the final words spoken by Evan before the crash.

"*No! He'll know we're here. He'll take you away from me!*"

She gasped, feeling again the fierce slap of cold water on her face as she tumbled through the roaring air and was swallowed by the river. She stared at Edric.

"It was the King's barge," Edric said, his eyes locked on hers. "And Drake was on board." He pointed to the amber pendant that hung against her throat. "I was supposed to give that to you on your birthday," he said, his voice trembling. "Once you were wearing it, Drake knew he would be able to pull you out of your world." He grimaced. "I wanted to destroy it, but once the Amber Stone was smashed, Drake would know that I'd betrayed him, so I had to warn you first. That was what I wanted to tell you that day. That's what I would have told you if we hadn't had the accident."

Tania's head was reeling. Gabriel had been kind to her ever since he led her away from her hospital bed, but had it all been pretense? She had been deceived first by Edric; had Gabriel made a fool of her as well?

She swallowed. "No one here wants to have anything to do with the Mortal World," she said. "Why is Gabriel so interested in it?"

"Because of Isenmort," Edric replied. "He believes he knows how to control metal, and how to bring it into Faerie without being destroyed by it."

"Why would he want to do that?"

Edric looked somberly at her. "For the power it will give him."

Tania frowned. "But he already has plenty of

power. Oberon has appointed him Regent while he's away. What more could he want?"

Edric stood in front of her with his hands on her shoulders. "Drake is insanely ambitious," he said. "You have to believe me when I tell you he can't be trusted."

Tania forced herself to meet his eyes. If Edric was telling the truth, it wasn't just her that Gabriel was intending to betray—it was the King as well, her family, the whole Faerie Court.

But who *was* this man standing in front of her? Evan? Or Edric? Why should she believe him now? Was she so desperate to believe he had loved her in the Mortal World that she'd believe more lies? She knocked away his arms and stumbled backward. "I can't!" she said. "It's too much! I can't think!"

His voice took on a hard, urgent edge. "Stop! We're in danger!"

He was pointing at the amber pendant. Tania suddenly realized it felt warm against her skin. She looked down. The stone was glowing with an inner fire, the amber light spilling out to stain her throat.

Edric caught her wrist in his hand. "Quick! We have to get out of here."

But before they could make a move, the door to the room burst inward with the crack and snap of splintering wood. A howling gale tore into the room, sending them stumbling back.

Gabriel stood in the doorway, his eyes fierce, his cloaked figure silhouetted against the sky.

XVI

"What treachery is this?" Gabriel hissed, and all the kindness Tania had grown used to was gone from his voice.

Edric stepped in front of her. "I have told her everything!" he said. "She will have none of you now!"

Gabriel gave a dismissive gesture with his hand and an invisible force sent Edric spinning across the room. Tania winced as his head struck the wall with a sickening thud. He lay crumpled on the floor, gasping for breath.

"Don't hurt him!" Tania shouted.

"Hurt him?" Gabriel echoed, his voice thick with anger. "I shall finish him! I shall put such an end to him that even the crows will find nothing to feast upon!"

Horrified, Tania ran over to where Edric lay and stood protectively in front of him. He was conscious but he looked dazed and in pain.

"No!" she said. "You won't."

Gabriel's eyes blazed and Tania was suddenly convinced he was going to do something dreadful to her. But then he seemed to change his mind and all the anger drained suddenly from his face. He smiled at her, but behind that smile, she could still see the dark stain of his rage in his burning eyes.

"Forgive me, Tania," he said. "Such was my wrath that I forgot myself for a time, but it is passed." He looked down at Edric, his expression dark with pain. His voice was low and full of distress.

"Why do you betray me so, Edric?" he murmured. "What lies have you been telling?"

Edric wiped his hand across his mouth. "No lies, my lord," he said. "I have only revealed to the princess the true reason why you wish to marry her."

Gabriel seemed surprised. "Indeed?" He looked at Tania. "And what are these *true* reasons?"

"To gain power for yourself," Edric said.

Gabriel looked at Tania. "This is foolish nonsense," he said quietly. "Can you not see that his wits are turned?" He gave a regretful sigh. "I guessed that it was so, and I had hoped to spare you from his pathetic deliriums. I fear his mind was damaged by his time in the Mortal World." He looked again at his servant. "Edric, Edric. If a man reaches for the sun, he will do nought but burn his hand. Do not seek that which is far above you."

Tania frowned. "What are you talking about?"

"Can you not see?" Gabriel said. "This man has fooled himself into believing there can be love between you and he. He wishes to have you for himself, and he would say anything to turn you against me, to make you doubt me."

Tania stared down at Edric, caught in a sudden uncertainty.

"When have I proved false to you, Tania?" Gabriel went on softly. "Have I tried to woo you, to rekindle our old love?"

Tania shook her head. "No . . ."

"And never shall, Tania. I brought you home for the sake of your father, my King, and for this Realm." He held out his hand to her. "Come away," he urged. "Let us bring this mischief to a swift end."

Edric staggered to his feet, blood threading down his face from a cut on his forehead. "No!" he shouted. "Don't go with him; don't believe him." He made a stumbling rush at Gabriel.

Gabriel lifted his hand and Edric stopped dead as though he had run into a wall. Gabriel's hand turned slowly, fingers outstretched like claws, and Edric's head began to twist awkwardly on his neck. His hands caught at his throat and stifled gurgling sounds came from his straining mouth. Tania stared in horror as he rose into the air, his feet kicking, his face contorted with agony.

Tania threw herself forward and dragged Gabriel's arm down.

With a choking cry, Edric slumped to the floor.

"Leave him alone!" Tania screamed.

Lightning flashed from Gabriel's eyes. "What madness is this, Tania?" he said. "What is this man to you? He is nothing! A slave, a chattel, a worthless piece of flotsam to be torn asunder and cast to the four winds at my pleasure."

Tania shook her head. "No!" she said. "You can't do that. Even if what you said about him is true, you can't hurt him like that."

"You would rather he was left free to spread his lies and malice throughout the Realm?" Gabriel said. "I am the King's Regent and I will not be mocked by this creature. I would have him dead at my feet first."

"There must be laws in this place," Tania said desperately. "If he's done wrong, then he should be put on trial. You can't just kill him."

Gabriel gave her a long, slow look. "Your compassion commends you, Tania," he said at last. "And for your sake, he shall not face the death he so richly deserves. Remember. All that I do now was done at your request." He slipped his hand under his cloak; when he drew it out again, he was holding a small glowing amber ball.

He held the ball out between finger and thumb, showing it to Edric. Its surface crawled like molten oil, and Tania could see wisps of steam rising from it.

"No!" Edric groaned.

Gabriel glanced at Tania. "This I do for you," he reminded her. His voice grew louder, echoing in the rafters. "Edric Chanticleer, I banish you to the Amber

Prison for all of eternity!" He hurled the amber ball down in front of Edric.

It smashed on the floor, exploding in a blinding blaze of white fire. Tania fell back, her arms up to protect her eyes from the searing light. She heard a despairing cry, cut off short.

She opened her eyes, but all she could see was the flare from the explosion.

"What have you done?" Tania whispered.

"I have passed sentence on Master Chanticleer," Gabriel said. "At your request, he is not dead. Indeed, fear not, Tania, for he shall never die."

Gradually, Tania's eyes cleared. A large sphere of amber light was floating just above the ground in the middle of the room, its skin moving like the filmy surface of a soap bubble. Crouched, trapped and immobile, within the sphere was Edric, his frozen hands clawing, his face petrified in an expression of dread, his blank eyes staring.

Appalled, Tania took a step toward the glowing sphere. She reached out a hand, but its surface was as hot as a flame. Thin yellow smoke coiled up from it and the ground beneath it was scorched and blackened.

She stared at Gabriel, disgusted by the look of triumph on his face.

"Let him go."

"That is impossible," Gabriel replied. "There is no way back from the Amber Prison."

"But he's still alive in there?"

"Ah, yes," Gabriel said. He spread his hands in a gesture of mock humility. "See how I bow before your desires, Tania. I am yours to command." He turned to the door and called. "Wardens! To me!"

"You mean you're going to leave him alive in there forever?" Tania gasped. "How can you do that?"

Gabriel didn't reply.

Two men in dark red livery came into the room.

"Take this filth away," Gabriel said to them. "The sight of him sickens me."

The men drew white crystal swords from their belts, and Tania watched in dismay as they used the sword-points to push the Amber Prison through the air, sending it gliding out through the open doorway. The last thing she saw was the tragic, grotesque sight of Edric's bent and hunched back, floating above the cobbled courtyard.

"Where are they taking him?" she asked, her voice dull with shock.

"To the dungeons," Gabriel said. "Cast him from your mind, Tania. He is no more."

She looked at him, her whole body tense, her throat taut and straining so that it ached to speak. "Was he lying? Please, I have to know."

"The question demeans you, Tania," Gabriel said, and his voice was all velvet again. "The man is a lowly servant, and you are a Princess of the Realm. Forget him."

"No," she said steadily. "I can't do that. If you're not prepared to treat him fairly, then I'll go to

Oberon." She was trembling so much that she could hardly stay on her feet.

"The King is far from here, Tania," Gabriel replied smoothly. "I am Regent in his stead, and my word is law."

Tania couldn't bear to hear him say another word. He had punished Edric more brutally than anyone deserved, too brutally for someone with nothing to hide.

What if Edric was speaking the truth?

She started to push past him to the door.

He caught her arm in a fierce grip. "Where are you going, my Tania?"

"Let go of me!" she spat, but his fingers dug deeper into her arm, and a cold glint came into his gray eyes.

"'Tis a pity indeed," he said softly. "Were it my choice, I would have wooed you by slow degrees until I held once more your beating heart in the palm of my hand. But I see now that the tattling of Master Chanticleer has turned your head." He smiled and his fingers bore into her arm until she gasped with the pain. "We will be wed, Tania, whether you wish it or not."

"Never!" she said calmly. "You can't force me to marry you, and as soon as I get out of here, I'm going to let my sisters know exactly what you are! Among us, I think we'll find a way to deal with a two-faced rat like you!"

Gabriel gave a breath of cold laughter. "Your sisters?" he said. "Your loving sisters?"

Tania stared at him, confused by the jeering note in his voice. He turned his head toward the door. "Come hither, my lady," he called. "Show yourself."

Rathina stepped into the open doorway. Her head was held high, but she avoided looking into Tania's eyes.

"Rathina?" Tania breathed. "What's going on?"

"You and Gabriel must be married," Rathina said, her voice clipped and abrupt. "It is for the best."

Tania stared at her, too shocked to speak. Why was Rathina siding with Gabriel like this?

"Watch over your sister," Gabriel told Rathina. "Make sure she understands the wise course." He turned to Tania. "If you defy me, Edric will die. If you agree to marry me, I will set him free. His fate is in your hands. Choose wisely, but choose quickly!"

He released Tania's aching arm and swept out of the room.

Two more of Gabriel's wardens escorted Tania and Rathina to Tania's bedchamber. Night had fallen and the room was lit by yellow candles. Tania stood just inside the door. She heard the sharp click of a key being turned in the lock. She was shaking with anger.

Rathina opened a window. "It is stuffy in here," she said. "Some fresh air will clear our heads."

"Why did you tell Gabriel where to find us?" Tania demanded, her voice knotted with fury.

Rathina stayed at the window, not looking at her.

"I did not tell him. Gabriel needs no spies to guide him to you, Tania." She turned and pointed at the pendant. "You carry the keys to your prison about your neck. While you wear the Amber Stone, you can never escape him."

Tania tore the pendant from around her throat. She threw it to the floor and stamped on it. There was a crack as it was crushed under her foot. Pale smoke drifted for a moment across the boards and Tania thought she heard the sound of a soft voice weeping. She lifted her foot. There was nothing left of the pendant but a scattering of yellowish brown powder.

"You should have done that long before now," Rathina said dryly. She walked over to a chair and sat down. "But it comes too late, I fear. Gabriel's wardens stand guard outside. You cannot get away now. Were I in your place, I would accept my fate with as good a grace as I deemed possible."

"You really think I should agree to marry him?"

"It would be wise."

"I don't believe this!" Tania hissed. "Why are you helping him?"

"Because it is the only way for you to save Edric's life." Rathina tilted her head. "Is that not your wish? Edric told me of his love for you. He believes that you love him, also. He begged me to arrange a tryst between you." She narrowed her eyes at Tania. "Do you have feelings for this servant man, or do you not?"

"Yes," Tania said in a whisper. "I do."

She had never stopped loving Evan. It was Edric she loathed for his apparent betrayal of her. But in the stable room, she had seen Evan again, heard his voice telling her he would never have betrayed her—and she had believed him.

She closed her eyes, her hands up to her face, feeling tears welling through her fingers. She heard Rathina walk toward her and felt comforting arms around her.

"Hush now, little sister," Rathina murmured, her mouth close to Tania's ear. "Do not lose heart. I am sorry for my part in this. I would not have aided Gabriel had I known how harsh would be his treatment of Edric."

Tania put her arms around Rathina's neck, too miserable to speak.

"Listen to me, Tania," Rathina went on. "There is a way in which you can escape from Gabriel and all the other heavy burdens of this place."

"How?" Tania choked.

"By stepping into the Mortal World."

Tania caught her breath. She looked up, wiping the tears out of her eyes. "What?"

Rathina nodded earnestly. "You did it once before," she said, "in this very room, five hundred years ago."

Tania stared at her sister. "Do you mean you know how I did it?"

Rathina shook her head. "I know not what powers you summoned up, but I saw you disappear. We just need to repeat the actions of that night. Do that, and you can leave Faerie forever."

"No," said Tania. "I won't do that. I have to save Edric. How can I save him if I go into the Mortal World and never come back?"

Rathina leaned forward, taking Tania's burning face between her cool palms. "Once you are gone again, Gabriel will have no reason to keep Edric imprisoned. I vow to you that I will do everything in my power to see that he is freed." Her voice became more urgent. "But that can only happen if you are gone from here, gone where no one can ever follow." Her eyes were huge as she stared into Tania's face. "Listen to me. You do not belong in this world. In your heart you know this to be true. You belong in the Mortal World, the world into which you were born, the world that you know so much better than you will ever know Faerie." Her voice dropped to little more than a whisper. "You know I speak the truth . . . *Anita*."

Tania blinked. It was the first time anyone had used her mortal name since she had come to the palace.

"All this is but a dream to you, Anita," Rathina said. "Go back, go home."

"I have to help Edric," Tania said.

Rathina gave a sympathetic smile. "And how would you do that?" she said. "Would you enter the dungeons and destroy the Amber Prison by the force of your will?" She shook her head. "Understand this,

Anita. The Amber Prisons can only be undone by those who have mastered the Mystic Arts. Believe me when I tell you that there is no power in all of Faerie that you could use to break the bonds of the Amber Prison. The only way you can help Edric is to *go back home*."

Tania stared at her sister for a long time. All her instincts told her that she couldn't abandon Edric, but what Rathina said made sense. And what could she do? If she stayed, Gabriel would force her to marry him. But if she left, she would lose Edric forever.

And then a possible solution struck her.

"You just said that there's nothing in Faerie that I could use to break the Amber Prison, right?"

"Indeed," Rathina said. "It is useless to attempt it."

"Nothing in *Faerie*!" Tania repeated. "But what about in the Mortal World? If I could remember how to cross between the worlds, I know something that I could bring back to set Edric free." It was obvious from Rathina's expression that she didn't understand. "Isenmort!" Tania cried. "Sancha told me that Isenmort is really dangerous here. If I bring back something made of metal, it might be powerful enough to break one of your Amber Prisons!"

Rathina shuddered. "But Isenmort is the death of all things," she said. "You cannot think to bring such a plague into this Realm. It would be our doom!"

"I'll be as careful as I can," Tania said. "But it has to be worth a try. And you're right," she continued. "I should use my power to leave Faerie, but only in order to come back."

She took a long, deep breath, trying to calm her mind.

"I can do this," she told herself. "I know I can." She closed her eyes and concentrated on home, on her mother and father, on their house. On her real— no, her *other*—bedroom. Picturing all those things as vividly as possible in her mind, she reached out her arms and stepped forward.

There was no rush of wind, no sensation of the floor melting under her feet.

She opened her eyes. She was still in Faerie.

Her sister was looking closely at her.

"Help me, Rathina," Tania pleaded. "Tell me what we did that night. How did I get into the Mortal World?"

"It is long ago," Rathina murmured. "Give me a moment to recall." She moved away and sat on a chair with her head resting in her hands.

Time dragged by.

"Rathina, please?"

Rathina lifted her head. "Believe me, I *do* want to help you." She took a slow breath. "The chimes of midnight hung in the air," she said, staring ahead with faraway eyes. "I was seated on your bed. You stood with your back to yonder wall." She pointed to where the wardrobe stood. "You walked toward me. The air moved like water and there was a sound like a distant wind, and then you were gone."

"I just walked toward you?" Tania checked. "It was as simple as that?"

"That is what I remember,"

"Okay, let's try it." Tania stood with her back to the wardrobe. Again, she filled her mind with thoughts of home. Mum and Dad. Jade and the gang. School. *Romeo and Juliet*.

With slow deliberation, she strode across the floor. Her knees bumped against the side of the bed. Nothing had happened.

She looked at Rathina.

"Are you sure that's all I did?"

"I remember nothing more," Rathina said. She frowned. "You must try again."

Tania nodded.

She stood with her back to the wardrobe again, farther across the room this time so that she wouldn't hit the bed. She could feel Rathina watching her closely as she filled her mind with images of her past life and then strode out across the room.

She came to the far wall and she was still in Faerie.

"Again!" Rathina said. "Do not give up!"

Clenching her fists with frustration, Tania turned and walked back—concentrating even harder this time, picturing her father's face. Her head began to throb with the effort. Her father. His eyes, nose, mouth, hair. The sound of his voice. Tania screwed her eyes shut, summoning up every last ounce of willpower, desperate to make the leap.

Her foot hit against something, a low stool that

stood at the foot of her bed. She stumbled sideways and fell onto her hands and knees.

"This is hopeless, Rathina!" she shouted angrily. "It's never going to work!"

There was no reply.

She opened her eyes.

She was still in the same room, yet everything was different, and Rathina was gone.

There had been no roaring wind, no wrench of nausea, no feeling that the world was dissolving around her.

But she was back in the Mortal World.

XVII

Tania looked around the unlit room, trying to work out where she was. It took a while for her eyes to adjust to the gloom.

Then she recognized the place. She was in the Queen's State Bedchamber in Hampton Court Palace.

She got shakily to her feet.

It was that easy? Just a simple sideways step, and here she was in the Mortal World again.

"Oh, yes!" She pulled her hair back off her face. "That's more like it."

She went to the window. Formal gardens lay under a starry sky, similar to the gardens of the Faerie Palace, but on a smaller scale and not as enchanting. Just as the stars above were similar, but not so huge and bright as the Faerie stars. There was a curious pale glow on the hem of the sky just above the horizon, a glow that she had never seen in Faerie. After a moment, Tania smiled, realizing that she was seeing the distant glimmer of thousands upon thousands of electric lights.

"London!" she breathed, her heart yearning for home.

No, not home. Faerie is home. This is the Mortal World.

She wasn't sure if she really believed that, but telling it to herself helped her focus on what she had to do.

"I will see my parents soon, but not just yet," she said aloud. "Things to do first."

She turned from the window and made her way to the open door. It led into a long, empty room with massive framed tapestries on the walls. She didn't recognize this as being part of the Faerie Palace. There should be a corridor outside her door.

She walked the length of the room, her footsteps echoing in the silence. Another doorway led to a much smaller room with no way out. Frowning, Tania retraced her steps, coming back into the bedchamber and leaving it via a door in the opposite wall, a door that did not exist in the Faerie Palace. She walked through three more rooms, all of them set up for twenty-first-century visitors: Glass panels covered the parts of the tapestries that were within reach, and there were small cards telling people not to sit in the chairs or touch the exhibits. Some areas were sectioned off with loops of red rope.

She came into a large room that was filled with oil paintings hanging on the walls. There were pictures of pale, blank-eyed people in formal Georgian clothes—definitely not Faerie paintings. It was weird the way Faerie things were mixed with mortal objects from other centuries. It was like a jigsaw puzzle where all the pieces fit together okay, but where some of the pieces belonged to a completely different picture puzzle.

Then Tania saw what she had been looking for.

In a far corner of the room, deep in shadows, stood a suit of armor. The arms were bent so that the gauntleted hands rested on the pommel of a long sword.

"Excellent!" she whispered as she ran across the room and stood in front of the armored figure. She reached for the sword.

At once, flashing tendrils of blue light exploded from the hilt. A blast of raw energy sent Tania skidding on her back across the polished floor.

Her arm tingled and her eyes were still dazzled as she sat up, shaking her head to get rid of the ringing in her ears. "That was the worst yet," she said, annoyed at herself for not remembering what would happen when she touched metal. She rubbed her arm. "It must be because I've been in Faerie for a while."

She eyed the sword thoughtfully. Obviously, she couldn't touch it with her bare hands, but she could use something to form a barrier between her skin and the metal. She gathered up the hem of her long skirts and pulled hard at the lining. A strip of silk came away. She tore out more of the lining, until she had a long ribbon of it in her hands.

She ripped the ragged silk band into two halves and then carefully wound the pieces around her hands until not even the tips of her fingers were showing.

"This had better work," she muttered. "Otherwise I'm in big trouble." She stared up at the closed helmet. "Behave yourself!" she said sternly.

She reached out again for the hilt of the sword, wincing as her silk-wrapped fingers touched the bare metal. This time she felt only a slight buzz in her fingers.

"Better!" she said. She carefully lifted the gauntlets and pulled the sword out of the plastic clips that held it in place.

"Yes!" she breathed, taking the weight of the sword. It was heavier than she expected, and she nearly dropped it. She balanced on her heels, lifting the sword in both hands. The fluted blade glimmered in the darkness. "You'll do nicely," she murmured.

She thought back to exactly how she had stepped from one world to the other. She had been walking forward. She had stumbled. She had taken a side step. . . .

Was that all it had taken to send her between the worlds? A simple side step?

"There's only one way to find out," she said.

But then she paused. Hampton Court and the Royal Faerie Palace were not identical. By stepping back into Faerie from this unknown room on the second floor, she might find herself outside the palace buildings, hovering in midair!

She had to reenter Faerie in a place she knew existed in both worlds. Holding the heavy sword in front of her, she made her way back through the galleries.

It didn't make much sense to reappear in her bedchamber. She'd still be locked in, and even if she could use the sword to hack her way through the door, the noise would give Gabriel's wardens plenty of time to prevent her escape.

She walked through the Queen's State Bedchamber and into the gallery full of tapestries. In Faerie this was the corridor outside her room. Gripping the sword in both hands, she took a deep breath.

She walked forward three paces then took a step to the left. The walls rippled around her and her ears popped.

She was in the candlelit corridor outside her chamber. She gave a breathless laugh. It had worked!

The wardens on either side of her chamber door stared at her in utter amazement for a moment, then one of them gave a shout and lunged forward, drawing his crystal sword.

Tania backed off, throwing up her hands to protect herself.

Throwing up her *empty* hands.

The sword had not come with her into Faerie.

Now what? Keep calm. Think!

She spun away from the guard and made a quick side step to the left. The candlelight quivered and went out. She thought she heard a faint crash as the warden fell headlong into the empty space where she had just been. She was back in the Mortal World. The sword lay on the floor in front of her.

She picked it up. She mustn't let that happen again. This time she would keep a really tight grip on it.

She took several steps along the room, making sure that she wasn't going to appear in Faerie too close to the wardens. She turned, tightening the fingers of both hands around the hilt of the sword.

"Okay," she said. "This time we're going to get it right."

But even as she took the side step again, she felt the sword hilt dissolve in her hands and heard the faint clang of it hitting the floor back in the Mortal World. Then she heard voices shouting.

"She is gone! Did you see her? What phantasm was it?"

"Methought it was the Princess Tania!"

"Nay, 'twas the specter of the dead Queen!"

"Hold fast! I shall fetch Lord Drake. This is miching mallecho; there is mischief afoot this night!"

Tania saw one of the wardens running away along the corridor. The other gave a yell of alarm, staring at her with goggling eyes.

"It is returned!" he shouted, brandishing his white

sword. "I fear you not!" he swore. "Be you demon spirit or evil phantom, I shall strike you down!"

Tania sidestepped as the crystal sword came slicing through the air toward her.

She stood forlornly in the twenty-first-century gallery, her shoulders slumped in defeat. The sword lay at her feet. She stooped and picked it up again.

"I don't know how to do it," she said, looking in desperation at the glimmering metal blade. "How do I get you into Faerie?"

"Stay right where you are!"

A startling streak of bright white light flashed around the room.

She whirled around. A beam of electric light shone directly into her face, half blinding her. Behind the bloom of the fierce white flashlight, she saw a uniformed figure.

"Now then, you just keep calm, miss, and we won't have any trouble." She heard the hissing click of an intercom. "Mike? It's Gerry. I'm up in forty-eight. There's a girl up here. You'd better call the police."

Tania lifted her arm to shield her eyes from the flashlight. "You don't have to blind me!"

The beam of light moved off her face and down her clothes. She saw the man's expression change to puzzlement as he stared at her Faerie dress. Then the light shone on the sword blade and his face hardened.

"Put that down, miss," he ordered. "Don't do anything silly. No one needs to get hurt."

"I can't," she said. "I'm sorry—I can't." She backed off. She had to get away from him and work out how she was going to take the sword into Faerie.

"Stop right there!" the guard said.

She turned and ran.

"Hey! Stop!"

She clutched the sword against herself as she ran. Heavy feet thudded behind her. The wavering beam of the flashlight danced over the walls, hurling her silhouette along the floor ahead of her.

She heard a panting voice. "Suspect is moving. Get up here, Gerry. She's got a sword."

Tania ran wildly through the rooms until she came to a zigzagging flight of stairs. She hammered her way down, almost tripping on the treads, but somehow arriving safely on the lower floor. There were several exits from here. She heard the echoing thump of booted feet on the wooden stairs. The flashlight beam raked downward, catching her again.

Gasping for breath, she pushed her way through a pair of double doors. She found herself in some kind of stone-walled vestibule. Ahead of her, glass-paneled doors led to a courtyard.

She ran toward the doors and shouldered through them. At once a shrill alarm split the air. She stumbled out onto a square of clipped grass. A wide pool of dark water filled the middle of the courtyard.

She knew this place. She had seen it before. But when—where?

"Tania! This way!"

The voice came so unexpectedly that at first Tania thought she must have imagined it.

"Tania!"

"Eden?"

"Come toward the light!" Eden called again. Her voice sounded distant but very clear, and it was coming from the far side of the courtyard beyond the black pool.

"What light?" Tania shouted. "I can't see any light!"

She heard the crash of the doors behind her. She glanced over her shoulder. The guard was barely ten strides away.

She ran across the grass, skirting the pool, searching for Eden's light.

And then she saw it, a dim-colored glow that hung against the far wall under a cloistered passageway.

"Quickly!" Eden urged her.

Tania raced toward the circle of glowing light. She knew exactly where she was now, and she knew what that light was. It was the Oriole Glass, the window that led into Eden's tower.

She jumped a low chain-link fence and darted under the cloisters. The round window shone brilliantly in front of her now, and she could see her sister's face through the glass panels.

She heard the guard shouting. He was almost on her, his hand clutching at her back. His fingers grazed her shoulder.

"Gotcha!"

Tania gave a final despairing spurt of speed. The blazing pool of colored light filled her eyes. Moments later she was in the air, diving into the light, bathing in its warm radiance, bursting through the window without any sense of impact and without breaking the glass.

She rolled across the floor, gasping for breath and feeling as if she had left her stomach back in the Mortal World.

But most amazingly of all, she still had the hilt of the sword grasped in her two hands. Behind her, the bright light faded. The rainbow of colors that had striped the walls faded to gray.

She staggered to her feet.

Eden stood in front of the Oriole Glass, holding a lantern in her raised hand. She was still dressed in her black robe, its hood raised to cover her hair, throwing her thin face into shadow.

"You are fortunate that I sleep but lightly," she said. "I know not how nor why, but the Oriole Glass was aware of your peril and opened a bridge between the worlds to aid you." She frowned. "How came you into the Mortal World?"

Tania looked at her. "I remembered how to do it," she said. "How to walk between the worlds. It was easy."

Eden raised an eyebrow. "And yet you were pursued and you could not find your way back into Faerie?"

Tania shook her head. "That's not true. I could get

back," she said. She lifted the sword. "But I couldn't get this to come with me."

Eden shrank back from the shining metal blade.

She gasped. "Keep that deadly thing away from me!" Tania put the sword behind her back.

"I heard the wardens abroad in the palace," Eden said. "They are searching for you. What have you done to incur Gabriel Drake's wrath?"

Where to start? There was so much to tell. Speaking rapidly, Tania poured out the whole story of Edric and Gabriel and the Amber Prison. Eden listened with an expression that grew more and more furious. Her eyes glittered fiercely.

"That young man will betray us all!" she cursed as Tania finished her tale. "Had I known the depth of his treachery, I would never have been persuaded to give him aid!"

Tania stared at her. "You mean you've been helping him?"

"I have, but it was against my wishes," Eden said, her face twisted in anger. "He forced me to teach him the secrets of the Mystic Arts. It was with those secrets that he was able to send his servant into the Mortal World in pursuit of you. He has grown powerful over the years, but we must do what we can to defeat him."

"No!" Tania said. "I don't care about that. I have to rescue Edric." She brought the sword around in front of her again. Eden recoiled as the blade gleamed in the lantern light.

"That's why I brought this," Tania explained. "But

how did it get through? I tried before, but it wouldn't come."

"The Oriole Glass is bound by many enchantments. That is how the Isenmort weapon was allowed to pass into Faerie."

"Good," said Tania. "Now, show me the way to the dungeons." She hefted the sword. "I'm going to use this to smash the Amber Ball that Edric is trapped inside."

Eden's eyes gleamed. "Indeed, it may well suffice. Come, I shall guide you there."

She led Tania from the room, keeping well away from the sword. Tania followed the slender hooded figure through the low archway and up the narrow stairs. They came to a bleak stone corridor, then passed through a door and down an even longer staircase of raw stone that ended at another low wooden doorway.

"Gabriel told me you'd gone mad," Tania said as they entered a dark corridor.

Eden smiled bleakly. "It would have suited his purposes to have you believe so," she said. "But fear not, Tania. I have not lost my wits." She sighed, speaking in a low voice, as if to herself. "Oft have I wished it were otherwise in the long watches of the night!"

They were in a part of the palace that Tania did not recognize—gloomy hallways and corridors of chill, bare stone without light or windows. There was another door, barred with a length of stout oak. Tania noticed that the door had no handle. Eden paused, muttering a few words and passing her hands in a complex pattern over the door.

It swung open silently into an ominous flickering half-light.

They came into a bare stone corridor hung with flaming torches. The ceiling was low, just high enough for Tania to walk upright. Eden had to stoop.

A man in black stepped out of a dark niche in the wall. He held a long pike in his hands. The sharpened crystal tip glinted.

"Who approaches the dungeons?"

Eden stepped up to him.

"Do you not know me?" she demanded

The man stared at her in confusion. "Yes, my lady."

"That is well," Eden said. "Sleep now, and dream of better places than this!" She reached out and touched his forehead with her fingers. He stiffened and became still, his glassy eyes staring past her shoulder as she turned to Tania.

"He will not awaken for many hours."

Tania went up to the frozen man. She waved her hand in front of his eyes. She grinned at Eden. "That's pretty cool!" she said. "You'll have to show me how that works some time." She looked carefully at her. "I thought you'd stopped using your powers. I was told that you haven't used them for a long time . . . not since Titania drowned."

Eden looked at her, and the horror and the

anguish in her eyes sent shivers down Tania's spine.

"The Queen did not drown," Eden said in a low voice. "Her death did not come by water, Tania. It was I who brought her to her untimely end. I killed our mother."

XVIII

Tania backed away from her sister, gripping the sword tightly in both hands. She had seen how easily Eden had dealt with that guard, putting him into a frozen sleep with just the touch of her fingers. If Eden was going to try anything like that on her, she'd have to get past the sword first.

"But I thought she drowned," she said uneasily.

"No, she did not drown." Eden sighed and drew back the hood of her cloak. Tania gasped. Eden's long, thick hair was snow white. "Do not fear me, Tania," she begged. "I meant no harm to our mother, and I have lived five hundred years in guilt and remorse for what I did."

"What happened?"

"The Queen and I spoke long with Rathina after you had disappeared," Eden said. "You played a fool-ish and a dangerous game that night, Tania. We guessed that you had stepped into the Mortal World and that you could not find a pathway back." She frowned. "You never should have attempted to walk between the worlds without seeking guidance first. Such powers are perilous indeed to the unwise and the untutored."

"I know that *now*," Tania said. "It's a pity no one thought to mention it at the time."

"Aye." Eden sighed. "We were remiss. I should have known better. You were ever an impetuous and wayward child."

"Go on," Tania urged.

"Our mother wished to pursue you into the Mortal World. But the King had forbidden it, terrified of losing anyone else he loved. So the Queen came to me secretly, knowing me to be well-practiced in the Mystic Arts. At first I refused. But the Queen was adamant, and so I relented." Her eyes closed tightly. "I summoned up the spirits of the Oriole Glass and constructed a charm of black amber for the Queen to wear. As long as she kept the charm about her throat, I would be able to draw her back. One last time, I begged her not to go, but she would not listen. She stepped into the light and was gone." Eden put her hands to her face. "I heard her scream, and when the light faded, I saw that the amber stone—the protecting charm—had fallen from her throat and lay on the floor at my feet."

"What did you do?" Tania whispered.

"Many times I opened the portal again in the vain

hope that our mother would be able to find her way home," she said. "But it was not to be. She is lost, indeed, and I fear that she was destroyed in her attempt to find you." She took a shuddering breath. "I dreaded the King's wrath, so I told the tale of a boating accident. And upon that day, when our father's grief caused time to stop, I renounced forever my powers and all my Arts. And so it would have remained had Gabriel Drake not come crawling to my door with his velvet threats."

"Gabriel again!" Tania muttered. "What did he do this time?"

"He guessed the truth about our mother's death from my decision to abandon the Mystic Arts. I knew nothing of his dark ambitions when he came begging me to open the Oriole Glass. All I knew was that he was desperate to find you and bring you back. I thought he acted out of love, but nevertheless, I refused to aid him. Then he threatened to tell the King the truth unless I did as he bade, and so I yielded to him. Even then, I would not work for him, but I showed him how to open the Oriole Window and how to construct the protecting pendants." She shuddered. "And then, patient as a spider, he watched and waited and brooded all the long years of our desolation until at last he found you and sent his servant through the glass to bring you back."

Tania let out a long, pent-up breath. "He's power-mad, isn't he?" she murmured. "He'll do anything to get what he wants!" She squeezed the sword hilt in her bandaged fingers. "But he's not going to get away with it," she vowed. She looked at Eden. Her face was white and drawn, and she seemed worn down by the effort of confiding her agonizing, long-hidden secrets.

"Show me where to find Edric," Tania said. "Let's get this over with."

Eden nodded and led her farther along the grim corridor until they came to a glittering door that seemed to be made of smooth black stone.

"This is the Adamantine Gate," Eden said. "You will find all that you seek beyond its portals." She looked at Tania. "But it is bound about with deadly invocations; no person may enter who does not know the words of power and protection. I have never needed to open this door, but I believe I know the words." She stepped close to the door and began to murmur under her breath.

Tania stood back, watching her. Several minutes seemed to pass, but still the door didn't open. Tania bit her lip. The longer this took, the more chance there was that Gabriel or his wardens would find them.

Eden's voice grew louder, speaking lilting words that Tania didn't understand. She made a double-handed pushing motion toward the door. The floor quivered under Tania's feet, but the door remained closed.

"I fear that Gabriel Drake has placed stronger closing incantations on the door," Eden said. "I have not worked these Arts for many years. I will need more time."

"I'm not sure we have more time," Tania said, glaring at the door. "Could you get out of the way, please? I want to see what a little touch of Isenmort will do!"

Eden stepped aside. Tania hefted the sword in both hands, lifting it over her head. She planted her feet wide apart and balanced herself for the swing. "Three, two, one, go!" she shouted. She brought the sword down on the black door. It glanced off with a ringing clang, sending shock waves up her arms and nearly throwing her off her feet.

There was a smell like bad eggs and a spurt of oily black smoke that jetted into the air like squid ink. The door fell open.

Eden stared into the black void with wide, horrified eyes.

"Let's go," Tania said, stepping over the threshold. Eden didn't move.

Tania looked back at her. "What's wrong?"

"It is an evil place. I cannot go inside," Eden said. "But I will remain here and guard the entrance. I will make sure that no wardens come this way." She looked at Tania. "But beware, there may be other guards within." Her voice became sharp. "Go, quickly!"

Tania nodded. "I won't be long." She peered into the utter blackness beyond the open doorway. "Can I borrow your lantern?"

"Yes, indeed. Take it and fare you well."

Tania took the lantern from Eden's outstretched hand.

"Here goes," she breathed. She held the lantern at arm's length in her left hand, the sword clasped in her right.

She was met with a bitterly cold draft of sour and fetid air. She did her best to ignore the smell. If a bad stink was the worst thing she encountered down here, then she'd be very lucky indeed.

"So far so good," she called back to Eden. There was no reply.

She walked deeper into the dungeon. The beam from the lantern trailed over dank, dripping walls of black stone. The corridor was low, with a barrel roof that barely gave her room to walk upright.

The passage ended in a small circular chamber with a round ceiling. Tunnels led off in several directions. Shivering with cold, she picked an exit at random.

Then she hesitated. She had no idea how far this dungeon went beneath the palace, and she wasn't about to let herself get lost down there. She had to make sure that she could find her way back. She would have to leave some mark. Putting the lantern on the ground, she used the point of her sword to carve a crude arrow into the stonework.

She found herself in another passageway, broader and with a higher ceiling than the first. The walls of this tunnel were pocked with shadowy niches, shoulder-width passageways three or four yards deep. Approaching one of them, Tania saw that a great black sphere hovered motionless in the air at the far end of the niche. The sphere was coated with filth and tattered cobwebs, but as she drew closer, she made out a faint yellowish light coming from inside the ball. She stared deeper into the sphere. Under the scab of grime, she saw the inert, crouched figure of a man.

She stepped back with an appalled gasp. The black globe was an Amber Prison. How long had it been there? Years? Centuries? What crime had that man committed that warranted such a dreadful punishment?

Shuddering, she carried on along the tunnel. Many of the dark niches were empty, to her relief, but still too many contained the awful black spheres—ancient Amber Prisons that had been left there to rot in the dreadful silence.

She came to another place where tunnels met and branched off. She gnawed her lower lip, staring into the half-circles of blackness. The place was huge. How would she ever find Edric?

"I have to find him," she muttered aloud. "I'm going to search until I do, and that's all there is to it."

She picked a tunnel, scratched her arrow on the stones, and continued her search.

Not all the Amber Prisons were in the same state of decay. Some were pitch black, but others still had a pale light in them. And occasionally she came across one where the trapped figure was clearly visible, outlined in the orange glow. Those were the worst, because she could see the agonized faces of the victims staring at her with their unseeing eyes. She learned not to look too carefully at those spheres. She just gave them a quick glance to make sure it was not Edric inside, then moved onward into the foul darkness—and onward and onward forever and ever and ever. . . .

"How long have I been in here?" she breathed, resting for a moment. Minutes? Hours? Time meant nothing down here. Her arm ached with holding up the lantern, and the sword dragged at her right hand. She was chilled to the bone, and her legs were starting to shake with tiredness. Much more of this, and she would just sink to the ground and give up.

"Edric!" she shouted, but her voice was swallowed up by the blackness. "Edric, where are you?"

. . . and Juliet is my sun . . .

"I wish I was," she mumbled. "I could use a bit of sunlight down here." She tightened her grip on the sword and walked down yet another of those vile tunnels.

She counted her steps to try and get some indication of time and distance. One hundred paces. Two hundred. Another junction. Another scratched arrow. Another tunnel. One hundred. Two hundred.

And then, stumbling along in a weary daze, she suddenly noticed an amber glow ahead of her that was stronger than anything she had seen so far.

Edric? Please let it be Edric.

Her heart thudding, she ran forward.

The light was seeping out of one of the niches. Hardly daring to hope she might have found him at last, Tania peered around the corner. The amber sphere glowed so brightly, she couldn't look at it for long—but she saw enough to recognize the face that gazed emptily out at her, clawed hands still snatching at nothing.

"I did it!" she whispered.

Tania put the lantern on the ground and stretched her left hand toward the thrumming yellow surface. The amber was quite cold now. She pressed her hand against it, staring at Edric's face.

"I found you!" she murmured. "I knew I would."

She stepped back from the globe, holding the sword in both hands.

"How am I going to do this without hurting you?" she said aloud.

And then she was aware of a new light—a hot, red flickering light coming from directly behind her.

"Halt, intruder into the forbidden place! Your life is forfeit!"

She glanced around in time to see the heavy, knobbed head of a crystal mace swinging toward her. She tried to duck, but the mace caught her a glancing blow on the side of her head and she stumbled to the floor, the sword springing out of her hands and clattering across the stones.

She lay on her back, her head throbbing with pain. A man in black livery stood over her, a flaming torch in one hand, the mace lifted for a second blow.

XIX

Tania managed to squirm out of the way just as the bulky head of the mace came crashing down an inch from her skull. She felt rough stone graze her cheek as she writhed away from the black-clad warden.

With a grunt of anger, he lifted the mace again. She kicked out, but although her foot made contact with him, he didn't even flinch. The air hissed as the mace sliced down, missing her by a hairbreadth as she tried to crawl across the floor to the sword.

A booted foot stamped down on her ankle. Tania cried out with pain as she struggled to get free. She strained her arm across the floor, trying to reach the sword. Her fingers touched the hilt, but she couldn't get a grip on it.

She twisted around so that she was on her back. The guard was holding the mace above his head in preparation for another blow. Summoning all her strength, Tania kicked at his shin with her free foot. He let out a howl and staggered back, his boot coming up off her ankle. She rolled onto her front again and flung herself at the sword.

This time she was able to close her fingers around the hilt. She hoisted it into the air as the mace came plummeting down. There was a shivering impact that sent shock waves along her arm, but the keen edge of the sword had split the crystal mace in two. The severed head thudded down beside her and the warden, caught off balance, reeled and fell against the wall.

She scrambled to her feet.

"Get away from me!" she shouted, flourishing the sword in front of her. "I'll use this on your head next! I will!"

The guard eyed her warily, the ruined stump of his mace hanging from his hand. She lifted the sword and made a move toward him. He thrust his hand out, shouting words she did not understand. Flickering amber lightning flared out from his fingers.

Instinctively, Tania brought up the sword to ward off the flashing threads of light. They sparked on the blade, hissing and dying in an instant.

The warden grimaced, throwing a curse at her before turning and fleeing along the corridor. The skittering red flame of his torch was soon swallowed up by the darkness. She heard his feet beating on the cold stone flags for a few moments, then there was silence.

Tania let out a long, shuddering breath. She had no idea if she really could have used the sword on a living person.

She turned back to the Amber Prison. Edric's glazed eyes stared out at her. She wondered if he could see her, if he had witnessed the way she had fought to rescue him.

One way or another, she would soon know.

She checked the silken wraps around her hands, making sure her skin was still protected. She lifted the sword.

"Carefully, carefully," she whispered. She had seen the effect Isenmort had on the door to the dungeons and on the warden's mace. She had to shatter the Amber Prison without hurting Edric.

She brought the sword up close to the globe and very gently touched the metal point to the amber surface.

A blinding flash bleached the tunnel ash white. Tania stumbled back, screwing her eyes closed. She felt the sword shiver in her hands and heard a sound like the tumultuous beating of huge, leathery wings.

Then there was a blast of furnace-hot air that knocked her off her feet.

She lay panting on the floor of the tunnel. The sword was lying some distance away from her. The lantern had been knocked over, but thankfully it was still alight. She got onto her hands and knees and picked up the lantern. Thick amber smoke rolled and boiled in the niche, and the tunnel was filled with a sharp, spicy smell. She couldn't see a thing.

Her stomach churning, she got to her feet and moved slowly into the smoke.

Edric lay curled up on the ground.

She knelt at his side. "Edric?"

There was no response.

She put her hand on his shoulder. "Edric?"

He gave a low moan and his eyes flickered.

He was alive.

She put down the lantern and struggled to lift him up. She managed to heave him into a sitting position, his head leaning heavily on her shoulder.

She rested her cheek against his hair. "Edric?" she said. "You have to wake up and help me. I can't do this on my own."

The voice was so soft that she only just heard it. "Tania?"

A thrill went through her. "Yes! Yes, it's me," she whispered. "I've got you out of the Amber Prison. But we're in the dungeons, and it's a long way out." She hugged him to her. "I'd carry you if I could, but I can't. You have to wake up properly."

His head lifted and his clear brown eyes gazed into her face.

"*But soft . . . what light . . .*" he murmured. "*. . . it is the east and Juliet is my sun.*"

She smiled. "That's not right," she told him gently. "Romeo says: '*and Juliet is* the *sun*' not '*my sun.*'"

"I'm never going to get that right." He sat up, wincing with pain.

"Are you hurt?" she asked, looking anxiously at him.

"Just stiff," he said. "And cold." He smiled at her. "I saw you fight that guard," he said. "I'll have to remember never to get on the wrong side of you."

"You saw that?"

Edric nodded. "I couldn't move in there, but I was still wide awake." His voice shuddered. "That's the real terror of the Amber Prison: Your brain works perfectly all the time, and you never sleep, not even for an instant."

She stared at him. "I saw other prisons. Some of them looked very old. Surely the people in there aren't still alive?"

A bleak smile lifted the corner of his mouth. "A prisoner in amber is trapped for eternity."

"Then shouldn't we try to free them?"

"Oberon doesn't imprison anyone without a good reason," Edric said. "These people are too dangerous to be let loose. The King of Lyonesse and many of his most deadly knights are incarcerated in here, and they were the most terrible enemies Faerie ever had to face."

Lyonesse? Tania had heard that word before. Then she remembered. It had been in the library. "Sancha was reading a book about the Wars of Lyonesse," Tania said. "Are these people prisoners of war, then?"

"They are," Edric told her. "The wars lasted for a thousand years, and Faerie was very nearly overrun before Oberon managed to defeat the King. That's why they can never be set free." He looked at her.

"That warden will be getting reinforcements. If we don't want to find ourselves facing a whole troop of them, we need to get out of here."

Tania put her shoulder under his arm and levered him to his feet, one arm around his waist, the other hand holding the lantern. He was wobbly, but he was able to stand. He tried a few steps and nearly collapsed again.

She looked at him in alarm. How was she going to get him all the way back to the Adamantine Gate?

She didn't have a choice. She *had* to.

"Come on," she said briskly. "Let's get going."

He put his arm around her shoulders and leaned on her, breathing heavily.

"It's this way," she said, indicating the way she had come. She decided not to let on how far it was.

"No," he said. "It's the other way."

She frowned. "How do you know?"

"I could see when they brought me here," he told her.

"Oh, yes. Of course." She turned and they began to walk slowly along the tunnel. This was the same direction in which the warden had run. She hoped they weren't walking straight into a bunch of armed guards.

Edric was only able to walk slowly, his full weight sometimes bearing down on Tania's shoulders. At first, they spoke to each other, but after a little while, his head hung down and he stopped talking.

Tania saw a square of red light flickering up ahead.

A black stone door stood wide open. The Adamantine Gate.

"I don't believe it," she breathed, almost laughing out loud. "I must have gone the long way around."

"I . . . must . . . rest. . . ." Edric mumbled.

"Not yet," she said. "This is a really bad place to stop, Edric. Soon, though." She helped him through the doorway and out into the torch-lit corridor.

"Eden?" She looked around. The corridor was empty. That wasn't good. She had been banking on Eden's help in getting him out of here. Her sister's ability to put the wardens to sleep with just a touch of her fingers would have come in really useful. She just hoped that Eden hadn't been caught unawares by Gabriel's guards—or, a nasty thought, by Gabriel himself.

"We'll just have to do it on our own," Tania said. She suddenly realized that she had left the sword in the dungeons. She had been so concerned with getting Edric to safety, that she had forgotten it—not that she could have carried it, anyway, with Edric to support and with the lantern in her other hand.

She looked back into the dungeon. Could she risk leaving Edric here while she went to fetch it?

She shook her head. No. Now that she was with Edric, she had no intention of leaving his side. They'd have to manage without the sword.

She just hoped that she could remember the way back to Eden's apartments. A door, a corridor, a long flight of stairs. Another door? Was that right? She wished she had paid more attention.

There were footsteps in the corridor, coming toward them. Tania froze, holding her breath, her arm tight around Edric's waist as he slumped against her.

The footsteps came closer. Not the hard clump of booted feet—the light patter of shoes, of someone walking quickly.

A figure appeared. Tania saw a red dress, long black hair, a familiar face.

"Rathina!"

Her sister broke into a run. "Tania, well met!" she said. "I was fearful for you when you vanished. I am glad indeed that you have returned safely. Fear not, I met with Eden; she told me everything. Quickly now, I will help you. We must quit this place before the wardens come."

She put her shoulder under Edric's other arm and between them they half carried him along the corridor.

"Where's Eden now?" Tania asked.

"I know not," Rathina replied. "She told me to come here and help you, then she was gone about some urgent errand." Rathina looked at Tania over Edric's lolling head. "Her hair, Tania, did you see her hair? It was *white*!"

Tania nodded. "I saw it," she said.

"'Twas ever black as a raven's wing," Rathina breathed, her eyes wide. "I have never seen the like."

They came to the wooden door that led off the torch-lit corridor. They managed to sidle through with Edric still held between them. Tania was becoming more and more concerned; at every step, he seemed to be growing weaker.

"We need somewhere to hide," she told Rathina. "I'm not sure I can remember the way back to Eden's rooms."

"I know a better place," Rathina said. "A secret place where none shall find us."

"Edric's ill," Tania said. "We need Hopie."

"I will fetch her once we are safe," Rathina said. She smiled. "Do not fear, little sister, I will lead you true."

Rathina took them by a quite different route than the one Eden had used. Tania quickly lost track of where she was, but she felt very relieved when they left the dark corridors and stairways behind them.

Edric was still able to drag his feet, one after another, but his breathing was labored and his chin had sagged onto his chest. Even with Rathina's help, Tania wasn't sure she could support him for very much longer.

"We are almost there," Rathina panted. "Do you see that door?" She nodded ahead toward a small arched doorway. "That will be your sanctuary while I summon help."

"Thank goodness for that," Tania gasped.

Rathina looked at her. "Do not despair, dear sister; all will soon be over."

The door led into a small windowless chamber

with austere white walls and hardly any furniture. Rathina pointed to another door that stood at the head of a shallow flight of steps.

"Beyond that door is journey's end," she said.

They hauled Edric up the steps and Rathina opened the door.

As Tania stepped through into the unlit room, she got the impression of a vast space opening out in the darkness, as though the walls and ceiling soared away to unknowable distances.

"Where are we?" she asked.

Rathina closed the door behind them before she replied. There was the click of a key turning in a lock, and suddenly Tania was bearing all of Edric's weight.

"In the Hall of Light," Rathina said, and there was a new, hard edge to her voice. "You have evaded your destiny for too long, Tania. But the true path of your life can no longer be denied."

Bewildered, Tania gently let Edric sit down on the floor with his back against the wall. She stood up again, holding the lantern toward her sister's face. Rathina was standing with her back to the door, smiling darkly, her eyes gleaming like diamonds.

"What are you talking about?" she said.

"Can you not guess?" Rathina reached out her arm. "Behold, your groom awaits!"

An eruption of amber light bloomed in the darkness. Tania spun around. The light was coming from a cauldron that stood on a low dais. And standing at the edge of the rising amber glow was the figure of

Gabriel Drake, smiling at Tania in dark triumph. Long sinister black shadows streaked up from his face, and his eyes were pools of darkness in which evil points of silver fire glinted.

"Well met, my lady," he said. "Never was a groom kept waiting for so long a time by his reluctant bride."

The shimmering radiance that came from the cauldron was not strong enough to light up the walls or the high ceiling, but Tania knew exactly where she was. This was the hall that Gabriel had shown her in the hand mirror—the hall in which their conjured images had performed the first ceremony of a Faerie Wedding, the Ritual of Hand-Fasting.

She looked at Rathina, saddened beyond words by her sister's betrayal. Instead of helping her and Edric to escape, Rathina had delivered them both straight into Gabriel's hands.

Rathina's dark eyes stared levelly into hers. "Did I not say it would be wise to do as Gabriel wishes?" she said. "You would not have done this of your own will, so I had to bring you here."

Tania stared across to where Gabriel was waiting for her in an ocean of shining amber air. There was no way for her to escape. Edric was only semiconscious. Rathina was guarding the door, and Gabriel stood between her and any other chance of getting away.

Gabriel held out his hand toward her.

A gentle, female voice sounded in Tania's mind, as if invisible lips had come up close to her head and whispered softly into her ear.

"Remember the words of the rhyme. . . ."

A shiver went up her spine. She knew the voice.

She didn't know *how* she knew, but she did.

It was the voice of her mother, Queen Titania.

Remember the words of the rhyme . . . ?

One alone will walk both worlds, Daughter last of daughters seven, With her true love by her side, Honest hand in true love given.

Suddenly Tania wasn't afraid anymore. She knew exactly what she had to do.

She put down the lantern and walked toward Gabriel with her head held high. Looking calmly into his face, she stepped into the glamorous amber light. The air quivered above the amber liquid as it seethed and roiled in the cauldron.

"Are you sure you want to do this?" she asked, her voice absolutely calm. "Are you really sure?"

Gabriel lifted the glass jug she had seen before and dipped it into the cauldron.

"It is the uttermost wish of my heart," he said.

"Very well, then," Tania said. "Let's do it."

A muted cry made her turn her head. Edric was on his knees, staring at her in horror. "Don't." He gasped. "Tania—no!"

"Don't worry, everything will be fine," she promised. "Rathina's right. This is my destiny. I've avoided it for five hundred years, but that's all over now. Trust me, it's for the best."

"You have made the wise choice, my lady," Gabriel said smoothly.

Tania turned away from Edric's look of horror. She couldn't explain to him why she was doing this— not yet. She unpeeled the silken bandages from around her hands then held one arm out over the cauldron.

She bit back her disgust as Gabriel's hand closed around hers. He lifted the jug above their hands. An expression of triumph and greed twisted his handsome face. She looked away.

She felt thick warm liquid flood down over their joined hands.

Her fingers tingled. A strange prickling sensation traveled rapidly up her arm and spread into her shoulder.

A heartbeat later, a powerful force blazed through her, searing her skin from the inside. It was as if she was becoming molten—her mind and body turning to liquid and flooding into the mind and body of Gabriel Drake. She gasped, staring into his face. But it wasn't his face anymore. It was her own face that stared at her across the glowing heart of the cauldron. Her face and his face, her eyes and his eyes—intermingled, melting together, becoming one.

And at that moment, she saw the full extent of his ambition.

She saw it as clearly as she had seen the images in the hand mirror.

She saw Gabriel bring into Faerie a bright blade of Isenmort from the Mortal World, and she saw him stab the King with it. She saw Oberon fall and die at his feet. She saw him seize the throne, blaming others for the King's death.

She saw him become the eternal tyrant of all Faerie. And she saw him lead Faerie armies into the Mortal World to extend his wicked rule.

And as their bodies and their spirits mingled, she knew that it was by the power of her gift to walk both worlds that he would be able to do these terrible things.

XX

With a cry of dismay, Tania tore her hand free of Gabriel's grip and staggered back from the cauldron.

"At last!" Gabriel shouted. "At last!" He began to laugh wildly, his head thrown back and his arms spread wide as his evil mirth rang out through the Hall of Light. Tania watched him through narrowed eyes. She could still feel where his fingers had been tight around hers. She looked at her hand. The amber liquid seemed to have drawn in, leaving only a faint golden sheen on her skin.

Smiling, Gabriel leaned both hands on the rim of the cauldron and stared at her. "Now, my lady," he said with velvet smoothness, his eyes glowing golden in the light, "let us put it to the test."

"Yes," she said, staring straight back at him. "Why not?"

Remember the words of the rhyme. . . .

He had not won yet.

She reached out her arm toward him, her hand open, inviting him to take hold.

He circled the cauldron, his black cloak swirling around him.

She didn't flinch as he grasped her hand.

"Are you ready for this?" she said.

His eyes glowed. "I have waited long for this moment," he murmured.

"Come on, then," she said. "Follow me." She walked forward. Gabriel moved with her, step for step.

She concentrated hard, and stepped sideways.

The Hall of Light trembled and her ears were full of racing air. The amber light of Faerie dimmed and all around her a darker place began to emerge.

She felt Gabriel's fingers slipping from her hand.

She turned and saw Gabriel falling away behind her, his form hazy as though she was seeing him through a coiling mist. He seemed to be caught in a rushing wind that sent his cloak streaming out behind him. His face was contorted with anger and frustration as his fingers clawed impotently at the air.

And then he was gone and she was standing alone in a darkened room in the Mortal World.

"Thank you, Titania," she whispered. "You were right."

. . . *With her true love by her side, Honest hand in true love given.*

That's what the rhyme said. Only one who truly loved her could share her gift to walk both worlds.

Gabriel did not love her, and so, despite the Ritual of Hand-Fasting, he wasn't able to move between the worlds with her.

She looked around. She was in some kind of office with a desk and a computer and filing cabinets. Venetian blinds hung at the window, and beyond them she saw a small paved courtyard lit up by a lamppost.

She was free of Faerie and of Gabriel. She could walk to the door and step out into the ordinary night of the Mortal World and never look back.

Except that she couldn't, not without Edric.

She sidestepped back into Faerie.

She had been half hoping that Gabriel might have gotten lost somewhere between the worlds, but he was there in the Hall of Light, crouched on one knee, gasping for breath and looking as though he had been caught in a hurricane.

Rathina was pressed against the door, her face white and her eyes huge and troubled. Tania ignored her. She ran to where Edric lay.

She came down beside him, smiling into his puzzled eyes. "You see?" she said. "I told you it would be all right."

His hand slid into hers. "But are you all right?"

"I'm fine." She turned to look at Gabriel. He was on his feet again, his face in torment. He had plotted for this moment for five hundred years, and it had all come to nothing.

Tania looked at him in quiet fury, and for the first

time she felt the power and the authority of the royal family of Faerie rise inside her. "You will regret what you have tried to do here, Gabriel," she said. "When my father the King returns, you will be dealt with."

Gabriel's eyes seemed to ignite with deadly white flame. "At the very least, you shall not live to witness my downfall," he snarled. He came swooping toward her with a murderous look on his face, his black cloak lifting above him like menacing wings.

Edric stumbled to his feet and forced himself in front of Tania.

"No!" she shouted.

It was too late. Gabriel sent Edric crashing to the floor with a single blow from the back of his hand. He towered over Tania, his face contorted with madness. He drew a small amber globe from his clothes and held it above her.

"Drink deep of the sleepless nightmare, my lady!" he spat. "Think of it as a gift from your cheated groom—an eternity of ceaseless suffering."

Tania screamed and threw her arms up as he flung the amber ball spinning through the air toward her.

A deep, echoing boom shook the hall to its foundations.

Tania opened her eyes to bright white light. The amber ball was hovering in the air above her, revolving slowly and shedding yellow steam. And then, while she was still wondering what had happened, the ball shriveled and vanished in a puff of smoke.

She stared around. The whole of the vast space

was lit up with an unearthly radiance that came from the far end of the hall. Gabriel was still standing above her, but he was staring at something in the heart of the brilliant light.

Lifting herself up on her elbows, Tania followed his gaze. The double doors at the end of the hall had been thrown open, and two figures stood in the doorway, sheathed in white light.

Oberon swept into the room, trailing light like a comet in the night sky, and Tania saw that the slender, dark-cloaked figure at his side was her sister Eden.

The King gestured toward Gabriel, and he was sent hurtling across the floor like a rag doll.

A warm, embracing force lifted Tania to her feet as her father approached her.

"Are you hurt?" Oberon asked, his eyes anxious.

"No, not at all," Tania breathed.

"'Tis well!" He turned to where Gabriel lay on the floor. Oberon lifted his hand and Gabriel was drawn up off the flagstones until he hung in the air, his feet clear of the ground, as if he was suspended from a hook.

"My daughter Eden has told me of your infamy," Oberon thundered. "Base and treacherous schemer. Your villainous intrigues will come to nought. You are a lord of Faerie no more. You are nothing! Be gone from my palace and from my Realm! The sight of you offends the very stars!"

A shrill voice screamed from behind Tania. "No!"

Rathina sped across the floor to where Gabriel was

hanging. She threw her arms around him, clinging onto him and staring back at the King.

"What madness is this?" Oberon demanded. "Rathina, stand away!"

"Never!" she shouted. "Do your worst, I care not." She looked imploringly up into Gabriel's face. "Wherever you are sent, whatever your fate, I will go with you!" she cried. "I shall never leave your side. All that I have done was done for love of you, and I will never abandon you, not even if dark eternity awaits!"

Tania reeled. All the time, her closest sister had been secretly in love with Gabriel Drake. Rathina had betrayed her in the hope of winning his affection. It was almost too much to take in.

Gabriel stared down at Rathina, his face full of scorn. "Spend an eternity of exile with you, my lady?" he snarled. "I would rather rot in an Amber Prison."

Rathina's face went ashen and she staggered as though she had been slapped. She stared up at him with horrified eyes. "You told me that you loved me," she shouted, spittle foaming at her lips. "You gave me your oath. You promised that if I helped you to win Tania's power, we would be together for all time."

"Did you truly believe that I could ever love you?" Gabriel spat. "It was but deception, my lady. I never loved you."

Rathina gave a despairing wail and fell to her knees.

Gabriel looked at Tania and a cruel smile twisted his lips. "It is a pity indeed that my hopes and plans have come to nothing, my lady," he said. "But I am comforted in the knowledge that you will never be content in Faerie. Your spirit is split between the worlds; you shall never find peace!"

Tania shuddered. His words sounded like a curse.

Gabriel spread his arms wide and looked at Oberon. "And now," he said. "I am at Your Grace's command."

The King's voice rumbled like an earthquake as he reached out a hand toward him. "Ill fortune devour you, Gabriel Drake. Thou art banished. Get you hence!"

Gabriel's eyes widened for a moment in terror, and then, without sound or movement, he was gone, as if he had simply winked out of existence. Wisps of black smoke hung in the air, holding the shape of the young lord for a few seconds, and then they too were gone.

Rathina let out a tortured scream and fell forward, sprawling on the floor. She glared at Tania, her face twisted with hatred and rage.

"This is your fault!" she hissed, pulling herself to her feet. "You should have been killed in the Mortal World—killed never to be born again." Her eyes blazed. "Did you think I urged you to use your powers all those years ago out of childish curiosity? No, sister, it was in the hope that you would die and leave me free to gain Gabriel's love."

Tania stared at her, too stunned to speak.

"I hate you!" Rathina spat. "I wish you were dead!" She gathered her skirts and ran from the room.

Eden shook her head. "Alas for poor Rathina." She sighed. "We should pity her, for she was more fooled by Gabriel than any of us. But there is nothing that we can do for her. She must bear her dishonor alone."

Sick at heart, Tania turned to Oberon. He was stooping over, his hand resting on Edric's golden hair. "Rise and be healed," the King said.

Edric's eyelids fluttered, then he stirred and stretched as if he was waking from a long sleep. He opened his eyes and met Tania's worried gaze, then a slow smile spread across his lips.

But soft, what light is this . . . ?

Oberon turned to Tania and held out his arms.

Tania put her arms around him as far as they would go, hugging him back. "How did you get back here so quickly?" she asked.

"Eden used the Mystic Arts to call to me," he said. "I rode swift upon the horse of air to be at your side. And it is good that it were so, for had I not been so fleet, much mischief would have been wrought this night."

A muffled sob made them break apart and look around. Eden was standing a little distance away, tears pouring down her face. Suddenly she dropped to her knees and grasped Oberon's hand.

"Forgive me, Father," she wept. "Forgive me for being the cause of the Queen's death. Forgive me for my deceit. Forgive me for my weakness."

Oberon reached down and drew his eldest daughter to her feet. He looked into her eyes for a moment then kissed her forehead. "You have borne a great burden down the long years," he said gently. "I cannot find it in my heart to blame you. You sought only to aid your mother and to find your lost sister. You would never have opened the Oriole Glass had you known your mother would not return. There is nothing to forgive."

Eden gazed up at him, her face filled with gratitude and happiness.

"I should be the one apologizing," Tania said. "If I hadn't let Rathina talk me into trying to walk between the worlds in the first place, none of this would have happened. All you did was to try and put things right."

"And in doing so, I disobeyed our father and caused the death of our mother," Eden said. "It is a hard thing to bear, even though it was love of you that brought me to it."

"I don't believe she is dead," Tania said. "I think she's still alive in the Mortal World. It's just that she can't get back here."

"That is not possible," Eden said forlornly. "She would have been vulnerable to the sicknesses and dangers of the Mortal World, just as you were. I do not believe that she can still be alive after so long in exile."

"Someone sent me my Soul Book on my sixteenth birthday," Tania insisted. "It must have been sent by someone who is in the mortal world but who comes from Faerie." She squeezed Eden's hand. "Don't you see? Who else could it be other than Titania? I'm sure she's still alive." Her eyes lit up. "And I'm going to prove it. I'm going back to find her."

A glimmer of hope appeared in Eden's eyes.

Tania looked at Oberon. His face was troubled. "I would not lose you again," he said. "The passage into the Mortal World is perilous."

"Not for me it isn't," she said. "I'm the seventh daughter, remember?" She smiled. "Don't worry," she said. "I can do this. I won't get lost this time. And when I come back, I'll have Titania with me."

Oberon put his arms around her, his voice a low murmur in her ear. "Never has a father been more proud of his daughter's courage, Tania," he said. "I understand the hold that the Mortal World has over you, but you must promise to return. I could not bear it if you did not come back to me again."

"I will come back," Tania promised.

"Then go with my uttermost blessings upon you," Oberon said. "But you will be vulnerable to the touch of Isenmort now." He held out his closed hand between them. A light flashed for an instant between his fingers, and when he opened his hand, two black jewels lay on his palm.

"They are black amber from my crown," he said. "The rarest jewels in all of Faerie. Take them, for they will protect you from the bite of Isenmort."

"Thank you," she said, picking the small black stones out of his hand.

"'Tis but a father's gift," he said. "May fortune go with you, Tania, and may you bring our beloved

Titania back to her home."

Eden put her arms around Tania. "I will watch for you every day until you return," she said. "A constant light will burn in the Oriole Window to guide your way home."

Tania hugged her tightly. "Say good-bye to the others for me, will you?" she asked. "Tell them I'll be back soon."

"I will."

Tania turned to Edric.

"I have to do this," she said. "There are other things that are just as important to me, but this is something I have to do first. Do you understand?"

"I understand," he said, his eyes filled with unspoken sadness. "I'll be waiting for you to come back."

"Thank you." She reached up and touched his cheek with her fingertips. "I needed to hear you say that."

She turned and gave her Faerie father and her sister a final loving look. She lifted her hand in farewell and made the side step that would take her into the Mortal World.

Faerie began to dissolve around her, but at the very last moment, she reached back and grabbed hold of Edric's hand.

"What were you waiting for?" she called to him. "A formal invitation?"

She gave a tug, and he stumbled after her.

A second later she found herself in that same dark office, but this time there was a warm hand in hers.

She turned and looked at Edric. He was standing beside her, wide eyed and gasping for breath.

... *With her true love by her side, Honest hand in true love given.*

She smiled at him. "You know what this means, don't you?"

"What?"

"It means you love me. And there's no getting out of it."

He grinned. "As if I'd want to!"

She opened her free hand. The black amber stones glittered darkly in her palm. "Oberon gave me two jewels," she mused. "Do you think he knew all along that I'd want you to come with me?"

"Maybe," Edric said. "But I'm glad he did. Drake took back the stone that he gave me when he sent me here to find you."

"Well, this is a replacement," Tania said, smiling. "And this time it's given with love."

Smiling, Edric took the jewel.

"Shall we go?" she asked. She led him to the door, turning the latch and pulling the door open. Together they stepped out into the courtyard. She closed the door behind them and took a deep breath of the cool dawning air.

Holding his hand tightly in hers, she looked out across the open end of the courtyard to a wide expanse of tarmac bordered with lawns and trees. It ended in a high red-brick wall with black wrought-iron gates. Houses and trees lay beyond, shadowy against a grainy blue-gray sky. It was all achingly familiar to her—or at least, to the part of her that was Anita Palmer. She was back in twenty-first-century London.

She looked at Edric. "Are you scared?"

"A little," he said. "That's quite a task you've set us, finding the Queen of Faerie after five hundred years."

"We'll find her," Tania promised. "Trust me, Edric. I know she's still alive."

Hand in hand, they headed toward the gates, and as they walked, the first rays of the rising sun lit up the sky at their backs and sent their shadows dancing down the pathway ahead of them.

Watch for Tania's next journey
between the Realms in

The Lost Queen

Book Two of *The Faerie Path*

Camden, North London

The van's horn blared loudly in the quiet of the early morning London streets: three short bursts followed by a cheery whistle from the driver.

Princess Tania, seventh daughter of Oberon and Titania, King and Queen of the Immortal Realm of Faerie, turned her head to look. The driver of the van was half leaning out of the cab, grinning at Tania and her companion as the vehicle sped by.

Tania laughed. She didn't mind the effect she and Edric were having as they walked along together; it was quite funny, actually, and that driver wasn't the first person to have reacted enthusiastically to their strange clothes. They had already been on the receiving end of several odd looks on their journey from Hampton Court in southwest London to Camden in the north of the city.

Tania knew why they were getting these reactions: Their ornate clothes would have blended in perfectly in an Elizabethan court, but they struck an odd note in twenty-first-century London. Tania was wearing a full-skirted, olive green velvet gown with long sleeves and embroidered panels picked out in leaf green and russet red stitching. Edric's clothes were similarly archaic: a dark gray doublet and hose trimmed with black brocade and with puffed sleeves slashed to show a lining of pearl white silk.

Edric smiled. "He probably thinks we've been to an all-night costume party."

"Probably," Tania agreed. "One thing's for sure: He'd never guess the truth." She paused and gazed into Edric's wide, chestnut brown eyes. A thread of wind caught his dark blonde hair and whipped it around his smiling face—the face of the boy she loved. A seventeen-year-old boy called Evan Thomas, who had turned out to be someone quite different—just as she had turned out to be a different person from the girl she had always thought she was.

Three days ago she had been Anita Palmer, an ordinary girl on the brink of her sixteenth birthday. Three days ago she had known nothing of the enchanted world of Faerie. She smiled to herself. Back then she had been only half alive.

Three days ago she had loved a boy called Evan, but now she knew who he truly was: Edric Chanticleer, a young courtier of the Royal Palace of Faerie.

The sharp click of heels on paving stones brought Tania out of her reverie. A woman was walking toward them, staring at them in amused curiosity.

"Hello, there," Edric said. "We've just come from the Immortal Realm of Faerie." He nodded to Tania. "She's a princess."

"Is she?" the woman said as she passed. "Good for her. The pair of you certainly brighten up the place."

"Thanks," Tania called as the woman walked on and disappeared around a corner.

Edric grinned. "You see? People are okay with the truth."

She looked thoughtfully at him. "So long as they think you're kidding," she said. "But that's not going to work with Mum and Dad."

Edric's face became serious. "No," he said. "I know it won't."

Tania glanced down at herself. "I can't turn up at home dressed like this," she said. "I'm going to have enough explaining to do without these clothes." She had been out of the Mortal World for three days since both she and Edric went missing from hospital following the speedboat accident—three days and nights for her desperate parents to fear the worst. She had to get back to them as soon as possible and let them know she was all right, but not in her Faerie gown.

Edric looked up and down the street. "The shops aren't open yet," he said. "It can't be much past seven o'clock. But even if they were open, we haven't got any money to buy clothes."

Tania frowned, thinking. "There's a charity shop not far from here."

"That won't be open, either."

"It doesn't matter." She gripped Edric's hand. "Come on. I know where we might find some things to wear."

St. Crispin's Hospice Shop, Camden
The charity shop had an assortment of items laid out in the window—everything from books and vinyl LPs to toys and games and ornaments. Deeper into the shop they could see racks of clothing and one shelf that appeared to contain nothing but folded crocheted blankets.

"Just like I said," Edric commented, peering through the glass. "It's closed."

"No problem," Tania said. "Come with me." She led him by the hand into a narrow alley that ran alongside the shop. A doorway was sunk into the wall about ten feet down the alley and up against the door, they found a pile of plastic bags, boxes, and bin liners.

"People leave stuff here for the shop when it's closed," Tania explained. "With any luck we'll find some clothes we can use. We can do a swap."

Edric crouched down and opened the nearest bag. He pulled out a garish green-and-purple knitted sweater. "What do you think? Should I try it on?"

"Over my dead body." She knelt at his side and started working at the knotted string that held closed the neck of another bag, hoping that the clothes inside would turn out to be more wearable than that purple-and-green sweater.

* * *

"Okay, I'm decent again," Tania said. She had
changed in the shallow confines of the sunken doorway while Edric had turned his back and guarded her
from the gaze of anyone passing the end of the alley.

He was already in normal clothes: a pale blue shirt
and a pair of blue jeans two sizes too big for him, held
up with a black leather belt.

Tania stepped out of cover. "Do I look all right?"
The choice of clothing hadn't been ideal, but she had
found a pink T-shirt and a calf-length, brown denim
skirt. She had discarded her red velvet Faerie shoes in
favor of a pair of white sneakers that fit reasonably
well.

Edric smiled. "You look lovely," he said.

She raised her eyebrows. "If you say so," she said.
She crouched and carefully folded her Faerie gown
into one of the bags. "And it's not like we're stealing,"
she said. "Just making an exchange." She looked up at
him. "Imagine their faces when they see this lot."

Edric reached down and she took his hand as she
stood up.

"You'll need one of these," she said, opening the fingers of her other hand. She had brought the two small
flat gemstones from Faerie in a pocket of her gown.
Now they lay in her palm, oval-shaped and glimmering
fitfully in the pale morning light: Black amber, the most
precious mineral in the Realm of Faerie.

Edric picked one of the jewels out of her hand.

"Remember," he told her. "You're as vulnerable to Isenmort now as I am. You have to keep this with you all the time."

"Yes, I know." For several weeks before she had entered Faerie, Tania had been getting electric shocks off anything made from metal. As the Faerie half of her spirit came alive, so had her susceptibility to metal—to the lethal substance known in Faerie as Isenmort. Oberon had given her these two pieces of black amber for protection; unless she kept one of them close by, the touch of metal could be deadly to her. She slipped the jewel into the pocket of her skirt.

"You haven't told me how I look," Edric said. "Am I respectable enough to meet your parents, do you think?"

She adjusted his collar and smoothed the creases on the front of his shirt. "You look just fine," she said. "But you can't come home with me."

Edric frowned. "I'm not leaving you to face them on your own."

"Yes you are," she said firmly. She lifted her fingers to his lips to stop him speaking. "Listen," she went on. "No matter what I say, Mum and Dad are going to blame you for what happened. I need to talk to them on my own—that's the only way this is going to work. If you come with me, it'll only make things worse."

Edric looked at her for a few moments without speaking. Then he nodded. "Perhaps you're right," he said. "But we haven't even decided what you're going to tell them."

"I wish I could tell them the truth," Tania said. "But I can't. They'd think I've gone insane."

"So we have to come up with a plausible reason for why you disappeared from the hospital and where you've been."

"I'm no good at lying," she admitted. "If we make stuff up, we have to keep it really simple otherwise Mum will suss it out in ten seconds flat."

"Okay," Edric said. "Nice and simple. You've already told them the story about my coming from Wales, haven't you?"

"Yes," Tania said. "And I thought it was true at the time. It sounded perfectly reasonable: You didn't get on with your stepfather so you came to London to get away from him."

"You can tell them you went to Wales to try and find me when I left the hospital," Edric said.

Tania nodded. "Yes, Wales is good. It could easily have taken me this long to get there and back. But we have to choose a particular place." She racked her brains—she had never been to Wales but one of her classmates came from a town in the northwest of the country, a small coastal town in Snowdonia. What was the place called? "Criccieth!" she said aloud. "That's it. It's up in the north of Wales. It could easily have taken me a couple of days to find you there. I'll tell them I wasn't thinking straight, that I was frantic with worry about you after you vanished. I went to Criccieth and found you at your parents' house."

"Tell them I had freaked out because I thought the

police were going to prosecute me about the boat crash," Edric suggested. "And you persuaded me to come back."

"Yes."

He looked anxiously at her. "Are you sure you wouldn't rather have me there with you?"

She shook her head. "Trust me, you don't want to be there. Stay with me till we get to the end of my street, then you should go to the hostel and keep your cell phone on. I'll call you as soon as I can." She grabbed his hand. "Let's go."

Tania and Edric stood at the corner of Lessingham Street and Eddison Terrace. Anita Palmer and her parents lived at number 18, down at the far end of the long residential street.

"I don't want to leave you," Edric said, holding both her hands in his.

"It's only for a little while," Tania said. "We can talk on the phone." She frowned. "What day is it?"

Edric thought for a moment. "Thursday."

"Then I'll see you at school tomorrow," she said. "Keep your fingers crossed for me that everything goes well."

"I will." He looked into her face. "I love you."

"I love you, too. But go, please."

He started to walk away.

"Aren't you going to kiss me good-bye?" she called.

He turned back and suddenly they were in each other's arms.

And then, far, far too quickly, she was alone on the street corner in the early morning light, watching him leave.

He turned and waved. She lifted her hand and waved back. She saw his lips move, mouthing, *I love you.*

I love you. She formed the words soundlessly.

Then he was gone.

She started to walk down the street. The sun blazed between two buildings, sending her shadow skittering away from her, filling her eyes with dazzling light and wrapping her in the warmth of the early summer morning.

Had it all been a dream, everything she had seen and done in Faerie? Her father the King. Her six sisters: carefree Zara; solemn-eyed Sancha; Cordelia with her beloved animals; Hopie with her stern gaze and healing hands; Eden, her unhappy eldest sister who had believed she was responsible for their mother's death; and poor deluded Rathina, who had done such terrible things for love of Gabriel Drake, who had never loved her in return.

Real? Not real?

Tania walked along the street she had known all her life, gazing amazed at all those strange, familiar houses, knowing as she approached the house she had always called home that the girl she had been was gone forever.

Tania's hand trembled as she reached for the doorbell; it felt odd to have to ring at her own front door, but then her missing keys were just another part of her old life—the life that had been stripped away from her over the past three days.

A thousand raw emotions churned through her. The pure joy of knowing she was about to see her parents again, and the apprehension over how they would react. The fear that things could never be the same again in her life, and the wonder and delight of knowing who she really was. The overwhelming intensity of her love for Edric, and the desolation of being apart from him. Memories of Faerie, memories of this world. All tumbling together as she stood under the porch and waited for the door to open.

Something in her wanted to run and hide—something stronger kept her there.

She saw a shadow approaching through the glass panels. The blood pounded in her temples.

Be brave! Be brave! Be brave!

The door opened and she saw her father's familiar round, gentle-eyed face. But the change in him was devastating. There were dark bags under his eyes, his skin was gray and his usual cheerful expression was gone, replaced by misery and despair.

Tania's mouth was parched. She swallowed painfully. "Dad . . . ?"

He gave a wordless shout, his eyes lighting up, his face stretching into a huge relieved smile. He jerked the door wide open and almost threw himself at her.

She gasped as the breath was squeezed out of her. She put her arms around him, her eyes shut, clinging on tightly, feeling his stubble against her cheek, smelling the familiar scent of his soap, her face buried in the collar of his dressing gown.

She had no idea of how much time passed as they stood like that on the doorstep.

Finally he let go of her enough to draw her over the threshold and close the door behind her.

"Mary!" he called, his voice shaking. "She's here!"

Tania tried to speak—to apologize—to explain—but her throat felt achingly tight and her voice wouldn't come.

Her father pulled her along the hallway. She saw her mother appear at the head of the stairs. She saw her grip the banister rail, her face a white blur through Tania's tears. She saw her mother's legs buckle under her, so that she sat heavily on the top step, her slender body wrapped in her old blue dressing gown.

Tania pulled loose from her father and scrambled up the stairs. She tumbled onto her knees in front of her mother and buried her face in her lap. She felt her mother's hands trembling as she stroked her hair.

"Oh, Anita!" Her mother's voice was ragged with emotion. "Where have you been? Where have you *been*?"

Don't miss the other magical novels in the Faerie Path trilogy!

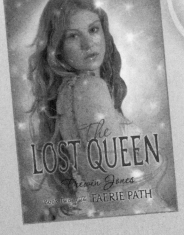

The Lost Queen
Book Two of the Faerie Path

Back in London, Tania learns that Faerie has been conquered by the evil Gray Knights — and only she has the power to save the day. But will she be able to defeat the Gray Knights and find the long-lost Queen Titania while still keeping her true identity hidden from the Mortal World?

The Sorcerer King
Book Three of the Faerie Path

When Tania returns to Faerie, she finds only devastation. The Sorcerer King, an ancient enemy of the Faerie Court, has been released. As the wicked sorcerer regains his power, Tania must prepare to fight a battle she might not survive. Can true nobility conquer evil?

An Imprint of HarperCollinsPublishers

www.harperteen.com